A Big Girl's Revenge

A Big Girl's Revenge

Ms. Michel Moore

www.urbanbooks.net

Urban Books, LLC
300 Farmingdale Road, NY-Route 109
Farmingdale, NY 11735

A Big Girl's Revenge
Copyright © 2019 Ms. Michel Moore

ISBN 13: 978-1-64556-179-8
ISBN 10: 1-64556-179-8

First Mass Market Printing April 2021
First Trade Paperback Printing April 2019
Printed in the United States of America

10 9 8 7 6 5 4 3 2 1

*This is a work of fiction. Any references or similarities
to actual events, real people, living or dead, or to real
locales are intended to give the novel a sense of reality.
Any similarity in other names, characters, places, and
incidents is entirely coincidental.*

Distributed by Kensington Publishing Corp.
Submit Orders to:
Customer Service
400 Hahn Road
Westminster, MD 21157-4627
Phone: 1-800-733-3000
Fax: 1-800-659-2436

A Big Girl's Revenge

Ms. Michel Moore

Dedication

MW-MW

12/28/15

Long Live Love

Bis as the World Is Round

Acknowledgments

As I have crafted numerous novels throughout the years, the list of people that support me has continued to grow. I'm so very thankful. And beyond all, I'm often humbled. Sometimes it all seems like a wonderful dream being blessed to do what you love. My husband, best friend, and rock, author Marlon PS White: You've been holding me down behind the scenes and have been since 1999. Now you have stepped out of the shadows and are doing ya own thing in this book industry. I love you big as the world is round and support your endeavors just as you've done mine. My mother, Ella Fletcher, has had my back in each and every way a parent should. She has stood by me and supported my dreams. She believed in me even when I didn't believe in myself. I know I don't say it enough, but I love you. My daughter, author T. C. Littles has been here to see my visions and assist me in making them reality. We have spent countless hours on the phone plotting and scheming how we can take over the world. One day we just might make it happen. (Smile) Thanks for my grandkids, Jayden and Lil Ella. My brother, Dwayne Fletcher, and cousin, Othello Lewis: it's always love. Rita Fletcher, continue to R.I.P. I miss you still. At Aretha Franklin's funeral, Jesse Jackson was posted beginning to end and never left her or the family's side. I remarked, "I wish I had a friend like that." Truth be told, I do. My best friend, Dorothea Lewis, is and has been my road dawg for decades. I love ya, Sis! Even when you clown, I will pull out my red nose and clown with you. (Smile)

It's several folk in this industry that have made my journey more than interesting, and each I hold in high regard. K'wan Foye was the first author that I considered my friend, and also the first author to sign his novels at my bookstore. Nikki Turner prayed for me when times were hard. Carl Weber blessed me with a deal and constant advice. Karen Mitchell and George Denard Breland are like true family. When the chips were down, Faye Wilkes, K'wan, Danielle Green, and Blacc Topp stepped all the way up. I will never forget the love you showed me and mines. We appreciate you. Nothing but respect and gratitude. People talk shit all day long, but these four backed it up. If you want to know the definition of loyalty, look no further.

To Monique Hall, Margret Waleed, E. Williams, Lissha Sadler, Racquel Williams, Spud Johnson, Eureka Jefferson, Ebonee Abby, Nika Michelle, Kenya Rivers, JM Benjamin, Shannon Holmes, Brenda Hampton, Amaleka McCall, La Jill Hunt, Ty Marshal, Danielle Bigsby, Avery Goode, Joe Awsum, Linda Brickhouse, and of course, my lil hometown soul sista for life, India-Johnson Williams: collectively y'all have had my back, shown love, and been nothing short of 100 from day one. In this industry, that's rare.

I still thank God for Sidi, Oumar, Mustafa, Henry, Porgo, Akieon, and the list goes on of the street vendors that showed me love when I first started. Blessings always to my friend, Hakim (Black & Nobel Books). A special thank you to Tonya Woodfolk, Johnnay Johnson, Stacy Jabo, Papaya, Jenise Brown, Ne-c Virgo for always traveling to my events. And to Qiana Drennen: you created

Acknowledgments

something great. DRMRAB was legendary. That book club and all its chapters impacted the paperback world in ways unimaginable. I salute you for that. To the other Detroit-based book clubs that rock with me, The Plot Seekers and EYE CU, thanks for the continued support.

Major respect to all who have always supported my bookstore, Hood Book Headquarters located in Detroit, and that supported the Detroit Hustle and Grind Book Fair. Lastly, to the Hood Book Ambassadors, Trina Crenshaw, Yolanda McCormick, Nia Smith, Krystal Robinson, Jay Knox, Desiree Bailey, La Kiesha Wright, Renita Walker, Kenya Johnson, Chanelle Patton, Eurydice Lofton, Martha Falconer, Tina Brown, Vickie Juncaj, Candance, Passion Beauford, T.C. Littles: you are the greatest book club and moral support a girl could ever have. I salute you all. We stay rocking that blue and orange. Ain't another betta than my HBA family!

God bless whomever is reading this. Make sure you check out the titles listed below.

Coldhearted & Crazy

Ruthless and Rotten

No Home Training

Tick, Tick, Boom!

A Product of the System

The System Has Failed

Acknowledgments

Homeless

Testify

I Can Touch the Bottom

Young & Hungry

Say U Promise Saga

Full Figured 9

Around the Way Girls 10

Get It How Ya Live

Girls From da Hood 13

Carl Weber's Kingpins: Detroit

Hustle Bag

When You Cross a Crazy Bitch

Stage Hustle

Married to the Shooter

. . . and many others.

Prologue

Once upon a time in a Detroit Westside ghetto, there lived a boy and a girl—or in hood terminology, a dude and a chick, whichever word you prefer to use.

Now the chick, Keisha Marie Jackson, might not have been the prettiest female from the Motor City, considering an awful case of acne often distracted from her pretty chestnut brown eyes. With her extra-thick waistline and double-cheeseburger-supersize-fries ass, Keisha was definitely not the skinniest. However, rest assured ole girl had her shit together business-wise. You know the type I'm talking about: good job, killer wardrobe, brand new truck, and a real go-getter attitude. She came from an upper-class privileged family—a two-parent household, huge home in a gated community, and a strict Catholic education at an exclusive all-girls' boarding school. She had the world by the tail and a bright, promising future. Wherever the big girl went, she surely slayed. Without question, she came, saw, and turned up with the best of them. Keisha was that deal and had no problem whatsoever letting folk know. Not cocky or arrogant, she was just confident. Her weight was just a part of her personality. She was good with it and owned it. But, never having truly been with a man before, that part of her life made her vulnerable to bullshit. Men were the kryptonite to her Superwoman shield.

Getting his honorary degree in the streets, Rico Campbell, the boy . . . here we go! He was a horse of a different color. Born to be trouble, thug ran deep in his veins. It was as if he maybe knew better but didn't choose to care. Abrasive around the edges in every sense of the word, he only attended school for the two things that mattered to him the most—free lunch and trying to push up on the females. Coming from a broken home, Rico suffered from a bad case of the three capital U's: Uneducated, Unemployed, and Unwilling to commit to any one woman. He had no home training. His attitude stayed negative. He wanted what he wanted by any means necessary. Considered a pretty boy by most, Rico rocked shoulder-length dreads, carved-out sideburns, and sagging jeans that were his trademark. His roughneck swag made him desired by every woman he met.

Unfortunately, Keisha was no different, and she would soon find out that even if a big black dick glitters like a motherfucker, it ain't always gold. The only thing that could save her from herself was herself.

Chapter One

It was exactly 4:53 in the a.m. and the occupants of the small, brick-framed house on Tyler and Linwood Avenue were awakened by the sound of the buzzing alarm. Five days a week like clockwork (no pun intended), it was the same routine in the two-person household. Keisha would break her neck trying to get to work on time, while Rico lay around doing what he did best—talking cash shit.

"Come on now. Hurry your fat ass up before I fall back out," Rico warned, stretching his arms and yawning. With blunt-burnt fingertips, he wiped the sleep out the corners of each half-shut eye. "I'm tired as hell. You know I had a long night!"

Keisha fumbled in the mirror with a comb and a bottle of spritz. Desperately trying to fix the sew-in her man had destroyed banging her body against the headboard in an attempt to bust his second nut, she frowned while sucking her teeth. "I'm hurrying, boy. Damn, if it wasn't for you wanting to have sex twice earlier this morning, I would've been ready. So, just chill out, okay? In addition, ain't nobody tell your slick behind to be out half the night doing God knows what and to who! It doesn't make any kinda sense."

"I do what the fuck I wanna do and to whoever the fuck I wanna do it to. You betta act like you know." Naked as the day he was born, Rico swung his legs out the king size bed. Still groggy, he grabbed the wrinkled blue jean shorts he'd worn the day before. Putting them on, he yawned once more. "And bitch, please. Don't tell me jack shit about chilling out. You gonna mess around and be walking up to Davison on your own! You feel me?"

"I'm just saying, Rico, dang." She slightly backed down, sensing an ass-kicking coming on.

Reaching over for his wheat-colored Tims, Rico angrily slid his sockless feet inside. Making his way to the bathroom, he yelled out as he took an early morning piss. "Keisha, don't nobody wanna be hearing all that lip. If ya keep running that big mouth of yours, I might stuff something else up in there. You understand me?"

"Whatever."

"Yeah . . . it's gonna be whatever."

"Rico, please."

"Okay, bitch. Keep talking. I told you the old Rico is back."

With dick still in hand, at six feet tall, he soon stood towering over a short-in-height but extra-thick-in-build Keisha. His overbearing presence, however, meant nothing at this point as she continued to low-key complain about their early morning freak-fest Rico demanded on the regular.

"Go on somewhere, all right? I'm already gonna be late to the bus stop." She hardly acknowledged his dick.

"So what?" He eagerly stroked his semi-hard manhood, wedging Keisha between the cheap imitation oak grain dresser and his body. "What's that supposed to mean to me? Huh? You running around here waking me up, bugging on some dumb shit and acting so worried where I was last night and who was getting this good dick, so what?"

Brushing past him, Keisha glanced at the digital blinking clock. "*So what* is if I miss that first bus, you know I'm gonna be late to work. My boss already warned me if I'm late anymore there was gonna be major consequences."

"Consequences!" Rico loudly laughed, searching for the half blunt he'd left on the nightstand. "How the hell the next person gonna regulate my woman's time?" With his shit still standing at full attention, he blazed up. "Ya ass belongs to me! I call the shots! Ya ain't banging that pale-face white cracker, is you?"

"Don't be stupid, Rico."

"Then real rap, fuck some consequences." He inhaled the last of the overpriced Kush then tossed the tail in the ashtray. "You know I got that good dick, don't you, Keisha. You better act like you know, bitch."

"Whatever! I gotta go."

Yanking the woman who practically worshiped him by her freshly ironed white blouse, Rico twisted Keisha's frame around. "Whatever this."

"No, stop, Rico. I'm gonna be late. My boss said—"

"Shut the hell up." His stale, hot morning breath filled her right ear as he shoved her upper body down on the top of the dresser. "Tell ya boss I'm running this here." Maliciously, he snatched Keisha's knee-length skirt up to her waist, revealing a heart-shaped tattoo on one cheek with his name inked dead in the center.

"Wait," Keisha protested, trying to rise up.

"Wait, wait," he taunted, mocking her cries while marveling at her flawless apple bottom. "Yo, let daddy put this good dick back up in that fat-ass pussy." Showing his Linwood/Dexter mentality, Rico swished around a huge glob of saliva. Opening his mouth, disrespectfully, the jobless neighborhood bully let the spit drop down on Keisha's huge backside. Smearing it on both sides of her plumpness, his hand spanked it repeatedly, making it appear to dance. "Hell fucking yeah. Now that's what I'm talking about." Enjoying the sight of her cheeks jiggling and the wetness oozing down her crack, he bit at the corner of his lower lip. The veins in his eight-inch curved penis pulsated, and the blood rushed quickly to the head.

"Please don't," she begged with each stinging smack echoing throughout the bedroom. "You hurting me. I'm telling you that hurts."

"Come on now, girl, stop fronting. As many dicks, tongues, and other bullshit that been up in this played-out cat of yours, I know this good dick right here ain't hurting you. You's a trooper, so shut up and start acting like one." Ignoring her tearful pleas, Rico savagely ripped one side of his live-in girlfriend's lace-trimmed thong, exposing her entire behind.

Raising his index finger up to his lips, he stuck his tongue out, licking it. Having no remorse or mercy, Rico violated Keisha's rear hole. Soon using two wet fingers, he stretched her once snug anus wide open.

"Make it jump for daddy," he demanded, watching her body jerk upward.

Yeah, this bitch gonna pay for popping off at the mouth.

"Is you banging your boss, you desperate ho? Huh? Is you?" he hissed as he relentlessly kept at it. "Tell me! Tell me!"

She wanted to turn around and smack the shit outta him or at least tell him he was a bald-faced liar and what he was saying wasn't true, but Keisha knew deep down it was. Since hooking up with Rico, she had been what most would consider a slut or a rat. She did participate in some of the most disrespectful sexual acts a person could imagine, and his asking was she banging her boss wasn't far from the truth. The fact was she did suck him off again the week before just for the hell of it all.

"Urrrgh, please, Rico, don't." Obviously in pain from his unprovoked, perverted attack, in agony she screamed, whimpering for mercy.

However, he couldn't care less. "Shut the fuck up, Keisha. I'm warning you. If you don't wanna miss the whole day at that stupid uppity job of yours, you better be still and treat daddy right."

"No!"

"What?"

"Rico, don't!"

"Shut the fuck up!"

"No, no, don't! My hair!"

"Fuck your hair!"

"You hurting my back bent like this!"

"Do you really think I give a sweet shit?"

"Stop! Why you doing this?"

"Damn, Keisha, shut the fuck up and get off into this big dick!"

Keisha struggling to get away only made Rico's shit throb harder and his sudden rage intensify. With one hand wrapped around his swollen shaft, he began rubbing the helmet-shaped head of his cock up and down her crack.

"Rico . . . don't . . . please." She tensed up, having one of her frequent migraines.

"Mmmm, this shit feel good as a motherfucker! Tell daddy you want this good dick. Tell me." Using the other hand, he snatched at her blouse, causing the buttons to pop off one by one and fall to the carpeted floor. No sooner had her sky blue lace bra been exposed than Rico groped her breasts, daring Keisha to resist his demands. As her oversized titties dangled, his dick grew what seemed like another half an inch.

Keisha had discovered Rico was bipolar shortly after their first meeting. However, his chiseled body and the long, thick-tongue work he'd put in between her thighs when in the mood was more than she could or would be able to resist. Those factors, along with the wishful thinking she could miraculously change Rico into a nine-to-five working dude instead of a petty, irresponsible street corner hustler kept her hanging on.

"Just hurry up," she whined, bracing herself for what was coming next. "I'm tired of this mess! I swear I'm tired! I'm fucking tired!"

"What'd you say? I know you ain't telling me what to do!" Pre-cum moisture formed on the tip as he roughly shoved his fully erect meat in her already moist hole from the rear. With his shorts now down past his knees resting on top of his boots, Rico showed her no mercy. "I call the shots! I done told your fat ass, I'm running the show! Now beg daddy to fuck you harder!"

"Noooooo . . . . .stop!" The hairy lips surrounding Keisha's pussy spread as Rico's body rammed hers with fast, penetrating strokes followed by slow, deep strokes to the left and right, then accelerating again.

"No? Fuck no! What I tell you about telling me no?" He went in deeper, waiting for an answer. "I can't hear you. Huh? What?" Shirtless, a tattoo-covered, muscular Rico watched himself in the mirror savagely punish Keisha's already sore cunt. "You want me to run up in your ass instead? Huh? You want all this good black dick in that tight hole. Is that what you want? Huh, is it?"

"Wait, Rico. Wait. Slow down," Keisha begged while panting, short of breath.

Every deep-rooted thrust he took, his facial expression changed as if he were performing for an audience or making a low-budget porno. Using his strong calves for support, Rico showed Keisha exactly who was boss in their small household. In and out, out and in. Slow stroking, then fast as hell, his loud moans and grunts intensified.

"Yeah, that's what the fuck I'm talking about. Give all that shit to daddy, you stanking-ass, nasty-mouthed bitch! Give daddy all that cat." Sweat pouring off his forehead, Rico pounded her pussy to the left then to the right. With no regard for the sexual pain he was inflicting, Rico treated Keisha's hairy snatch no better than he would a five-dollar whore in the street.

With each position change of his harsh, penetrating movements, Keisha could feel his pipe stabbing the raw inner walls of her shivering body. It was if she could feel him in her womb and touching her spine. Getting tingling chills when Rico's big nut sac touched her skin, she wanted to scream out in pain and, strangely, maybe a little in passion; but she refused to give Rico's disrespectful ass the satisfaction.

Easily caught up in his own arrogant world, his huge ego needed no encouragement. Squeezing his left hand around her thick waist, he had malice in his heart. Disrespectfully, Rico used his right hand to twist Keisha's weave in between his fingers.

"Urr, urr, yeah, hell yeah! Don't move, bitch. Right there—right fucking there. You like this big black log daddy got, don't you? Don't you?" He grunted as if he would really get a response to his strong-arm tactics, which were nothing short of rape. "Tell daddy you love his good dick. Tell me you want it, bitch. Tell me."

Keisha couldn't catch her breath to respond. Even if she could, what would she say to the man she once proclaimed to love so much? Frustrated and tortured, as Rico mounted her like a wild dog, her upper body broke down and collapsed. No longer squirming or fighting the inevitable, she gave up. Every hole in her body belonged to Rico, and before the morning was over, she knew his freaky ass would abuse them all with his dick, his finger, his tongue, or whatever other object he chose to violate her with.

With her arms stretched out, Keisha's perfectly manicured, square-shaped nails clawed the sides of the wooden dresser that was now rocking back and forth. The more brutal force Rico used in banging the cow shit out of her, the weaker her knees and ankles became. Realizing she was going to be once again late for work, Keisha zoned out as Rico smushed the side of her jaw onto the top of the dresser.

Face to face with a hairbrush, a bottle of cheap knockoff perfume, a can of oil sheen, and a small tube of vanilla-scented lotion, the newly promoted assistant office manager at Compuware knew she was as good as fired.

Maybe I can suck my boss's dick again in his office or let him watch me eat his wife's pussy like last time I was late. Thoughts ran through Keisha's mind at a fast rate, wondering how she could keep her paycheck. Unbelievably, if she were fired this time, it would be the third job she'd lost since originally hooking up with Rico and ultimately leaving the carefree lifestyle of her parents' house. *Why me? I try so hard, God, so why me? I hate him so much!*

Maybe if Rico hadn't totaled her truck, she'd have a chance to make it to work on time. Possibly, if she wasn't responsible for paying all the bills, she could afford to take a cab. But, thanks to her so-called man and his roguish behavior, it was a wrap. She'd definitely miss her bus, probably ending another hard-earned, much-needed job.

"You like this good black dick, don't you? You daddy's little slut, ain't you?" He pounded as sweat poured down from his forehead, dripping onto her spread-wide ass cheeks. "Ain't you?"

Keisha didn't respond, causing a good shit-talking Rico to go in even harder with his banging and the hurtful, cruel insults.

I hate everything about him. I swear I do. I just wonder why I keep allowing all this bullshit. I wonder why I put up with him. I had so much good going on in my life before I met his silly ass. So what I'm a little thick? I know I could've still did better than him. One day he gonna pay for treating me no better than shit on a stick. I don't deserve this. I'm better than this no matter what in the hell he say. Keisha's mind was racing with thoughts of resentment. With every movement, she felt enraged.

Rico was, of course, in the dark. Having been the dominant leader throughout their troubled relationship, he knew Keisha would never plot on him, let alone have enough courage to call herself leaving him.

"Why you so quiet, big girl? Huh? Huh? You usually a loud-talking bitch. Where's all that lip, with ya bumpy-faced ass? Where it's at?" He eased his dick out her hole, looking down on the thick, creamy cum that had accumulated on the shaft. Roughly, he slammed it back in, making her body shake and the dresser move. "You

wasn't quiet when my boy and his ho-ass cousin was
running up in you, was you? You was screaming and hol-
lering like there ain't no tomorrow—begging for more."

With their red nose pit-bull, Kilo, now in the bedroom
with his tongue hanging to the side, watching his master
beat it up, Keisha didn't want to say anything out of the
way to her so-called man to piss him off any further. Last
time she did, Rico let the dog lick her pussy while he
recorded it on his cell phone. Rico coldheartedly sent it
to all his friends and hers. He even posted it on YouTube,
but thankfully, someone reported it as obscene before it
received a lot of views.

*I can't keep living like this! I just can't! I'd rather be
dead.* Ashamed of the true freak she'd become and still
very much relentlessly addicted to Rico's perverted dick
game, the once good girl was speechless. Struggling to
endure all eight rock-hard, curved inches of the DLA-
certified thug beating it up from the rear, Keisha Jackson
tightly shut her eyes. Lost in the darkness, her mind
drifted back almost a year prior; back to the day she first
met her supposed soul mate and man of her dreams, Rico
Campbell; back to the day she wasn't considered a slut, a
tramp, and a ho.

Chapter Two

*I think I'm Big Meech . . . Larry Hoover . . . whipping
work . . . hallelujah.*

It was the hottest day of the summer season. The
sounds at River Rouge Park were banging from every car
and rimmed-up truck that crept through the main strip.
Half-dressed females and wanna-be thugs were out and
about. The three-day weekend Detroit's own homegrown
rap group Rock Bottom was famous for sponsoring was
finally winding down. The first night was an off the chain
concert at Chene Park, followed by the annual picnic.

Dressed in beige-colored army fatigues and Timberland boots, the tightly knit DLA clique was representing
in full force. Sure, there were people hailing from the
Eastside as well as the West, but Dexter Linwood Area
guys were definitely holding the spot down. That's what
they did in Detroit . . . held wherever they went down.

Rico Campbell, Swazy, and the rest of the crew posted
up on the north end of the crowded festivities. Packing
chromed-plated nines in their waistbands just in case
a nigga wanted some, they downed the rest of the keg
they'd chipped in for. Belching three or four times in a
row, an out-his-mind Rico quickly sobered up at the sight
of one of the roundest, most perfectly shaped asses he'd
seen all afternoon.

"Shit, where you been all day?" Rico leaned off the grill of the silver-and-red-trimmed F-150 he was pushing. Moving his thick, freshly twisted dreads out his face, he made his way over to the small group of giggling females. Not sure of exactly who he was talking to, all the girls blushed while praying they were the lucky one in question.

"You fine as a motherfucker," he slurred, half out his mind.

"Who, me? You talking to me?" Keisha was admittedly shocked, to say the least, when Rico grabbed her hand, turning her completely around, inspecting the total package.

Lusting at her wide hips and extra plump blessing from God, Rico, always horny, grinned. He tugged at his pole that was bulging through his camouflage pants. "Yeah you, ma. Damn, what's your name, big girl?"

"Keisha," she nervously answered as her heart raced.

"Well damn, Keisha, what you got up when you leave here?" Rico was drunk as shit and high as hell. He'd been talking trash to women all afternoon and collecting numbers. Now, the three-day Rock Bottom weekend was ending, and he needed a hot and ready bed warmer for the night.

Rico never had a problem getting a female to give up her goodies, but keeping them around was a different thing altogether. Even though he was more than official in the bedroom department, his ridiculous, rude, and most times over-the-top behavior would result in any half decent, self-respecting, sensible female to get the fuck on. So, whether light-brown-chocolate-complexion-with-a-bad-case-of-acne, slightly overweight Keisha was his type or not—it was the chase of the game Rico loved. He collected pussy like some people collected loose change in a jar.

"Umm, me and my girls going down to the IHOP on Jefferson near the Isle, then maybe the casino." She sheepishly twirled her long micro-braids around her fat fingers, hoping his attention was not a joke.

"Oh yeah, for real?" Rico took the time to check out her friends, quickly sizing each female up one by one.

Damn, these some huge hoes. No wonder they going to eat. That's probably all they hungry asses do. He realized they were all pretty much big-boned, to put it nicely, but at that point, it didn't matter. He wanted to run up in Keisha's wide ass from the back, so he thought he'd give it a shot with the fellas.

"Well, umm, let me see what my dudes got up. We might roll out with y'all."

"Okay." Keisha giggled with her girlfriends at his suggestion. They all hoped for the best response, but expected the worst.

As the anxious, chunky clique, dressed in their summer's best Lane Bryant outfits, waited underneath the cool shade of the tree, Rico went to work on his crew.

"Come on, y'all. Niggas is bailing up out this motherfucker left and right with bitches," he reasoned while pulling up on his sagging fatigues. "We might as well chill with that big-booty freak over there and her girls. Look at they desperate asses," Rico whispered low key in an attempt to persuade them. "You know we can all hit tonight. Come on, now. Don't leave ya manz hanging."

Swazy, Rico's main man and the soberest out the crew, laughed out loud, not giving two shits if the big-boned bitches heard him or not. "Dawg, is you blind or what? That last cup of Old E got you blew back way too far.

Big girl that need the Proactiv and 'em is some ugly throwaways. I ain't sticking my dick up in none of they big-bear husky asses. You can forget that, my dude. On everything I love, you on your own on smashing that."

Keisha and her friends might have been overweight and not missing any meals, but the group definitely wasn't deaf. Catching serious attitudes, they were immediately offended by Swazy's insensitive name-calling. Used to playing second fiddle to all the extra-skinny, model-type chicks that ran the streets of Detroit, they didn't say a single word. Instead, rolling their eyes, they all turned away, heading toward the parking lot. Rico, stalking Keisha's wide hips swinging from side to side, felt his little head swell, convincing his big head she really wasn't that tore up in the face.

"Yo, wait up, girl."

"For what?" Keisha momentarily paused as her girls continued walking. "So your boy can say more rude, outlandish garbage?"

Rico jogged over to her. Standing face to face, he moved his dreads out his eyes. *Shit! What the fuck!* In the sunlight, he realized Swazy was right. Ole girl wasn't all that cute, but still, her thick body was kinda slamming.

"Damn, girl, why is you tripping? I ain't say that shit. I still wanna hang with you."

"You do?" Keisha, 22 and still somewhat a virgin, was overjoyed a guy as handsome as Rico was interested in her. "Well, do you wanna meet us down there at IHOP?"

"Listen, I need to dip to the crib for a few, then I'ma get back up with you. Just put your number in my cell." He handed her his iPhone. "And put Sexy Key for your name."

Practically snatching the cell out his hands, Keisha happily did as instructed with her "big girl crew" looking on with anger and disgust. "Well, call me later. I'm gonna go drop them off as soon as we finish eating."

"Oh, that's you?" Shocked, Rico motioned toward the gold-colored Yukon Denali the now disgruntled clique of women were standing next to.

"Yeah, that's me." Keisha, Grosse-Pointe-raised and spoiled by her rich parents, was used to brothers from around the way only caring about her plump, oversized ass or the whip she was driving. So, his reaction to the costly truck or his boys' comments about her overall appearance was nothing new. Although, by the looks of the expensive jewelry Rico was rocking and the shiny F-150 he was posted on, Keisha assumed he had his own share of hood riches. Fine as he was in her eyes, even if Rico sold crack to pregnant women and small kids on the playground to get his money or set innocent animals on fire, Keisha couldn't care less. He seemed to want her, and desperate to be loved, nothing else mattered.

Saying their temporary goodbyes, Rico schemed while watching Keisha walk away and then roar off in her truck.

Damn, what these niggas talking about? I'ma be pushing that motherfucker quick, fast, and in a hurry. Ole girl seem like she got that serious bread. I'm about to use the shit outta her dumb ass! If she wanna be with a guy like me, she gotta be dropping that bread. Her goofy ass gotta pay like she weigh.

Once in her truck, Keisha exhaled. Her heart was racing and her throat was dry. She felt chill bumps. She couldn't believe she'd just been chosen like that. She always dressed nice, and a few guys from her father's job used to try to push up on her, but to her it was all fun and games. Their whistles or failed attempts of flirting were just that: fails. Keisha didn't know if they meant it or were just trying to low-key get on her dad's good side. Nevertheless, this experience was different, much different. As she drove, she gripped the steering wheel, feeling as if she'd just hit the lottery. Naïve to real game, she had no idea that it was just the opposite.

"Girl, I know damn well you didn't give that two-bit-ass thug your real number!"

"What you mean?" Keisha raised her brow.

"I mean after all that foul-mouth shit he was talking on the sly, I wanted to slap the fire outta his mouth my damn self. So, I know you was offended, 'cause he was directing that garbage basically directly at you," one of Keisha's friends protested. "Big girl this, big girl that. I swear dudes these days be killing me. Running around Instagram liking all those skinny females' pictures when they know all along they trying to go large."

"Yeah, I guess you right, but—"

"But nothing. Old boy was trying to pretend he all right with thick-boned females, but him and his boys was laughing. Like we all some sort of jokes or something."

"He seemed nice. And real talk, I am a big girl, and so are you. So, what's wrong with that?"

"Nice? Is that what you call some drunk, random-ass thug that called you a big girl to your face? Ain't a damn thing wrong with being thick. I love all my curves. But that fool wasn't trying to be cool. He called himself dissing you and all of us."

"Do you think so?"

"Girl, I know so. I can't believe after all that money your parents wasted on school you can't see that bullshit! I'm shocked you ain't peeped that out."

Keisha was tired of the impromptu lecture. Reaching over, she turned up the radio. Allowing the loud music to drown out her friend's negative, ill-toned conversation, she maneuvered her way through traffic and out of the park. Finally coming to a red light, Keisha glanced up in the rearview mirror on the sly, then over at her best friend.

Hmph, she just jealous he didn't step to her. For once, the fine-ass nigga chose me and not her. Bitches can't never be happy for the next female. What's wrong with him calling me that? I'm fly as fuck anyway it goes.

The next few days, the ill-matched pair was practically inseparable. It didn't take ladies' man Rico long to discover his assumptions were one-hundred percent correct. Keisha did have a bankroll. Having a good paying job, her finances were in order and her credit was A1. Growing up on the streets of Detroit, Rico was gonna get his by any means necessary. The fact that Keisha was getting most of her dough from her well-off parents still didn't matter to him. Their money spent just as well as hers, and his main objective was self-satisfaction.

"Girl, why you keep dealing with him?" another friend asked her, holding a lunch menu at Friday's. "I thought you knew better than to let some low-life Negro from the hood play you like you worthless. You act like you ain't hear that bullshit him and his boys was saying that day at the park."

Waiting until the server left after bringing Keisha and her friend two glasses of raspberry lemonade, she responded, "Remember, he didn't say none of it, plus he's not playing me. We have fun when we hanging together." Keisha blushed, only having had her young pussy slightly licked before meeting Rico, but never any real penetration. "Plus, dang, I'm not even gonna tell you what else we have fun with. You just hating on us."

Keisha's friend was not trying to hear shit else her girl was saying. "Look, crazy, stop being so naive. And hating? Bitch, please. Are you serious? Even Ray Charles can see what that shady perpetrator is up to. He's straight up using you. You don't even know that fool. He might be a murderer for all you know."

"Girl, please." Keisha took out her cell phone, showing her friend all the text messages Rico had sent to her over the past few days, proclaiming his love in one sentence, then *let's go shopping* in the next. "Look, he on my shit. Every thirty minutes he's checking up on me and asking where I'm at. Now, do that seem like a murderer?"

"Every thirty minutes?" She shook her head with a smile on her face. "Where they do that at?" Sitting back in the booth, hungry as hell and ready to order, Keisha's husky friend laughed at her quick devotion to Rico as well as her stupidity. "Naw, my bad. You right, Keisha. He don't seem like a murderer. I'm wrong. He seems like a slick con man trying to watch where his money flow. Them texts ain't nothing but a hood fool running game before he run your pockets. He using your dumb ass. Wake the fuck up. Damn."

"But he loves me."

"He got you so twisted you don't know what the hell love is."

"Girl, when we together, it feel so right."

"So what? When niggas on dope shooting up and crackheads get a rock, I bet that shit feel good too."

"So what you saying?"

"I'm saying everything that feels good ain't good for your naïve-acting ass!"

"I know but—"

"But nothing, Keisha. That dreadlock hood Negro using you. Why you acting so slow?"

"I'm not." Keisha tried defending her and Rico's new relationship.

"Well, have your parents met him?"

"You mean my father?"

"Of course your father, fool. You know like I know your mother is crazy soft like you, but Mr. Jackson . . . "

"I know."

"Well, has he?"

"No, but—"

"Well, forget what I'm saying and my opinion." Her friend took a sip of her lemonade. "Get back with me after your dad meets him. You must've forgotten all the days and nights I used to spend at your house."

"I'm not scared of him meeting my father," Keisha skeptically replied. "Rico loves me. It's gonna be all good."

"Well, with all your father's money you keep spending on that fake hood nigga, we'll see. Rico loves you my fat ass. Girl, please, let's just eat."

What her friend was saying did have some truth to it, although Keisha would never admit it out loud. Every time they'd go to dinner, Red Lobster, Outback Steakhouse, or even White Castle, Rico didn't go in his pocket. If it was the movies, Keisha had it. Each trip to the liquor store, no problem, the party was on her. When they had sex, it ultimately cost her room fare. He ain't even have jack shit on getting the pussy. Much to

Keisha's surprise, even when big, shit-talking, "I'm the man" Rico was forced to return the rented Ford F-150 she originally thought he owned, she had to cough up the late fees to cover the bill. And as for the jewelry he was rocking, hell, it belonged to one of his homeboys. What was in the dark quickly came to the light and surfaced. Rico's fine ass was broke as a motherfucker and fake as a three-dollar bill.

Maybe she is right. Maybe he really don't care about me. What if all I am to him is a meal ticket? Oh my God, I hope not. I hope he's not trying to run game. Keisha silently puzzled as she dipped a chicken finger into the ranch dressing. *Matter of fact, I'm not even gonna feed into what anyone else has to say. I'ma be his girl and he gonna be my man. We were made for each other—period.*

True to the game of hustling hoes, nickel-slick-talking Rico dicked her down so thoroughly the first time he hit the virgin pussy, it was no doubt in his mind good girl Keisha was willing to do whatever he asked. Just to make sure he could really run her pockets, Rico decided to give her the full special treatment. Driving her truck to Palmer Park late one night, he parked in the lot near the swimming pool.

"Why we here, baby? There's no one else at the park this late." Keisha, confused and concerned, glanced over both shoulders, seeing nothing but darkness. "You must have to pee or something."

"Naw, I wanna look at the stars with you. Is that all right?" Rico was running his game, and by the gullible expression on Keisha's face, the corny bullshit was working. "Come on, babe, let's walk."

Pushing the button on the automatic locks, they both jumped down out of Keisha's truck. Setting the alarm with the spare set of keys now belonging to him, Rico took her hand. Filling Keisha's head with a gang of lies and misconceptions about him falling in love with her at first sight, the ghetto Romeo led her into the woods.

"I'm scared, Rico. It's so dark. Let's go back," she whispered with each step on the gravel walkway. Constantly looking back, a scared and sheltered Keisha was starting to panic. At that point, it began to dawn on her what her friend had said days before. She didn't really know that much about Rico. Besides meeting a few of his boys, he never had mentioned his family or where he went to school, or even if he had kids. "Let's go back to the truck—please, baby."

Rico tied his dreads behind his head so Keisha could see his face in the moonlight. Raising his navy blue linen shirt she'd bought him at Somerset Mall the day before, he smiled, revealing the handle of his ever present nine pressed against his ripped abs.

"You good, ma. You with me. Don't worry—I got us. You trust me, don't you?"

"Yeah, Rico, I trust you." Still hesitant about her surroundings, Keisha continued following him because unlike his false claims, she was falling in love with him. After all, he was her first, and as open as she was, love was all that mattered.

But Rico had been around the block hundreds of times. He was a veteran and good at playing the game. Since he'd been getting pussy from the ripe age of twelve, the females around him would cake. Clothes, jewelry, sneakers, weed: no matter what Rico wanted, if he could get it from a dumb broad, why not? Besides, it didn't take much work on his behalf, because most of the females he ran into didn't have that much to offer. However, Keisha's pockets were the mother lode, so he wanted to add extra insurance to getting blessed. She already craved riding his dick, so now she'd experience his true showstopper.

Coming to a gigantic boulder wedged in the ground, Rico sat Keisha down as the late night breeze slightly blew the leaves.

"Look up at them stars. They bright as hell, ain't they?"

"Yeah," a still wide-eyed Keisha answered, swatting at a mosquito. "But I'm scared. It might be wild animals out here. Dogs, rats, or oh my God, even snakes."

Listen to this stupid bitch, he thought to himself. Rico took a small bottle of Paul Mason out his pocket, twisting off the cap. Downing the double shot in one good swallow, his mindset went into total game mode.

"Lean back," he gently commanded her.

"Huh?"

"You heard me. Lean back and close your eyes."

Feeling Rico's rough hands start to touch her thick body in places not even she knew existed, Keisha's breathing increased and chills vibrated throughout her inners. No longer worried about being attacked by wild animals or Rico, she let her guard down. First, there was the unsnapping of the top button on her shorts, followed by the sounds of her zipper going down. Her mind was racing. The wetness of Rico's long tongue touching hers, mixed with the adrenalin rush of his hands cupping her now semi-exposed ass, made Keisha feel like she was in heaven.

"Oh, Rico, don't."

"What, you want me to stop?" he sarcastically asked, shoving his hand in between her legs, making her jump. Slowly fingering her tight, freshly untouched virgin pussy, Rico smirked, knowing that after tonight she'd be his puppet on a string for real.

Wiggling around in a fit of ecstasy to remove her shorts altogether, Keisha could only moan in passion. "Umm . . ." As her eyes rolled in the back of her head then refocused to see the top of the trees and a cluster of stars, the surface of the rock felt cold on her naked ass cheeks.

Oh my God! It feels so good. Don't stop! Don't stop!

Just as Keisha thought his strong fingers had taken her soaking wet snatch to a sexual point of no return, he slowly eased his hands on both of her trembling thighs. Having no trouble spreading them wide, bad boy Rico finally took his naïve victim to the next level of ecstasy.

"Did you like that?" He devilishly smiled.

"Yes."

"Yes what?" Rico rubbed his hard pipe through his jeans, never taking his eyes off hers.

"Yes, daddy."

"Now that's what the fuck I'm talking about. My bitch knows my damn name. So say it again."

"Daddy."

"One more time, you big bitch," Rico demanded, gritting his teeth.

Normally, Keisha would be offended by any man calling her a bitch, but she had been around Rico for some days now and knew he was calling her that out of love. Dumbly, she figured it was kinda his term of endearment for her.

"Daddy, daddy, daddy," she eagerly replied to "bitch" as if her parents had named her that at birth. Expecting the DLA thug to drop his pants and pound his throbbing meat inside of her in the middle of the dark Palmer Park Woods, Keisha's body suddenly felt an indescribable surge. Caught off guard, her mouth opened wide, but no words could escape, only thoughts.

Oh, shit! Oh my God! Oh, yeah! Damn! Shit! She was out of her mind as Rico's tongue licked her cat as if it was an ice cream cone on a scorching hot summer's day. Raising her head to look between her legs, all Keisha saw was the top of Rico's dreads. Instinctively, her hands reached downward, holding onto his thick ropes.

Oh, yessss! This shit feels so good!

"Umm, umm," Rico hummed, vibrating her raw walls as his dreads became untied, falling to his shoulders. Every motion of him deep tongue-fucking Keisha was calculated.

Yeah, she all into this bullshit now. I'ma make this big bitch cash me out later for sure. Noticing her lower body rise off the rock to meet every wet, long lick, Rico took two fingers of each hand, using them to stretch apart her fat, protruding, hairy lips. Staring at her inner bright pinkness in the moonlight, Rico's mouth devoured her surprisingly tiny clit, sucking it gently while teasing it with the tip of his tongue.

Keisha screamed out his name twice. "Rico! Ohhhhh . . . Rico!" Her raspy voice echoed throughout the woods.

Reaching one hand up, he instantly covered her mouth still going in, eating her out. "Shhh . . . " He came up momentarily for air. "Lay back, close your eyes, and cum for daddy." When he was sure Keisha was gonna be quiet, he removed his hand, grabbing her left 36DD breast. Pinching her nipple, Rico bobbed his head back and forth, face completely buried in the moist, nappy dugout.

Finally, Keisha climaxed, creaming as if she were a man. "Oh, yessss . . . !" exhausted, she tried desperately to catch her breath.

With a mixture of Keisha's cum-filled juices and his sweat dripping from his mustache, Rico stood to his feet. Conceitedly, he leered down at a seminude Keisha sprawled across the huge rock. Proud he'd made another female call out his name, he slow-stroked his dick while tugging at his balls.

"Okay, now, nasty bitch, play with yourself!" he commanded in a heavy whisper. "Stick those fingers up in that hairy, fat-faced monkey." In the darkness of the wooded area surrounding them, Rico shook his Mr. Good Bar, as Keisha had nicknamed it, in the humid night air as she lusted. "You wanna taste this good dick, girl? You wanna suck it? You wanna drink this hot milkshake I got?" Tightening his grip, jerking up and down, then down and up, moments later, Rico shot off a warm stream of thick nut on Keisha's pudgy stomach.

As the slimy cum slid down from her belly button, Keisha, already turned out by his thuggish freakery, rubbed it into her skin as if it were lotion. Then, on Rico's command, she licked her hands clean. The bad boy womanizer knew at that point, the world of easy living was in his reach. Keisha was gone.

The next few weeks after that mind-blowing tongue banging went just as Rico knew they would—in his favor. Dumb as the day she was born, missing days at a time from work to cater to Rico's every whim, a head-over-heels-in-love Keisha showered him with just about every gift imaginable. His wish was her command. Anything he'd glance at, even in passing, she would purchase for him: a 24k gold chain with a rapper-size cross, a pair of Cartier sunglasses, two pair of Jordans, a new Playstation, some True Religion jeans, or a few Polos. She even bought a thirty-two-inch flat screen for his two-year-old son that all of a sudden he mysteriously announced he had. It hadn't been thirty days since she first met him at Rouge Park, and Keisha was caking beyond belief.

Rico's close friends, including Swazy, were still talking shit about how ugly in the face and chunky Keisha was; however, Rico fired back that her pockets were just as big as she was—so it was all good. He had no shame walking hand in hand with her anywhere in Detroit, because bottom line was he was getting paid. Fuck what the next male or female thought about her face was his general mindset. As long as she was paying, he was staying.

"Dawg, I'm telling you, she be cashing me out on the regular. No matter what in the hell I say, the big bitch do it, no questions asked. Dude, this is the American Dream, I'm trying to tell you! Keisha and her parents got more bread than the law allow. Her daddy supposed to be some wanna-be big-time commissioner or something."

Swazy continued smoking the blunt Rico had blessed him with. "Nigga, don't tell me shit! I don't give a fuck who her people is or what she paying. Her face is wrecked. I know you must be hitting it from the back."

Rico reached into his jean pocket, pulling out a small knot, courtesy of Keisha. "My nigga, I'm hitting it from the front, the back, the side, and the middle, you feel me? Now ,if you wanna get on this here money train, a brother can get you hooked up on one of her girls. All them big birds got that bread."

Choking off the potent weed, Swazy laughed, strong-arm hogging the blunt. "Naw, dude, I'm tight on all that. Just keep getting Baby Bop to buy more of these good-ass trees."

"Dawg, you could be getting your own trees from one of her friends instead of working valet at that stuck-up club you slaving at."

Swazy laughed. "Dude, I'd rather park a hundred cars for a hundred different nickel-tipping old white motherfuckers that pull up to work than live like you. Why don't your ass try getting a job, guy?"

Rico smiled from ear to ear. "Yo, I got a job, full time, and her name is Keisha Jackson. And you know what else? I don't have to wait till income tax time to shop like a baller. I get mines every day, playboy."

Chapter Three

Sunday afternoon rolled around. Keisha had pleaded with Rico all week long to come to dinner at her house. She wanted her parents, especially her strict, overbearing father, to meet the man she'd been spending all her time with, not to mention the man running up her credit card bill. Rico was hesitant to be put on display in the upscale suburbs, so he tried coming up with every excuse in the book as to why he couldn't make it to the place Keisha called home. Spoiled and intent on getting her way, Keisha desperately made him an offer he couldn't refuse, promising an ounce of weed and a rental car for the weekend. Rico gave in to her wishes.

Pulling up in the long, cemented, flower-lined, U-shaped driveway, Keisha parked her truck near the entrance in the company of several other equally expensive cars and trucks. Turning off the engine, she took a deep breath, secretly crossing her fingers.

"Okay, baby, this is it. This is where I live."

"Goddamn, girl. You live in this big crib?" Rico looked around the gated property, feeling like a fish out of water.

"It's not all that big," she replied, casually downplaying her family's wealth.

"Shit, it's big enough, ma, and damn, who pushing these cold-ass whips?"

"Just come on, silly. It's almost five, and my mother has Sandy serve the appetizers at five on the nose."

"Who in the fuck is Sandy?" he asked, wondering if that was her sister or something like that. If it was, maybe he could hook her up with Swazy so he could financially get all the come-up Rico was getting.

Keisha assumed Rico would bug out even more if he found out her family had a chef and a part-time maid, so she just let that question go by unanswered.

Walking through the front door of the mini-mansion Keisha called home, Rico knew immediately he was out of his league—huge ceilings, crystal light fixtures, and linen tablecloths. Sure, his clothes were up to par, Keisha made certain of that much; however, when it came to manners and common sense, the DLA street thug would be on his own. Keisha could only pray Rico would be able to step up to the plate and not say or do any dumb, out-of-the-way bullshit she'd seen him display at times they'd been out in public.

"So, this is the young man you've been keeping company with. Hello. It's so very nice to meet you." Mrs. Jackson greeted Rico with a smile and a mid-evening peach-flavored martini in her hand. "I'm Keisha's mother."

Rico almost gagged. He wanted to throw up in his mouth, now up close and personal with how Keisha was gonna look in twenty years or so. It wasn't a pretty sight in his eyes.

Sticking out his hand to shake hers, he spoke. "Yeah, wat up, doe, Mrs. Jackson? How you?"

"Oh, Mother, he's just teasing around with you." Keisha interrupted, nudging his shoulder. "Aren't you, Rico?"

"I would hope so." Mr. Jackson walked in the room, giving the visitor, his daughter's new boyfriend, a disapproving stare for speaking to his wife in that street slang-inspired manner. "That conduct is not acceptable in my household. We speak English."

Once again, Keisha jumped in, praying the spontaneous heated attitudes in the room would vanish. "Daddy, this is Rico Campbell," she gushed. "Rico, this is my father, Executive County Commissioner Lorenzo James Jackson."

Remaining silent, ignoring the introduction altogether, Rico checked out the expensive statues, pictures, and other knick-knacks that were placed just so. He felt the obvious heated tension in the room as well as the shade Mr. Jackson was throwing his way. Not used to being judged, Rico became arrogant as well as defensive, and it showed.

We speak English! Rico mocked Keisha's father in his mind. *Who in the hell this guy think he talking to?*

Keisha's mother also sensed her husband growing angry, and like her daughter, tried to intervene. "So, you guys were running a tad bit late. We were just about to be seated for dinner. Excuse me, Rico. Would you like to wash your hands and freshen up?"

"My hands is already clean. What is you trying to say, lady? Shit!" Still feeling some sort of way about Keisha's father checking him, he abruptly lashed out at a stunned Mrs. Jackson's hospitality. "And I see y'all watching me like I'm gonna steal some of this ugly stuff y'all got around here."

"Now, hold it one minute, son!" Mr. Jackson was going to put a stop to Rico's outlandish behavior before he went any further. "I will not tolerate that type of language in my home! Keisha, where did you find him at, the city dump? Is this the type of individual you've been spending all your time with? This-this-this bum!"

"Who in the fuck you calling a bum?" Rico dropped one of the tiny knick-knacks he was holding to the floor. Instantly, he took offense, and the two men squared up.

"You—whatever your name is," Mr. Jackson quickly replied, infuriated and not backing down. "You have my daughter out running the streets all times of the night and days at a time. Now you come into my home behaving like an animal. It's obvious you have no home training to speak of."

"Damn, what's wrong with you? You mad I'm getting some of that old school money you trying to keep to yourself? Or is you pissed off that I'm bending your daughter over regularly, getting that fat, tight-ass pussy of hers?" Rico's voice got louder and louder with each passing disrespectful word. "Which one is it? 'Cause I'm doing both, trust."

"Are you insane?"

"Naw, old man, is you?"

"You must not know who you're talking to."

"Wow—you saying that shit like you the president."

"Listen, young man, you're treading on dangerous ground. I'm warning you. You're making a serious mistake."

"Come on, you ain't the Mafia." Rico turned to Keisha, further ridiculing her father. "You ain't tell me your sperm donor was a comedian."

"Rico, shut up," Keisha snapped, frowning.

"Oh, okay, so now you calling boss shots like this ancient motherfucker."

"That's it!" Mr. Jackson feverishly announced.

Short of coming to blows, the two men violently argued as Mrs. Jackson, glass still in hand, horrified, wasted no time in calling the police to remove Rico from the premises. She couldn't believe her ears and the godawful things Rico alleged he was doing to her only child.

"Yes, the young man is being overly aggressive and extremely disrespectful. I'm scared he's going to become physical as well. Please send help right away. Please."

Not believing what was taking place, Keisha was in shock things had gone to the South so fast. "Rico, please. Please, stop it. What's wrong with you?" she cried out, tugging at his arm as Sandy, the chef, emerged from the kitchen with a meat cleaver in tow.

"What's wrong with me?" Rico snatched his arm back, knocking Keisha toward the doorway where Sandy was standing. "Bitch, what in the fuck is wrong with you and yours? Y'all think cause y'all live in this big-ass crib y'all can look down on a nigga. Well, fuck all of that and that commissioner of whatever garbage. That bullshit don't mean jack to a street nigga. Y'all ain't no better than me or mines."

"Naw, it's not like that, Rico, I swear. You need to calm down. Everyone does."

Smushing her in the face like she was nothing, Rico turned his attention back to Mr. Jackson.

"I want you out this house now," Keisha's father demanded, still not backing down to the common thug and balling up his fist to defend his daughter's honor.

"Fuck you, old man. I'll leave when I'm ready."

Keisha tried once more to intervene but stumbled backward as each man in her life got closer to exchanging blows.

Just as Rico cuffed up Mr. Jackson, throwing him into the wall of the foyer, Sandy raised the cleaver to protect her longtime employer and his family. Luckily, the police bolted through the front door. If this was Detroit, it might've taken hours for the police to show up, if they even came at all. However, this was the Caucasian-infested suburbs where playing with an individual acting up wasn't in their department's DNA. Sure, Commissioner Jackson and his family were just as black as Rico appearance-wise, but his vast wealth made him green to the white man, and his political position made him and his family's safety a priority.

They dragged the defiant young hooligan out to the yard. The neighbors, along with Keisha's parents and Sandy, shook their heads in disgust as Rico yelled out every obscene vulgar word in his limited high-school-dropout vocabulary. He even called a hysterical Keisha a couple of "fat bitches,", "stankin' hoes" and "dirty sluts" before it was over.

"I had your daughter on her knees right before we came. Tell your father how you deep-throat this motherfucker, Keisha, and call me daddy. Tell him that!" Handcuffed, stomped out, then tossed in the rear of the patrol car, Rico kicked at the windows as an embarrassed and enraged Mr. Jackson vowed to press charges.

When the cops drove off, Keisha stood mute. She knew the man whose milky warm cum she worshiped was now more notorious in her parents' eyes than Public Enemy Number One. Despite Rico's barrage of insults and threats against her family, Keisha grabbed her purse and keys. Obviously hoodwinked and loyal to the salty taste of his nut, she tossed her purse onto the passenger seat and jumped in her truck to follow.

"Keisha, wait just one minute, young lady. Did you hear how that hooligan spoke to you? Have you lost your mind? He's no more than a common thug!" Mr.

Jackson held the door of the truck. He was disappointed in his daughter's recent choices and dark changes in personality. Obviously, it was due to her dealings with Rico. He promised Keisha, right then and there, as long as she chose to run with the likes of that lowlife goon, she'd be financially disowned and was as good as dead to them. "Keisha, I'm not playing around with you. I know you think you're grown, but that type of street element is beneath you. He doesn't love you like I do—like we do. What are you thinking? We raised you better than this—better than him!"

"Daddy, it doesn't matter what you say. I love him," she screamed, ready to pay Rico's bail no matter what the cost. "And he loves me too. You just don't know him. I don't know what happened just now. He's not like that. I promise he isn't."

"You are restricted from seeing him," Mr. Jackson ordered as his well-to-do white neighbors looked on, wondering what their gated community was coming to. Luckily, in hopes of avoiding a scandal, his nosey reporter neighbor wasn't in the crowd.

"Daddy, I'm grown and I love him!"

"Listen, sweetheart, no normal person just flips out like that." Mrs. Jackson, distraught, spoke up, trying to coax Keisha to come to her senses. "It's obvious you don't know him either. Maybe he's on drugs. And maybe he has you on drugs, too. Is that it?"

"Drugs? What?" Keisha, too stubborn to see the true Rico, pulled the truck door shut, ready to leave.

"Now, Keisha Marie Jackson, I'm warning you. You drive off in this truck, running behind that low-life fool if you want to." Mr. Jackson had had enough of trying to bargain and negotiate. Tight-lipped, he stood out of the truck's path. "I promise you a couple of cold days in hell before I let you back into my house."

Keisha was blinded by love and the power of Rico's long, curved dick. Strung out, she wasn't going to let no one, including the strong bond she and her father always had, come in between it.

"I gotta go." She forced a smile at her sobbing mother and Sandy before starting the truck and screeching off.

Rico loves me!

As Keisha continued being bent on top of the wooden dresser, now being recklessly banged in the ass, she momentarily snapped back to her senses. The months she'd spent hanging with Rico were nothing more than a waste of her young life. Almost destitute, now living from paycheck to paycheck in the griminess of the Detroit ghetto, she thought about everything she'd given up to be with him in such a short amount of time—her parents, her friends, her truck, and even her cherished virginity.

Most importantly, raising her head to see Rico laughing at her excruciating pain in the mirror, Keisha realized she'd even lost her own self-worth. Crazy as it seemed, Rico didn't rob her of those things. Dumbly chasing the almighty good dick Rico always claimed he had, Keisha gave them to him on a silver platter.

Why did I bail him out that day? She wished she could turn back the hands of time and take back most, if not all, the degrading things she'd done for Rico, all in the name of love. *Why didn't I listen to my friends when they said they saw him at the club kicking it with other females? Why did my ass really believe when I was slaving at work for a paycheck to pay our bills, he let Swazy smash a chic in our house and that was her bra I found stuffed in the cushion? Damn, I guess that wasn't his used condom that was disrespectfully thrown under the driver's seat of my truck back then . . . Yeah, right!* Resentful of her stupidity, Keisha fought with her demons as Rico took every shit-covered, throbbing inch out her rear end, shoving it back into her swollen cunt, and started to grind.

"That's enough. Stop!" she shouted, trying to stand up. "I want you to stop! I'm not playing, Rico!"

"Bitch, please. I'm calling the shots. I done already told your ugly ass that, so you might as well relax until I bust." With a balled-up fist, Rico socked her in the back of her head, making her collapse back down onto the dresser. "And I done told you about that smart mouth of yours already this morning."

Keisha felt dazed, shutting her eyes once more, re-membering more of her horrible life since hooking up with Rico—especially the evening she'd bailed him out after the confrontation at her parents' home.

"I swear I'ma kill your motherfucking father. That wanna-be white nigga is as good as dead!" Still infuriated from spending the night locked up then mysteriously released, Rico took his personal property out the large manila envelope. Re-lacing his Pradas as Keisha drove toward the hotel room they'd been staying in, he reached over, violently smacking her across the face.

"Argggh, why you hit me?" Grabbing the side of her jaw, Keisha swerved toward the curb, almost crashing into a parked car. "What's wrong with you? What did I do?"

Rico laughed but was very much still pissed as the veins pulsated on each side of his temples. "Are you fucking serious? Your dumb ass is the one that took me over to that motherfucker. If it wasn't for you wanting me to meet your fake old dude and that ugly mama of yours, I would've been chilling at the club or some shit, not posted on a hard metal bench surrounded by a bunch of hard-leg niggas."

Fed up with him talking so disrespectfully about her parents, Keisha finally spoke up. "Look, Rico, my mom and dad were only trying to be cordial to you. You're the one who blew everything out of proportion acting all crazy, embarrassing me, them, and yourself. You were wrong. You ruined everything."

"Oh, yeah?" Rico laughed once more before putting his chain and cross back around his neck and tossing the now empty envelope out the truck window. "Is that right? You think I was wrong? Is that what you said?"

"Yeah, dead wrong." Keisha got even more brazen with it. "And because of me bailing you out, my father said he was cutting me off and was done with me. We've always been super close, and you destroyed that bond, probably forever."

"Fuck your old man. I told you dude is gonna get his. Talking down to me like he's some sort of kingpin!"

"You need to stop acting so damn stupid."

"What?"

"You heard me, Rico."

"Bitch—you done lost your mind."

"No, I haven't! You out of control."

"Who out of control?"

"You, Rico—that's who. My girl was right about you."

Rico waited until Keisha reached the next red light, bringing the truck to a complete stop. Before she could say another word, he lunged over to the driver's seat, ramming her head against the window.

"What you mean, your girl was right?" He shoved harder, pressing his fingers into her cheek. "I spent the night in jail, and your punk ass out here talking reckless shit about me with them fat, ugly friends of yours?"

"Naw, Rico," Keisha cried, never having been treated like this before. "It wasn't like that. I promise it wasn't. You gotta believe me. It wasn't."

"I don't believe jack."

"It's true. I swear."

"Yeah, right. I was stuck in jail, nursing a swollen lip because of them ho-ass police, and you was out here letting your family and friends dog me."

"Oh, Rico, please. You gotta believe me. I love you! It wasn't like that at all. I'm on your side."

When Rico saw the way she was begging for his forgiveness, his mind started working overtime. "You know what? Just drop me off at the hotel room and get the fuck on."

"What?" Keisha was stunned as he suddenly released his painful grip, switching up his demeanor altogether. "What you mean? What you saying?"

"Yeah, you heard me. Get the fuck on. I'm done with your silly ass. Go on back home to your daddy. I'm tight on you."

Keisha didn't know what to say or do next. The guy she was so head over heels in love with had cursed her mother, attacked her father, and had just smacked her up. Any hood-raised female's reaction would've been obvious: either stab the nigga in his sleep with a butcher knife or get the fuck on altogether. However, Keisha's suburban upbringing and low self-esteem had her at a total loss.

"Wait, Rico, I'm sorry. Let's just talk, please."

"Naw, Keisha, I'm good." Rico knew she was sprung, and he played the game like a champ. "Just drop me off at the room." He started searching through his cell phone contacts, acting as if he were going to make a call. "I need to be with a female that's down with me. Go live your life. I'll be all right."

Begging Rico to stay with her and give her a second chance to be that down-ass chick she thought he was about to call, Keisha started to hyperventilate while she was driving. So emotionally in, she had to pull the truck over for him to take the wheel and drive.

"Please . . . Rico . . . give . . . me . . . a . . . chance." She struggled to breathe through the magnitude of tears and an almost unbearable migraine. "I . . . love . . . you . . . so . . . much!"

By the time Rico pulled up in the parking lot of the Red Roof Inn and jumped out the vehicle with the engine still running, he knew he had her hook, line, and sinker.

Keisha didn't care if someone drove off and stole the truck that was in her father's name. Not bothering to turn it off and take the keys, she was trailing behind Rico, still pleading her case. Rico eased up on the mental torture he was putting Keisha through, knowing what pimp player stunt he was about to pull. He told her to go get her keys and purse and come inside the room so that they could talk.

Unfortunately, when the young, ill-matched pair got inside the hotel room they had been sharing for the past month, streetwise Rico was the only one doing the talking. Twenty minutes of him berating her and a few phone calls later, there was a knock at the door.

"What up, doe?" A shirtless Rico smiled, flinging the room door all the way open and standing to the side.

"Hey, what up doe with you?" a thin-framed female with a short cropped hairstyle came inside. "I was just thinking about you. Where you been hiding, stranger? And is that a new tattoo?" She slowly rubbed his chest with familiarity.

Not really in the mood to do too much talking, Rico cut the greeting short. "Listen, babe." He opened his muscular arms, pulling her close to him as a red-eyed, dumbfounded Keisha looked on. "Let a nigga get some of that wet tongue of yours."

"Dude, what in the fuck happened to your lip?"

"Trust me, it ain't shit. Just kiss a nigga."

As they swapped spit, Keisha grew instantly jealous. She was on ten but knew not to say a word. The girl was thinner than her, much prettier than her, and seemed to have more of a ghetto edge, just like Rico. She wanted to jump up from the mattress, ball up her fist, and go ham, but she held her composure. Just minutes ago, the once-proud female was on her knees, crawling around the carpet, begging for Rico's forgiveness for her smart mouth. She'd promised Rico she'd be down with anything as long as he didn't break it off with her. Keeping quiet was her first test of the night, but certainly not her last.

"Lay back on the bed and open your legs," Rico smoothly urged the mystery girl who was wearing a short blue jean miniskirt with no panties on. "Then play with that pussy. You know how daddy like it."

Doing as she was told, no questions asked, the petite skank was now sprawled out on the bed directly next to Keisha, who still had yet to say a single word.

Rico, now somewhat a puppetmaster, was doing enough talking for all three of them. "Now, Keisha, take off your clothes and eat my homegirl's pussy for me."

"Huh? What?" Keisha, stunned at what he'd just said, jumped to her feet. As her jaw dropped, she knew he had to be kidding, telling her that bullshit. She wasn't a lesbian and had no desire to hold another bitch's hand, let alone eat some random hood ho out. "What you mean, Rico?"

"You heard me," Rico arrogantly insisted, not cracking a smile through his swollen lip. "I thought you was down for whatever? What happened to all of that 'I'm with you,' 'I can be who you want me to be,' 'Give me another chance' fucking shit you was talking? I guess that was some game you was running, huh? You ain't really trying to be down with a nigga like me, is you?"

"Yeah, but . . . " Trembling, Keisha looked over at the bed, frantically trying not to make direct eye contact with the girl's fingers that were moving in and out her own pussy. Her thoughts were twisted. The girl and Rico seemed to already be fucking mentally. Feeling like a fish out of water, Keisha was beyond distraught at what was taking place.

Why is he doing this to me? Why? This ain't right. Who do he think he is? Her thoughts were bouncing off the walls as she stood frozen in her tracks. *I need to just leave him alone. I need to just stop dealing with him altogether.*

"Get the fuck on, Miss Goody-Goody. Go your ugly ass back home to your rich daddy!" Rico eased his zipper down, dropping his pants to the floor. Stroking his growing dick, he headed toward the bed, arrogant as ever. "I knew you ain't really love me. Now shut the door on your damn way out."

Seconds later, Keisha was speechless as her supposed man, Rico, had his head and shoulder-length dreadlocks buried deep in between the next woman's legs, making her moan the same way she did when he treated her to his unique head game. The room was spinning. She couldn't think clearly. She couldn't breathe.

I can't lose him! I can't! Oh my God! Oh my God! Oh my God! Why is he doing this to me? Desperate to keep Rico satisfied and his eight inches in her life, the shy-about-her-naked-body female stripped down to her bra and panties, joining her man's side. *If I don't do this, he might leave me. I can't lose him, but this is so wrong!* Before Keisha knew it, she'd taken Rico's place in between the girl's legs and was devouring her first taste of hot pussy. As Keisha licked away at the female's snatch, she caressed her legs and thighs, getting herself turned on. *Damn, her skin is so soft and smooth.*

It was not half as bad as she thought it was going to be. The originally skeptical Keisha was soon making the girl, whose name she still didn't know, squirm more than Rico had when he was eating the pussy. When Keisha felt the girl's legs clamp down around her neck, she increased the speed of her sucking on her clit and the force of her finger fucking her insides. Within seconds, she was tasting another female's juices drip down her chin.

After ultimately getting his way, Rico stood smugly over to the side, commanding both females, who'd never met before, to do every nasty thing he could think of. An hour or so in of watching them eating each other out, shoving every comb, brush and even a pair of unplugged flat irons inside of their hairy pussies, he wasn't done. Degradingly instructing Keisha to tongue-fuck his girl's asshole after she had shitted, Rico was feeling like he was the man. Throat-banging them both simultaneously, Rico finally couldn't take it anymore. Chills were vibrating his entire body.

"Yeah, I'm cumming, I'm cumming! Daddy about to bust!" Snatching his manhood away from the other chick's lips, he shot his hot, thick, streaming load directly in Keisha's face.

"Naw, you cum-thirsty ho. Close ya mouth. Don't swallow it," Rico urged, squirting every drop of nut out his dickhead then shaking the rest damn near in her eye. "Smear that shit on all them fucked-up-looking bumps of yours. Then maybe your skin can look as clear as her fine ass does." He dogged Keisha even further, giving the other female a sloppy kiss.

When he was completely satisfied in every sexually perverted way imaginable, Rico made Keisha go into her purse and give the female, who he finally announced was his baby mama, some money for herself, as well as some extra ends for his son.

"You ain't got no problem with me and her taking the truck and hanging out, do you?" Rico started getting dressed. "Because if you do . . ."

"Naw, Rico, naw, I don't mind." Scared of what he was gonna say next if she disagreed, Keisha kept her true emotions to herself. She was so in love with Rico and his mannish ways, nothing else mattered but him not breaking up with her.

"Good, that's daddy's big bitch!" He smacked her across her wide ass. "Now crawl your slutty, good-pussy-eating self up in the bed and go the fuck to sleep. I'll be back to hit that sloppy pussy some more later. Now tell me you love me."

"I love you, Rico."

Leaving Keisha alone in the sex-aroma-filled hotel room, Rico brazenly left with his son's mother, telling the woman who'd just hours earlier bailed him out of jail for cuffing up her father to also be ready to go shopping in the morning if she really loved him like she claimed she did.

Dumbly wrapped in the bed sheet that smelled like the next bitch who'd just left with her supposed man, Keisha did as she was told. Turned out by Rico's helluva eight-inch dick game and now, a strangely overwhelming thirst to eat some more pussy, she played with herself, imagining a female squatting over her face until she drifted off to sleep. That night might've been Keisha's first experience being with a female and having a three-some, but definitely not her last.

Bright and early, when Rico finally returned, Keisha was up, dressed, and ready to take her new "daddy" shopping.

Chapter Four

"Hey, bitch, you hear me talking to your faking ass." Callous in his intentions, Rico snatched a hold of Keisha's hair, drawing her once again back to reality. "Stop acting like you don't like all this early morning good dick I'm blessing you with." With brutal force, he threw her down on a pile of dirty clothes. "Move, Kilo! Get the fuck on!" he yelled at the pit bull that immediately rushed over, sniffing at Keisha's dripping wet cunt. "Maybe I'll let you get sloppy seconds on this slut again one day." Rico laughed, using his leg to kick the dog out his way. "But not this day."

"Stop, Rico! No, stop!" Keisha tried unsuccessfully to fight Rico from him climbing on top of her and continue getting his rocks off.

I let this bum nigga tear up my damn truck and have the cops knocking at my door. I know the hangup calls on the house phone are for him. Why am I being so stupid? Why?

"Rico, you hurting me. Now stop. I'm not playing. Stop!"

"Ease up on all that whining and treat daddy right before I get heated."

"You're not my damn daddy. You're nothing like him." Keisha thought about the several times throughout her ongoing rocky relationship with Rico she had tried to mend fences with her estranged parents. But her father was a man of his word. He ran his household with an iron fist. When he vowed not to have anything to do with his child as long as she was dealing with Rico Campbell, he meant it. Keisha's mother, weak-minded as her daughter, had no choice but to follow her husband's lead to keep the peace in her own household.

Sandy, the family chef and Keisha's friend and confidant, opened the rear door, allowing Keisha to sneak in and hopefully retrieve some of her personal items her father had been holding somewhat hostage. Time and time again, whenever she attempted to call the household to speak to him or knock on her own front door, Mr. Jackson's reaction was the same.

"If you're still dealing with that Rico Campbell character, you are still dead to me!"

Keisha couldn't blame her father. She knew repeatedly by Rico's mean-spirited actions, he was right. She was too good for him, but at this point, she was so far deep into the shady and perverted sexual world of pleasure, she didn't know which way to turn. Now, sex was like an addiction to her, and no matter what it took to climax, Keisha was with it.

"Oh, Keisha," Sandy sobbed, wiping her tears with an apron that hung from her plump frame. "I miss you so much."

"I miss you too, Sandy. And Mom—where is she?"

"Her and your dad is upstairs arguing about something. You know how he gets."

Keisha quickly flashed back on some of her parents long, heated, and verbally hurtful battles throughout the years. She felt immediate remorse for the pain her mother was probably suffering. Her father, the esteemed County Commissioner Jackson, looked good on paper to his constituents and the general public; however, behind closed doors, every family has some low-key bullshit within its confines. The Jackson family—mother, father, daughter, and even longtime chef, Sandy—were no exception.

"Yeah, Sandy, I know."

"Well, I gathered some of your favorite things Mr. Jackson put in storage or tried to throw away."

"Thank you, Sandy." Keisha hugged her always-sympathetic buddy. "You stay having my back no matter what, even when I was a kid."

Only thirteen years older than Keisha, Sandy had always been around since Keisha could remember. Her mother, now deceased, had been her father's household chef growing up, and Sandy, an excellent cook in her own right, carried on the tradition upon her mother's untimely death.

"Here, hurry and put them in this bag and leave before he comes. I'll try to sneak you more next week. Your father is going away to New Orleans then for a conference."

"On business? Is mother going?" Keisha peeked around the corner and up the long staircase, easily overhearing her father's loud tirade concerning her mother's use of sleeping pills and the fact that she was losing too much weight in all the wrong places.

"Keisha." Sandy gave her the side-eye, indicating not much had changed since she'd left home.

"Never mind, Sandy. I don't know why I even asked."

"Keisha, why don't you just leave that no-good boy alone and just come back home? I miss you so much, and so does your mother. She needs you. We both do." Trying her best to keep her voice down, Sandy filled Keisha in with as much family gossip and as many reasons as she could as to why she should abandon the idea of being with Rico and return home. Sandy knew life under Mr. Jackson's roof wasn't always pleasant, but it beat the alternative of being young, black, uneducated, and unemployed in Detroit.

"I can't, Sandy. I just can't." Keisha took a deep breath, reliving the horrors of all the sexually promiscuous acts she'd taken part in and continued to crave. "One day maybe—but not now. I have to get myself together first and prove to Daddy that I can make it on my own."

With an armful of her belongings in tow, some she hoped to pawn to pay the rent to "make it on her own," Keisha crept back into the kitchen area. Exchanging hugs with Sandy, almost out the door, she was surprisingly met by her father, who'd come down the back stairs.

"Oh, Daddy," she stammered. "I, I, I was . . . "

"Was what, Keisha?" He blocked the doorway, folding his arms. "What are you doing sneaking around this house? Who let you in here—Sandy?"

"Umm, umm . . . " Not wanting to confirm, throwing Sandy directly under the bus, Keisha stood mute.

Mr. Jackson hastily removed most of the stuff from his daughter's arms, setting them on the kitchen table. "Just where do you think you're going with all of these clothes?"

"Daddy, they're mine. I just wanted to . . . "

"First off, all of this stuff—" He pointed to the pile, nodding. "My money paid for. So, you taking them out my house and to that shack I heard you were now living in with that filth is not an option! And look at you!" He shook his head in utter disgust. "You look like an unkept ragamuffin. Your hair, your nails, those shoes . . . and it's beyond apparent you haven't been to the dermatologist since you started running with that boy! I should've prosecuted him!"

"Daddy, please." In tears and ashamed of her overall appearance, Keisha lowered her head. "I'm trying."

"We gave you everything a child could ever want or dream about, and you threw it all back in our face for some hooligan. Now get out of here and be thankful to your mother's begging I'm still allowing you to drive that truck that's still in my name." Mr. Jackson stepped out the way, holding the door open. "But believe you me, the very first time a payment is a day late, I'm going to have it voluntarily repossessed."

"Daddy, I thought you loved me. I thought I was your special girl. You always used to say that, didn't you?" Throwing her arms around her father's neck in hopes of an impromptu reconciliation, Keisha tightly held on.

Not budging an inch in his stern demeanor, he coldly pried his distraught daughter's hands off him. "Keisha, you heard me—go!" Mr. Jackson was irate, slamming the door shut, forcing his once-angel to stand on the other side, listening to him make Sandy verbally pay the tab for letting her inside.

She left that night empty handed, with nothing to pawn to help her pay the overdue bills. Rico, lazy, selfish and a dog, degraded Keisha even more, loaning her to a weed man for a night of his sexual pleasure in exchange for some cash and a half of an ounce. Feeling worthless and knowing her father's disappointment, Keisha went along with it—even somewhat welcoming some new, strange dick in her reckless, out-of-control life.

***

"You are not my daddy," Keisha repeated loudly.

Rico was amused at Keisha trying to all of a sudden grow a set of balls. "You right, Keisha, I ain't. 'Cause your daddy ain't shit but a fake wanna-be white motherfucker that tried to get a nigga hemmed up. He lucky I didn't go back out there and beat the piss outta his old punk ass then make your ugly mama suck me off."

"Fuck you, Rico."

"Naw, fuck you." He spit in her face like she meant no more to him than a piece of trash. Then he grabbed a hold of both her legs, pulling them apart. Dropping to his knees, he leaned over, stuffing all eight inches into her hole, then roughly went in. After three or four good hits to her guts, he stopped and stood to his feet.

With her blouse ripped wide open, her breasts displayed outside her lace bra, and her skirt hiked up to her stomach, her eyes rolled in the back of her head. Keisha physically felt like shit on a stick. Exhausted and defeated from the harsh pain of Rico's dick fucking her forcefully and raw every which way but loose, she wanted nothing more than to ball up on the floor and die. She hated the person who she'd now become and hated Rico even more for instigating her now overly promiscuous behavior.

"Please, Rico, I can't anymore," Keisha barely muttered through her dry lips. "I can't take this."

"You take what in the hell I say you take. How many times I gotta tell your dumb ass that?" Rico responded with his still very much rock hard cock in his hands. "And after I go take another leak, I want you to suck the nut out this motherfucker, then go get me some weed. A nigga need a blunt in his life."

The clock was ticking on the amount of verbal and physical abuse Keisha was willing to take from the man she once loved so much and was convinced that loved her. Lifting her arm and hand to touch her matted hair, she wiped Rico's spit off her face and his musty perspiration from her breasts. She tried to raise her body but couldn't find the strength. Wanting to get up and run out the room and even the house, for that matter, Keisha's body wouldn't allow her. Her legs were weak, and her inners felt like it was throbbing and irritated, yearning to be soaked in a bathtub of hot water.

Listening to the sounds of Rico pissing a few yards from where she was laying at and still talking cash shit about what he was gonna do to her next, Keisha turned her head into the pile of clothes, trying to drown out his annoying voice. Clutching a striped button-up she'd purchased for Rico some months back in what she thought were happier times, Keisha stared across the room. With his long, pinkish-red tongue hanging to the side of his mouth, Kilo's hairy face was staring back. Rico's forever present sidekick was anxious to get back at her moist but sore, purring pussy like Rico had allowed him to do one drunken night they partied with some of his boys, but wisely obeyed his master, staying away.

Hearing the toilet flush and footsteps coming, Keisha closed her eyes and braced up for more of Rico's sexual tirade. In the darkness, she remembered back in the days, when things were kinda good and Rico kinda treated her nicely—that was until he got angry. When he'd get pissed off, he was out of control.

Chapter Five

The Valentine's Day Soul to the Bone concert featuring, Robin Thicke, Brandy, and Fantasia was right around the corner. It was being held at the Fox Theater. Rico and Keisha had been planning on the outfits they were gonna wear for over two weeks. If a Negro in Detroit was gonna show out, gatored up, mink to the ground, bad bitch on his arm, the famed Fox Theater was where it all went down. With Keisha being the only one working to pay bills for the small house they'd rented and Rico spending every spare dollar she made on weed, getting his high-priced layaway out was more than a notion.

Thankfully, Keisha's mother had sympathetically snuck out most of her expensive clothes, including a few mink jackets and a pair of custom-made high-top gator boots from the house she once called home. For Keisha, thick, big-boned or not, her having something to wear the night of the concert really wasn't a problem. She could go into the archives in her closet and still be one of the best dressed of the night.

However, jean-sagging, Timbo-wearing, I-wanna-drink-and-smoke-all-day-and-fuck-random-hoes Rico couldn't. Not accustomed to anything but running the Detroit streets and acting a straight fool, he wasn't interested in going outside of his element. He'd proven that character flaw early on in their relationship at Keisha's parents' home. The majority balance of the layaway belonged to Rico but was automatically Keisha's responsibility. If she wanted to go to the concert and have any part of a good time, she knew she had to make sure her man looked as good as, if not better than, her and every other Negro and trick that walked through the doors of the theater.

"Didn't I tell you not to wear that gaudy jacket?" Jealous he didn't have a fur to rock, Rico practically ripped Keisha's lightweight mink bomber off her back, throwing it in the corner of the bedroom. "You trying to upstage a nigga or what? Is that how you doing it now?"

"Naw, Rico, it ain't nothing like that. I was just trying to look good for you." She followed him into the living room.

"Yeah, right." Resting his foot on the arm of the couch, Rico rubbed a cloth across his big block gators Keisha had slaved hours at her job to be able to purchase. "Your horny freak ass probably on the prowl for some strange pussy to suck on, ain't you?"

He eased behind his woman, knowing if they both played their cards right, they could hook up with some freak tricks at the concert to get down with. Rico had plenty bitches on his line, but it turned him on the most to have his main chick, Keisha, go out and bring him some new ass to run up in. He wasn't into swinging, but more into just getting off on the power that came with making his sexual partners do exactly what in the hell he said.

Rico was serious about his body, staying in the gym working out. An old head from around the way schooled him back in the day that even if you dead broke, pockets on empty, a woman, whether she was pretty or not, would take care of a dude that took care of his body. Crunches, sit-ups, and keeping his locs well maintained; Rico still had random females dropping bread on him. Most knew he lived with Keisha, but some didn't. But the one thing that all the females he banged had in common was that they didn't care one way or the other, as long as Rico kept dicking them down with the eight inches he had in between his legs. It was no shame in his game. Rico Campbell would beat it up and eat it up.

Since the months they'd been together, he'd easily fucked at least fifteen or twenty pounds off Keisha. She'd transformed into a brick house, body-wise, and got more than enough attention and complements on her plump ass. Yet, her complexion—no amount of nut she constantly got shot in her face, no matter from what different dick it came from, was helping. She was still a "blocker," meaning from a block away, she was a dime.

The night of the concert, Rico was looking like a bag of hundreds, and Keisha, with the weight she'd lost in all the right spots, looked like a dime in her own right. As heads turned to watch the seemingly hood rich couple, a set of familiar eyes locked with Keisha as well as Rico.

"Oh, hell naw."

"Oh my God, Rico. Is that my father?"

"Hell fucking yeah. What in the hell his old, fake ass doing here?"

"He's on the Restoration Board for the Downtown Detroit Empowerment Zone. He attends most of the events held in this area." Keisha caught a glimpse of herself in one of the many beveled mirrors that lined the alcove. "I used to come with him."

As a small crowd of other politicians and concertgoers tried to get pictures taken with their elected officials surrounded Commissioner Jackson, Keisha struggled to keep her eyes on her father's exact whereabouts.

"Look at that dude over there acting like he own this motherfucker! I should—"

"Damn, Rico. Leave it alone and be thankful he didn't press charges that day you bugged out!"

"Is you back on blaming me again?" Rico turned his attention to Keisha, who was practically standing on her tiptoes and jumping upward to see where her dad had disappeared to and if she could maybe see her mother and at least say hello. "Hey, bitch. Do you hear me talking to you?"

Embarrassed by the loud, insulting tone and nature of Rico's voice, Keisha tried her best to get him to shut up before they drew any more unwanted attention than they were receiving. "I'm sorry, baby, please!"

Out of nowhere, Keisha's friend Kim walked up. "Hey, girl, I didn't know you were coming! Damn, you looking good."

"Hey, Kim. What's going on?"

"Nothing much. Down here getting my shine on." She flossed, flaunting her new weave and tight-fitting dress. "I see you shining too, in spite of—"

Knowing Kim was referring to him by her sour expression, Rico blasted her. "Damn, a lot of horses had to die for that fucked-up mop on your head."

"What?" Kim fired back, ready to go to war. "Listen, hood filth, I ain't the one."

"Man, get your Big-Bird ass the fuck outta here."

"Rico, please." Keisha tried to intervene, but Kim was on a roll.

"Negro, you got her fooled, but not me. But trust your days are numbered."

"Oh, you threatening me, bitch? You trying to carry it like that?"

Acting as if she was looking at a watch, Kim raised her wrist. "Tick-tock, broke Negro, tick tock!"

"Broke? Ho, I'm about to come the fuck up."

"Boy, bye." Kim waved her hand, dismissing Rico's wishful claims. "The only way you gonna come up is you hit the lottery off one of them thousands of stupid numbers you got Keisha's low-self-esteem behind playing for you every day."

"Yeah, right. Don't hate on my girl 'cause she got a good thang. Bitch, just say you just want some of this good dick right here Keisha done told you about! Don't front." He yanked downward on his manhood. "With your lonely, funny-built ass."

"Lonely? Never that." Kim looked herself up and down. "Look, you wanna-be player, I fucks with men. Grown-ass men with something going on for themselves. Men with more than a blunt and a forty on their agenda."

Before things got further out of control, thankfully, Swazy interrupted them. Dressed in black pants and a red polo shirt with the word *valet* stitched across the right side of his chest, Rico wasted no time clowning his best friend.

"Yo, what up, doe, slave boy?" Rico teased, popping Sway's collar for him. "What's the deal?"

"Nigga, it ain't nothing. Down here making that bread while you spending yours."

"Mine?" Rico sarcastically bragged, putting his arm around Keisha, who rolled her eyes almost to the top of her head. "Why work for something if you can get it for free?"

"Well, whoever's," Sway replied, taking notice of how much Keisha had transformed since the day he'd first seen her at the park.

"Hey now, Keisha," Swazy greeted her. "How you doing tonight? And how are you?" He also acknowledged Kim, who he hadn't seen since the day he clowned her, Keisha, and their other overweight friends.

"We good," they both answered.

"Yo, girl, how you put up with this fool?" He pushed at Rico's shoulder.

"I know, right?" Keisha smartly replied as people started to stare for all the wrong reasons.

"Bitch, shut the fuck up!"

"Rico, why you so rude?"

"Why you so ugly?"

"What?"

"You heard me, Keisha. All that makeup ain't helping hide them bumps and that face! Don't fool yourself. You still one ugly trick. You just got a fat ass!"

"Damn, dawg, calm down. You tripping."

Rico picked up on Swazy giving his girl the once over and decided to teach her a lesson in getting smart with him out in public.

She wanna act all tough 'cause her old dude here. Yeah, all right.

"You's right, dude. My bad. But come here and let me holler at you for a minute."

Relived Rico was out of her face, she tried to find her father. Scanning the theater, he nor her mother were anywhere in sight. *Damn*, she thought, knowing she'd possibly missed an opportunity to reconcile. *They gone.*

"Keisha, why you let him talk to you like that? Are you crazy or what?"

"I know Kim, but—"

"But my ass! You a fool!"

"I know, I know, but have you seen my father and mother tonight? My dad was just over there."

Before Kim could answer, Rico returned to Keisha's side, causing Kim, still very much caught in her emotions, to walk away from the couple without even saying bye.

The rest of the night at The Fox Theater, thankfully, went on without Rico bugging out anymore. The concert was wonderful, and so was the overpriced restaurant dinner Keisha paid for afterward. The fact that the couple hadn't found a stray female to come home with them still didn't put a damper on Rico's sudden unusually good spirits. But that was only because he had a back-up plan in place, one that Keisha didn't know about but soon would.

Once-good-girl Keisha had been involved in all types of over-the-top sexual acts since becoming linked with Rico: threesomes, foursomes, toys, taking it in the ass— which once required her getting stitches—role playing, getting fucked with household objects, and even having three dicks inside her at once, but little did she know this night was going to be way over the top, even for Rico.

"That was fun, wasn't it?" Keisha kicked off her shoes, plopping down on the couch. Slowly, she started to rub her sore feet. "We need to go out more often. I just wish I could've talked to my parents."

"What the fuck ever." Rico was already buzzing from the cheap wine at the concert and a few shots of Remy VSOP at the restaurant. Blazing up a blunt he'd just rolled, Rico was gonna be on one real soon and feeling extra nice. "Check this out. Keisha, don't get too comfortable. I got company falling through, and need you to look out."

Keisha knew what he meant by "look out," and wasn't in the mood, especially after being deliberately snubbed by her father. "Naw, Rico, I'm tired. I worked all day, then the concert. I'm about done."

"What?" Rico coughed several times from hitting the intoxicating weed. "Hold tight. I know your ass ain't talking back, is you? Is that how we doing it now? What, you acting funny since you seen your daddy?"

Keisha gave Rico a long, cold, hard stare. She might've been with them getting some wild freak shit to jump off earlier in the night, but now she was truly exhausted, physically and mentally. Eating one of the many females' pussies that Rico insisted in cheating on her with, or letting his boy hit it, was not on her agenda for the rest of the night.

"Look, I'm going to bed. I gotta be at work at seven thirty tomorrow. You know I don't even have ninety days yet, so they looking for a reason not to hire me in. And as for my father, don't start."

Rico wasn't trying to hear what Keisha was saying. The fact that her job was the one thing that helped pay the bills and keep a roof over their heads meant nothing to him. Sure, he'd make a little bit of extra money selling weed that Keisha had to purchase for him from jump, but he'd spend that hanging out with his buddies at the local strip club or smoke up all the profit. If she lost this job, Rico would just sit back and wait till she got another one. Them being evicted wasn't an option for Keisha, since she couldn't go home to her family as long as she was with him. And since Rico knew she wasn't about to leave him, he was tight.

"Stop whining. You heard what I said, didn't you? Now, go in there, take a damn shower, and scrub that dead fish smell off your pussy. Swazy and his cousin A.J. from down South is on they way over. I know you ain't trying to make me look bad in front of those dudes, is you?"

"Naw, but—"

"Look, Keisha, stop stalling and go. Damn!"

"What if I say no?"

"What if I come over there and knock the shit outta you? How about that?"

"You straight foul, Rico," she mumbled, not brave enough to say it any louder.

"Say what?" Momentarily he stopped smoking.

"Nothing." Keisha could tell by the expression on Rico's face he wasn't in the mood to be defied. She'd given into his every sexual whim for months on end, no matter how perverted or over the top, so now he was spoiled. Not wanting to get her ass jumped on again and risk showing up at work with yet another black eye or busted lip, she headed toward the bathroom, slamming the flimsy door behind her.

"I don't give a fuck if you knock that motherfucker off the hinges, you dumb bitch. That's just one more thing you gotta pay for to get fixed, so go ahead and do you."

Chapter Six

Swazy and his cousin, both buzzing, arrived. Even though Swazy still thought Keisha was tore up in the face, that still didn't stop him from hitting the pussy, especially since it was free. In their world, the only shit better than new pussy was free pussy. After introducing Rico to his family, Swazy made himself at home. He and A.J. both sat on the couch and smoked a dime bag of weed they'd brought with them. Grabbing the remote, Rico turned on the television to the twenty-four-hour video channel. With the loud banging sounds of the music flowing throughout the house, he excused himself to go see what was taking Keisha so long to come out and greet their guests.

"Damn, girl, what you in here doing?" He pushed the bedroom door all the way open. "I know good and well you heard Swazy and his cousin come in!"

Wrapped in a pink bath towel, with tears flowing down her face, Keisha looked up at Rico, hoping for some sort of a reprieve from what he'd planned for her. Sensing nothing but coldness in his eyes, she spoke.

"Rico, I can't. Please, baby. I've got a headache."

"So what else is new?" He laughed. "You always got a headache, so stop fronting. I done told you what was up before these niggas even got here, so why you stuck up in here tripping? Bring that fat ass of yours out front."

"But . . . " She tried one last time, pressing the palm of her hand on her forehead.

"Okay, Keisha. I'm about five seconds from breaking my foot straight off in your ass! Now come the fuck on. I'm not bullshitting."

Rejoining Swazy and an anxious A.J. in the living room, Rico reassured them that the party was definitely still on and popping. Five minutes later, still wrapped in a towel, Keisha shyly came out the bedroom and sat down in the chair, practically on Rico's lap. She'd got down with Swazy before, so she knew what he was about in the dick and tongue department, but his big, country-fed cousin looked like he was ready to rip the frame outta her ass.

"Hey, Keisha. What up, doe?" Swazy blew the smoke from a Newport in the air. "You good?"

Wanting to say "fuck naw" and get the hell out her house, Keisha knew better and just shook her head.

"Hey, girl. How you doing?" A.J. couldn't help but noticed the huge backside Keisha was working with. Used to females down South being blessed with a nice-size ass, he automatically got excited, knowing what to expect. "Damn, shawty, you looking real sexy-like over there in that towel." He licked his lips and gripped up on his growing manhood in anticipation of what he knew was about to jump off. "You don't mind me saying so, do you, partner?" he asked Rico out of common courtesy, not wanting to overstep his boundaries.

Rico, feeling like a boss, was amused. "Come on now, A.J. You's family now, my dude. Trust, me and Swazy is like this." He crossed his fingers. "We tight. We share and share alike—don't we, nigga?"

Swazy, who was focused on the video playing, barely looked away from the screen. "Yeah, fool, sharing is our middle name."

"Yeah, well, I showl hope your girl feel the same way about sharing. Do you, Keisha?" A.J. smiled, showing off his gold tooth.

Tightening her towel, Keisha didn't answer. She just took a deep breath, wanting the night to be over so she could get to sleep and hopefully make it to work on time.

Almost throwing her off his lap, Rico roughly nudged her in the ribs. "Keisha, you hear that nigga asking you a question. I know you ain't deaf."

Keisha could tell by the harsh tone in Rico's voice that he was going to a place in his mind she didn't want him to go. Making him mad would only make it worse, so she gave up fighting the inevitable and went with the flow.

"Naw, I don't care about sharing, I guess." She faintly grinned.

"Well, stop fronting and go on over there and get them knees dirty for my manz." Rico stood to his feet, pushing Keisha in the middle of her back. "Make him feel at home up in this motherfucker."

A.J.'s dick was already rock hard and standing at attention. Eager to get right to it, he leaned back on the couch, getting comfortable. "Is y'all sure y'all want a brotha to go first?"

Rico took the pack of cigarettes off the coffee table and lit one. Throwing the lighter to the side, he shrugged his shoulders and laughed. "Dawg, company first. Don't worry. My girl good to go for all of us. Ain't that right, Keisha?"

On her knees in front of a more-than-ready-to-get-some-head A.J., Keisha glanced over at Rico and snarled at what he was making her do.

"I said ain't that right, Keisha?" Rico blew the smoke from the Newport extra hard.

"Yes," she replied, untying the string on A.J.'s track pants and removing his huge, country-size pole. He had at least a good half an inch on Rico's dick. Her eyes grew wide.

"Yes what, ho?" Rico was trying to play the big-fella role, especially when he noticed the enormous size of A.J.'s dick and for the first time felt a little inadequate.

Before Keisha could answer, "Yes, daddy," she was taking all of A.J. down her throat with complete ease. When she had first got with Rico, she was somewhat of an amateur in the sex department, scared to touch the dick, let alone be aggressive. However, now gifted, Keisha went in. Slurping, licking, sucking, head bobbing from the left to the right and the right to the left, she had their country guest in a daze, almost speaking in tongues. Not being able to sit still, A.J. raised his lower body off the couch to meet each deep gulp Keisha now happily took.

She was easily gaining the attention of Swazy with her skills. He stood to his feet, dropping his own pants. With Rico looking on, secretly pissed at the way "his woman" seemed to be enjoying sucking A.J. off, Swazy snatched the towel from around a thick-boned Keisha. Watching her wide ass bounce up and down and jiggle while she swallowed his cousin's dick, Swazy got down on his knees behind her. With one hand balanced on her protruding dunk, he used the other to guide his stiff meat down Keisha's crack. All into it, Keisha reached her hand backward and started to finger her own wet, hairy snatch.

Swazy's dick grew harder as the veins started to bulge. Sensing what he wanted from past experiences, Keisha then used both hands to reach back and spread her cheeks wide open. Not being able to stand it any longer, Swazy gladly accepted the invitation, shoving his throbbing, helmet-shaped dick head into her asshole. With as much force as he could, Swazy tried to ram through to the other side.

Keisha didn't care, still holding her cheeks open so Swazy could keep handling his business. Every time Swazy went in harder from the rear, it made her take even more of A.J.'s blessing without so much as gagging.

A.J. didn't miss Keisha using her hands to stroke him, because she was throat-fucking him royally. Every few seconds, in his Southern swagged-out voice, he would yell out she was the best he'd ever had. And Swazy, who never really wanted Rico to get with her in the first place, was also screaming out Keisha's praises.

The cousins talking shit seemed to fuel her to get even more buck wild with it, throwing her ass up higher in the air for Swazy's pleasure while burying her head deeper on A.J.'s dick.

With all three of them apparently in their own freaky world, rhythmically banging to the beat of the video now playing on television, Rico got heated, feeling left out the loop and questioning Keisha's loyalty to him. Sitting back in his favorite chair, he tried his best to mask his contempt for Swazy, A.J., and especially Keisha. He couldn't care less about the fact that what was taking place in front of his eyes was all set in motion thanks to him.

Who these cornball motherfuckers think they are, getting wild up in this bitch? And this goofy broad acting all the fuck in for this country Bama nigga, with his gold-tooth-having ass! Infuriated, ready to bug out, Rico had enough game about his self to keep his fronts up. It was no way in hell he was gonna let any of them see him sweat even though he felt some sort of way. *I swear I'ma beat the brakes off this stankin' bitch when they leave!*

He got up to go to the bathroom, but the trio never noticed Rico's absence. Standing in the mirror, Rico turned on the cold water in the sink. Cupping both hands together, he bent down, splashing his face. Hoping the water would help snap him back on his game, he used a hand towel to dry off before re-entering the living room where Keisha, his longtime meal ticket, was being cum drained by his best friend and his random-ass country relative.

Relieved they'd all finally had enough, Rico resumed trying to be a puppetmaster no sooner than Swazy called out, "I'm about to bust" for the second time.

"Hey—y'all niggas hungry or what? 'Cause I can have her hook us up some yard bird."

Exhausted and about ready to pass out from pleasing his boys, Keisha shot Rico a *damn you, nigga* look that A.J. and Swazy both easily picked up on. Having just been served some of the best, freakiest no-strings-attached free sex they'd both recently encountered, the cousins were ready to bounce.

"Naw, dawg—we good. We can just grab something at the Coney." Swazy disappeared into the bathroom to wash his shit-covered dick.

"Man, I can't say y'all city boys don't know how to offer a dude some good, down home Southern hospitality." A.J. leered at Keisha as she bent over, picking the pink bath towel off the floor. "Shit, if I had a girl back home that was that official on her head game like Ms. Keisha, I might fuck around and wife the shawty!"

Seeing Keisha wink at A.J. and him smile, showing that damn gold tooth, Rico felt some sort of way once again. "Yo, Keisha, take your good-dick-slurping ass into that kitchen and hook up some grub!"

Snatching at her forearm, Rico dragged her into the other room, pushing her up against the refrigerator. "Just what in the fuck is you doing out there? I told your hard-headed ass to serve my boys up, not flirt."

"But . . . "

"But what? What you about to say to get your ass kicked now?"

Keisha looked into Rico's weed-induced red eyes and decided to quit while she was ahead. She knew with him, there was no winning. So instead, she wrapped her towel extra tight and took out a bag of wingdings to deep fry. With stinging carpet burns on each kneecap, she begrudgingly started to prepare the late-night meal.

"Hey, y'all sit back and chill out. Old girl in there hooking us up on the food tip, some chicken and fries." Rico regained his composure, going back into the living room, handing his boy and A.J. both cans of ice cold Red Bull and a small bottle of Ciroc.

Swazy and his cousin were both sitting on the couch with their heads laid back. Rico, who had not participated in the fuck-fest, was the only one in the house that was full of energy. Throwing in a DVD, they were only ten minutes or so into *Belly* before A.J. was knocked out, snoring like he was at home. Swazy was fighting to keep his eyes open. Rico wanted them to know that the double-teaming gangbang they'd just put down on his woman meant nothing. He had to keep the party going at least until the chicken was done cooking and at least until he proved to them he was the boss. The fact that he made Keisha give it up to them simultaneously was not enough.

Having finished all the weed he had and also the bag they brought, Rico suggested they run a few blocks over to cop a bag to blow so they'd be extra hungry.

"Come on, dawg, that shit right around the way." Rico finally convinced Swazy to get up from the spot he was posted in since coming back from the bathroom.

"Yeah, all right, dude. I guess a nigga can smoke a little bit more, 'cause that chicken is smelling good as a fuck! And I am in the mood to smash some shit," Swazy remarked, glancing over at his still sleeping cousin. "Yo, let me wake this giant motherfucker up! His ass been on that Greyhound all day bringing that work up here, and after that shit Keisha laid on him, I know he about done."

Standing by the kitchen door, Rico saw that Keisha, still wrapped in the towel, was only half done frying the chicken and had yet to even drop the fries into the skillet. "Swazy, man, let that big-ass Bama nigga sleep. We'll be back before he even know we was gone."

Barefoot, constantly re-wrapping the pink bath towel around her sore body, Keisha was beyond tired. It was undoubtedly one of the longest nights in her young life. She continued to cook as Rico demanded.

I'm sick of this bullshit life. I just wanna go home. I don't know why I'm letting myself be caught up in this lifestyle. Dealing with Rico is way more of a liability to me than an asset!

Tearing the plastic bag of frozen fries open, she dropped the entire contents into hot grease. Stepping back so she wouldn't get popped, she was suddenly met by A.J. Now standing backward in his arms, Keisha felt something strange come over her. It was the same feeling she had when she sucked her boss and his wife off for the hell of it. It was also the same feeling that took over her body and mind when she let the Comcast man tie her up with black cable cord and bang her with a remote. None of those times or numerous more was Rico making her get her freak on; she was just turned out on getting off by any means necessary.

"Damn, girl, you in here throwing down like you was raised in the South. Let me find out you a country girl at heart. I might take you home in my suitcase," he joked, massaging her shoulders.

A.J.'s Southern swag was overwhelming, and Keisha felt at total ease. Her adrenalin rose, and her heart started to race. She didn't speak or say a word. Slowly, she seductively turned around, stood on her tiptoes, and slid her tongue in A.J.'s mouth, moving it around like a snake toying with its prey. Keisha soon felt his oversized hands grope both of her ass cheeks through the towel.

"Damn, shawty, it's like that?"A.J. felt her up.

"I guess so." Keisha devilishly smiled.

With the intense heat radiating from the deep fryer and the skillet, the two of them acted as if they were some star-crossed lovers in some sort of low-budget black made-for-DVD flick instead of two strangers that'd just met and had some freaked-out sexual experience minutes earlier. Exchanging spit, it was not long before A.J., strong as two bears, lifted Keisha up in his arms, sitting her down on the kitchen cabinet. Being thick as Keisha always was, Rico, although strong, was not strong enough or maybe just not that into her, to risk throwing his back out to pick her up. Rico was all about pleasing himself, not a female. That was, unless he was running game.

Pushing a loaf of bread, a bag of rice, and a few cans of green beans out the way, A.J. caressed Keisha's plump titties and sucked her inner thighs before diving full-faced in between her legs. Licking her already swollen and sensitive clit like it was a Popsicle, then eating her out like it was a huge plate of homemade grits and gravy that he was accustomed to, A.J. never once let up till he felt the hot cream flow from her hole and coat his lips. Mesmerizing Keisha even more by once again kissing her inner thighs, he smiled, feeling her tremble in ecstasy and her body collapse on the counter.

"Look, li'l mama." Conniving in thought, he grinned, coming up for air. "A bad-ass female like you need to leave that piece of shit buster you with and upgrade. Join up with my crew and me. We making that bread down South! Niggas I know would really put some money in your pocket—a few racks a week. Ask Swazy what's good with me. He'll tell you how we get down in the Dirty."

Keisha realized A.J. thought she was no more than a mere prostitute and was trying to recruit her to whatever he had going on down South. A normal female would be insulted, but now a freak to her heart, she found it flattering and a testament to her head game skills.

Moments later, they were interrupted by the sounds of Rico and Swazy coming back into the house. This accompanied the need for Keisha to take the chicken out of the fryer. Jumping down off the countertop, Keisha quickly tightened her towel. Using the spatula, she started to remove the chicken, placing each piece on a strainer to drain any excess grease. A.J., not knowing the true extent of her fear of Rico, stayed in the kitchen, admiring Keisha's voluptuous shape. He had no idea whatsoever, especially since Rico had just allowed him and his cousin Swazy to hit it, that Rico was heated.

"Oh, you up, huh?" Rico asked A.J. while giving Keisha, who was looking suspect, the evil eye. "What, you helping my girl cook now or what?"

"Yeah, man, I'm up. Shit, I don't even remember dozing off. I guess a nigga was more tired than I thought." A.J. was making it more than clear he wanted more of what Keisha had in between her legs and that out-of-the-ordinary head game she was working with. "Ya girl wore me out."

Rico barely cracked a smile, adjusting his gun in his waistband and tying his dreads up in a bun. Keisha did all she could to take his mind off tripping.

"The food is ready. You want me to fix your plate and bring it to you?"

"Naw, bitch, I ain't fucking hungry no more." Rico spazzed, caught deep in his emotions, on the verge of snapping. "You can leave the shit on the stove, or better yet, throw it the fuck away. Give that shit to Kilo."

Swazy knew his best friend and could tell he was about to nut up. Without bothering to split or twist up the bag they'd just went half on, Swazy told his cousin they were about to just be out. "Yeah, Rico, me and cuz about to head back around the way to the weed spot. It looked like them fools 'bout to get a serious-ass dice game going on."

"Oh yeah," A.J. interjected, pulling a knot out his pocket, staring at Keisha, who was grinning on the sly. "Maybe I need to get down on that shit. After all, tonight damn straight seem like it's my lucky motherfucking night! What you think, Keisha?" He bragged, now seeming full of energy.

Rico immediately peeped game and walked over, smacking Keisha to the ground on point and principal. As she lay on the floor, holding the side of her face, A.J. started to come to her aid but promptly stopped due to his cousin.

"Naw, dude, don't get involved in they dumb shit! A slut like her ain't worth the trouble. If she ain't like that type of shit, she'd break out!" he sensibly suggested, grabbing him back by his arm.

"Yeah, well . . . " A.J.'s country captain-save-a-ho upbringing made him despise to see a woman abused, unless, of course, it was by his huge ten inches.

With appreciation in her eyes for A.J. even caring, despite Swazy's cruel words, Keisha wished they would just stay to prolong whatever Rico had in store for her. Swazy, however, wasted no time heading for the front door, shoving A.J. outside onto the porch.

"Naw, cuzzo, leave that shit alone and get in the car. I done told you her crazy ass off into that fool Rico. You think it's just by chance me and you got to freak the bitch tonight? Hell naw! That nigga be having that bird do all type of wild, off-the-meter madness and flat out, she be with it."

A few seconds later, Swazy was pulling away from the curb with A.J riding shotgun, still worried about Keisha's well-being.

"Just what in the fuck was y'all doing while I was gone?" Rico stood towering over Keisha, ready to hit her again.

"Nothing, Rico, I swear." Keisha was lying through her teeth but would say just about anything not to get smacked once more. "I was in the kitchen cooking the chicken. He had just come in the doorway when you and Swazy came back. I promise. I swear."

Drawing his sneaker back with malice, he kicked her dead in the left side of her ribs. "Why I don't believe your good slick-talking ass, huh?"

"Urggg . . . " She tucked her body into a ball to protect herself from Rico's assault. The towel she was wrapped in came loose.

"What in the fuck?" Rico leaned down, snatching the towel all the way off, leaving Keisha buck-asshole-naked in the middle of the living room floor. "Open your legs," he demanded, using his foot to open them for her. "What in the fuck is all that?"

Whimpering in excruciating pain, Keisha couldn't get the words out of her mouth. *What is he talking about? Dang!* repeated over and over in her confused thoughts. *What now? What did I do wrong?*

"You and that Bama was fucking while we was gone!" Rico exploded, dragging Keisha, naked, across the floor by one leg, causing carpet burns on her ass to match the ones already on her knees. "You think I'm stupid or what?"

"No, Rico! No!" she painstakingly screamed out. This time, she was telling the truth. She hadn't actually had sex with A.J. Yeah, she'd gave him some head in the living room while Swazy hit her off in the ass, but as far as A.J. getting the pussy, it didn't go down.

What is he talking about? Damn, what now?

"Don't *no* me, bitch! You lying! Look at that bullshit! You think a nigga blind or what?" Rico spit on her, which was a bad habit he'd now made regular. "You gave that big, goofball nigga my pussy without my permission in my motherfucking house!"

Confused, knowing Rico wasn't looking through the kitchen window to see what went down, Keisha replayed what truly jumped off between her and A.J.

Hell naw! Throughout the commotion, she wasted no time remembering she and him didn't bang. Yeah, his tall, country ass returned the favor of some head, but as big as his dick was, she'd remember having the pleasure of having all that meat stuffed inside of her.

"I didn't have sex with him, Rico, I swear. I promise I didn't." She crawled into the corner of the room, using the entertainment center as refuge from his attack.

Having had enough of her playing games, Rico disappeared into the kitchen, coming back out with the now unplugged, still very much hot deep fryer.

"Okay, Keisha. I'm done fucking around with you. Now, I'ma ask you one last time."

She had mentally suffered over the past few months and had been terrified of the physical abuse he'd often put her through, but nothing could compare to what he was about to do. "Please, Rico, don't! Don't!" Finding the courage to get to her feet, she tried to run toward the front door.

With hot chicken grease splattering out onto the floor from the fryer, he recklessly chased behind her. "You must think this shit a joke." He blocked the doorway as she defensively used her hands and arms to cover both bare breasts and her face. "And seriously don't try to keep running or I'm gonna throw all this shit right on your goddamn back."

Frozen out of fear of Rico keeping his word, Keisha stood motionless, not daring to move and not saying a word.

"I see all them hickeys between your legs! Now, how that shit get there . . . space fucking magic?" Rico set the fryer on the dining room table. "You wanna explain?"

Hickeys? Keisha puzzled. *Oh my God!* It then dawned on her that A.J. must've left some marks on her legs while he was sucking on her thighs. "Rico, wait, wait, let me explain!"

"You fucked that monkey while me and Swazy was gone, didn't you? You gave him the pussy." Rico yoked her up by her throat, infuriated and feeling insecure about the size of A.J.'s dick in comparison to his, causing her toes to barely touch the carpet. "Tell the truth, bitch, and don't lie. I'm warning you." He reached both hands up to her neck.

Trying to break Rico's strong grip, Keisha decided to confess what she and A.J. had done "Listen, listen, please!" She clawed at his fingers, gasping for air, struggling to speak. "I didn't have sex with him. The only thing I did is let him eat my pussy. I promise. That's all."

Rico finally had the answer he was looking for and let her go. "I knew that shit. That lame, nothing-ass nigga." He balled up his fist, punching Keisha dead in the stomach. With her bent over gasping, he walked on the other side of the room with a strange expression on his face.

Keisha, naked and bewildered, reached her hand up on the wall to steady herself. "Please, Rico, don't! I love you!"

"Bitch, please. You don't love nobody but your damn self! Running around here, giving niggas the pussy in my crib as if it ain't shit. Damn. And you really think that shit gonna be all good, huh?" Opening the bag he and Swazy had just copped, he rolled a blunt.

A terrified-to-move Keisha watched, not knowing what to do next. After blazing up and hitting it twice, he let the blunt hang between his lips as he went over to the back door. Taking the chain off and unlocking the two deadbolts, he pushed the black iron gate open.

"Kilo, Kilo . . . here boy." He whistled.

What is he doing? I need to get away!

Keisha tried running into the bedroom and locking the door but couldn't in time. Rico was on her trail, with Kilo now barking beside him. Not having to use much force, he thrust the door open. Raising his arm, he backhanded Keisha, causing her to fall across their bed. Watching her cry while still trying to explain, he grabbed both her legs, dragging her to the end of the mattress.

"Don't move, bitch, or I swear I'll kill you." Swinging the closet door open, he took out a handful of belts. "Move, Kilo—move!" He kicked at the dog, which was under foot. Connecting two belts into one, he used them to tie Keisha's legs open on each footpost.

Taking his gun out of his waistband, Rico set it on top of the dresser, prompting Keisha to believe he was going to kill her for real this time.

"Rico, please, please, please! Don't shoot me, Rico, don't," she pleaded, raising up, trying to stop him. Instantly, his fist met her in her left eye and another backhand.

"Shoot you? Come on now, trick. You ain't worth my bullets," Rico proclaimed as she lay bruised and battered. "I got something better in store for your non-loyal ass. Something you'll never forget."

With Keisha's legs stretched out, Rico leaned over, taking the lamp off the nightstand. Removing the teal-colored shade, tossing it to the side, he clicked on the light.

"That shit you did was real fucked up." Holding the bright, heated bulb near Keisha's lower body, he could easily see the passion marks A.J. had obviously left along with her swollen cunt. "You and that nigga got me twisted. I let him get some head, and as soon as I was gone, y'all played me like I ain't shit." Rico was yelling as saliva spewed out. "Well, guess what, slut? Since your slick ass like head so much, I'm about to hook you up."

"Rico, I'm sorry," she pleaded as he set the lamp back on the nightstand. "Please, baby, I'm sorry."

"Sorry for what? That you played me as soon as my back was turned?"

"I'm sorry I let him do that."

"Yeah, right, Keisha. Who you playing mind games with? You liked that bullshit."

"No. I swear I didn't."

"Whatever, bitch. I know you a freak."

"Rico, please. I'm sorry. I'm sorry. I was just in the kitchen cooking."

"Yeah, right, then all of a sudden his head just managed to slip between your legs."

"It wasn't like that, Rico. I swear it wasn't like that."

"You wanna embarrass a nigga so bad and disrespect me all over getting that stankin' cat licked? Well, I got something real proper for that ass."

Re-lighting his blunt, he called Kilo over to the edge of the bed. Grabbing him by the collar, he led his nose and mouth to Keisha's exposed cunt. Within no time, Kilo was going in on the pussy. Using his long, pink-and-red tongue, he slurped up and down from the top of her clit to her open asshole. She had not taken a shower after sexing Swazy and A.J.. Kilo licked both of their scents off Keisha's shaking body. She was scared the animal was going to eat her pussy whole and tried not to move despite the strange, demented pleasure she was starting to feel.

Rico knew his woman and knew what kind of facial expressions she'd make when she was really into it. *This ho feeling this freaked-out bullshit!* Sitting back with his iPhone, recording the whole tripped-out thing, he started coaching her from the sideline.

"You like that shit, don't you, Keisha? Don't you?"

"Nooo . . . " She moaned, desperately trying to fight the feeling. "Please, Rico, make him stop."

"Yes you do, bitch. Don't lie." He inhaled more of the blunt, bugging out on Kilo going in like a porno star getting paid. "You like his ass licking that stankin' motherfucker. Say it, Keisha. Say it. I can tell. I know you."

In denial, biting the side of her hand as her toes curled was the only thing keeping Keisha from yelling out "Yes!" The more Kilo sucked, licked, and tongue-fucked her hairy, soaking wet hole, the more she couldn't take it. In a strange fit of ecstasy, using both hands, she reached down, holding both sides of the dog's huge head. Gyrating both wide hips, Keisha met Kilo's every sloppy, foaming-at-the-mouth tongue stroke until she finally exploded, having multiple orgasms. As her legs appeared to have convulsions, Keisha exhaled. Kilo, on the other hand, had never tasted a woman's pussy and wasn't done yet. With his small, red penis poking in and out at a fast rate, Kilo was in pure dog heaven.

Sinisterly amused by Keisha's constant pleas to make the animal stop, Rico let his four-legged best friend keep going in on the now creamy twat until he got tired on his own. Still holding his cell phone recording, Rico knew exactly what other type of true punishment he was gonna inflict on Keisha for her sexual betrayal, especially since she seemed to get so much satisfaction out of Kilo giving her head.

Chapter Seven

It was almost six thirty in the morning when Keisha was awakened by Rico, drunk and high, stumbling in the house and passing out cold on the couch. Having untied her legs after realizing he'd left, she'd taken a long, scorching hot shower, desperately trying to scald away her freakish sins. Some, she'd voluntarily committed, and in others, she was forced to participate. Whatever the case was, her conscience was kicking her ass far worse than Rico, in the flesh, ever had done.

Lying in the same bed he'd let the dog violate her in, part of Keisha wanted to get a butcher knife and stab it straight through Rico's back. Another part of Keisha's brain was urging her to go heat up that same grease he'd threatened to burn her with and let him see how it felt. Lastly, the once-good-girl ethics she was raised with encouraged her to just tiptoe out the door with the clothes on her back and get as far away from Rico Campbell as humanly possible. Getting to work on time, if at all, was out of the question. Mentally, not to mention her battered and bruised face, Keisha knew she couldn't make it, so she sat still.

Interrupting her mind fighting with her demons, she heard her cell phone ringing in her purse. Not in the mood to talk to anyone, Keisha ignored it. Five minutes later, it rang again, and every two minutes after that.

What could be so important? She dragged her body out of bed and over to the stool that sat by the dresser. Finding her purse wide open and sitting on the floor instead of the stool where it usually sat didn't mean anything to her at that point. Rico had probably been in there stealing her loose change as he typically did when broke.

Sixteen missed calls, seven voice messages, and eleven texts! What in the hell? Keisha didn't know which one of the alerts to respond to first. Before she could get a chance to hit the small neon green envelope-shaped icon on her cell and read one of the eleven texts, the phone rang again. Seeing it was her friend Kim on the screen, she immediately pushed TALK.

"Hey, girl, what's going on?" Keisha, weak and mentally drained, was groggy. "What's up?"

Screaming through the phone, Kim's voice annoyingly seemed to echo throughout the room. "What's up? What in the hell you mean what's up? Have you lost your damn mind? What's wrong with you?"

"Huh?" Keisha, nursing a major headache, was taken aback, not knowing what her friend was talking about.

"Don't 'huh' me, bitch. I know you and that stupid-ass creep you deal with is off into some ridiculous bullshit, but you done crossed the line. Who does that?"

"Does what, Kim? Crossed the line?" Keisha was still puzzled, running her fingers through her tangled hair. "Crossed what line? What is you talking about? Tell me."

"Why in the fuck would you send that mess to my fucking email and text? Who in the hell does that, and matter of fact, where they do that ratchet shit at?" Kim was going hard in the paint on her once close but recently distant best friend. "You need help. Both of y'all retarded motherfuckers do. Have you spoken to your father? I know he pissed."

Before Keisha could get some true clarity in what Kim was referring to, her other end rang. "Wait, Kim, wait," she begged. "This is my job on the other end probably wondering where I'm at."

Clicking over before Kim could say another word, Keisha tried using a super-soft voice to maybe buy her a sick day. "Yes—hello."

"Good morning. Keisha Jackson?" the office manager firmly inquired.

"Yes, this is she." Keisha coughed twice, trying to make it sound good.

"Well, Miss Jackson, this is a courtesy call to inform you that we no longer are in need of your services here as of this morning."

"But I—" Keisha was on her way to try to negotiate when she was cut off.

"In light of the disrespectful circumstances and the morality policy in your signed contract, we will mail your personal belongings along with your final paycheck. You are no longer allowed on company premises. Is that understood?"

"Excuse me?" Keisha rubbed her nappy head, confused. "I know I've missed more than my fair share of days, but is it customary to mail a person's belongings?"

The office manager was trying to keep it brief and not get off into sordid details, but she felt that woman to woman, she had to set Keisha straight. "Miss Jackson, although your work here is very impressive to say the least, when an employee or any individual sends the type of group email to the entire staff like you did, one would really think you'd be much too embarrassed to even show your face! Now, have a good day."

Clicking back over, Keisha was met by Kim still nutting up.

"Why, girl? Why? I feel like I don't even know you anymore."

"Listen, Kim, please slow the hell down and tell me what you're talking about. My manager just called tripping too. I'm confused."

It dawned on Kim at that point Keisha wasn't playing dumb; she really didn't know what was going on. "Okay, girl, did you send me an email and a text late last night?"

"Last night?" Embarrassed to tell her what she was really doing, or had done to her, last night, Keisha just answered no. "I've been 'sleep since last night since we got back from the concert."

"Well, check your sent box on your email account while I hold on." Kim waited for her friend to check using the other screen of her Android cell.

"Oh my fucking God! Oh my God! Oh my God! Oh, no! Oh my God!" Keisha started screaming, running from one side of the room to the other on ten. "Naw, naw, naw. Oh my God! Naw. Why? Why? Oh my God!"

Kim could hear the shock in her girl's voice and knew she obviously didn't mean to send her that should-be-private bullshit.

"Kim, Kim, Kim, I can't believe he would do that. Why would he? How could he? Oh my God." Keisha discovered that not only did Kimberly receive a video of Kilo giving her head in the bed, but every single person in her cell contact list and Gmail account had too. "I can't believe this. Oh my God!"

Distraught, Keisha started to think about each person that must've gotten the shocking, perverted freak peep show by now.

*My mother! My Father! My Uncle Samuel! Shit . . .
All the people at work! My little cousin! All my former
classmates! Damn, the people at the temp agency! Shit!
Shit! Shit! Oh my fucking God! The entire church youth
group I used to belong to! How fucking could he do this
to me? How?"* Feeling nauseated and sick to her stomach,
Keisha started to hyperventilate.

"Keisha! Keisha! Listen to me! Keisha!" Kim tried her
best to calm her down over the phone. "You need to just
get your clothes and come on over here. Leave that grimy
lunatic. You done did enough charity work on his bum
behind. I told you he wasn't about jack shit. Leave that
ho-ass lame."

"I know." Keisha pushed her hand close, holding her
chest while trying to catch her breath. "I am. I swear I
am. I just gotta handle something first; then I'll be there.
Don't worry."

"Before you go, I need to tell you something else."
Kim knew Keisha was going to go even more bananas;
however, she knew she had to expose the whole truth.
"That slimeball put that shit on Facebook, Instagram,
Snapchat and damn YouTube. I reported the garbage and
got it took down and removed as soon as I saw it, but it
ain't no telling how many motherfuckers seen it. I swear
you better leave that nut. If you don't, just forget my
damn number. I mean it. Don't even call me anymore
with ya Rico drama."

Wanting to curl up in a ball and die, Keisha's mind
was telling her to just end it all. How could she face
anyone she knew again? Detroit was big, but it wasn't
that big. Even if she tried to stay out the way, nine
outta ten she'd run into somebody sometime that knew
somebody that knew something about what Rico had
made her do—let Kilo eat her out.

Spending the next ten tormenting minutes listening to "shocked, angry, amazed and extremely disappointed in her" voice messages and reading the same sentiment in every text, Keisha felt her heart sink to the floor every time she'd push erase.

"Oh my goodness Keisha how could you?" Her mother uncontrollably cried. *"How could you? Baby, you need help—some spiritual guidance! I'm praying for you!"*

"Girl, you out cold!" Cousin Greg laughed all the while leaving his message. *"A dog? You out cold, cuz! You wildin'!"*

"You need to have your head examined! You need to be ashamed of yourself!" one of her former classmates, baffled at what she'd viewed, yelled out. *"Why would you send this despicable trash to me and the rest of the girls in the reunion committee? Needless to say, you're off the committee! Most likely to succeed? Yeah, right!"*

"Damn, Keisha, it's like that? A fucking dog? You straight tripping!" a guy who'd she met at one of her temp jobs commented through his laughter. *"I seen that shit on your Facebook page too!"*

"Take my number out your phone!" one person after another angrily demanded.

All her family, friends, colleagues, and just random folk she knew whose contact information was in her cell responded to the outrageous video Rico posted. It had Keisha's head pounding like it was on the verge of exploding. Lastly, and most heartwrenchingly, she repeatedly listened to the one left by her father.

"Keisha, I don't know what your mother and I have done to you to make you treat us both so disrespectfully. Why send this type of filth to us?" His voice cracked with each passing word. *"We raised you better than this.*

Your poor mother is devastated. Your uncle and all your cousins apparently received the same email. She's embarrassed, and so am I." The humiliation he felt for his daughter and the person whom she'd obviously become since leaving his strict household was almost unbearable for him to accept. *"Maybe that hot-headed, no-good fool has you on drugs or something. I don't know. But I do know, from this point on, you are no longer a part of this family. If you thought I was playing before, you can rest assured, I'm extremely serious now! Please, Keisha, don't contact your mother or myself ever again. You've hurt us both enough for two lifetimes. I'm glad I didn't acknowledge you last night. You are an utter disgrace. I warned you it would be a couple of cold days in hell before you stepped back inside of my household, but now hell could freeze over!"*

Having had enough of Rico and his spiteful, selfish actions, Keisha slipped her sore body into a tracksuit. Lacing up her Air Max, she stood in front of the mirror, getting a good look at what she once believed to be her beautiful face, which was now bruised and seemed to have aged five years since starting her relationship with Rico.

Hell bent on revenge, she eased over toward the other side of the room with the least noise possible. Pressing her ear against the door, she listened for any movement from Rico in the living room. Hearing none except for his snores, she cracked open the bedroom door. Tiptoeing like a panther, she focused on her "man," fast asleep on the couch. Keisha's eyes quickly scanned the room to find a weapon to use.

This nigga gonna pay! Right fucking now! Wrapping her hands around a small-in-size-but-heavy-in-weight

African warrior statue she'd bought from a festival at
Hart Plaza that past summer and a butcher knife from the
kitchen, Keisha snuck up on a sleeping Rico.

The Night Before . . .

*All of a sudden she wanna think for herself—make
moves on her own? That ugly ho got a lot of nerve letting
that country-Bama big nigga eat that stankin' pussy
without my permission—freak bitch! If it wasn't for me,
she'd still be big as a house and green to the streets!*

Convinced he was about to do no wrong, Rico down-
loaded the scandalous video he'd just taken on his cell,
sending it to Keisha's. Walking around the bed where
his woman was still tied to the footpost, passed out cold
from exhaustion, Rico removed her purse off the stool.
Rambling through it, he found her phone, along with a
couple of twenty-dollar bills wrapped around the ticket
stubs from the concert the night before. After stuffing the
money in his back pocket, he touched the envelope icon
on her cell, bringing up her already-read text messages.

Not the slight bit interested in being nosey and reading the old texts from her inbox, he pushed RETRIEVE,
downloading the one he'd just sent. Saving the media file,
he then forwarded the unbelievable 2:21 minutes he'd
labeled *We're Getting Married!* to every contact in her
phonebook, as well as her email account. Next, he put
the scandalous, soon-to-be infamous film on Facebook,
YouTube, and any other social media site he could think
of.

*Let's see the next time this dumb ho think for herself!
She called herself getting down on me; well, the last*

laugh is fucking mine! This shit gonna hit WorldStar quick, fast, and in a hurry! Tossing her cell back in her purse and throwing it onto the floor, Rico left the bedroom. Grabbing several pieces of fried chicken Keisha had left on a plate on the stove and another Red Bull, he was out the door—gun in waist.

Jumping in Keisha's badly-in-need-of-an-oil-change-and-new-tires truck, Rico backed out the driveway. With Keisha's gas money for the week tucked in his rear pocket, he proudly pulled up at the weed spot, where the dice game was going on.

Yeah, good! Everybody still up in this piece throwing 'em! Leering through the vehicle's tinted window, Rico grinned with contentment. Wiping the chicken grease from his lips and the crumbs off his pants, he downed the last of his energy drink. Snatching his cell off the passenger seat, he was more than ready to go inside.

Parking behind Swazy's car, Rico knew with the wild shit he was about to show the fellas inside the trap house, it'd be one of those explosive what-in-the-fuck moments Negros in the hood lived for. He would no doubt be the talk of the streets for days to come, probably weeks.

Minutes after going inside the crowded dwelling, Rico shut the entire dice game down with the aid of his iPhone, pushing REPLAY more than nine or ten times. Every person that eyeballed the brightly lit, outrageous video starring Keisha and Kilo were left practically speechless. First, because what freak-ass female in Detroit would let a dog eat her out, then be all off into the bullshit? Then, lastly, why in the fuck would Rico tape his supposed woman and show it to all of them? *Where they do that at?* was the main sentiment of all the dudes, chiefly A.J., who Rico made sure was first to see it.

"Man, ain't that Keisha?"

"Wow, you deep! That's ya woman?"

"Nigga, you sick in the head!"

"Boy, you wild for this one here!"

"Man, what in the fuck she do to you?"

"If that was my sister, I'd body your ass for this shit!"

With a bad taste lingering in his mouth, Rico wanted to chin-check A.J. for that slick, behind-the-back kitchen stunt he knew he'd pulled, but he decided not to let his country ass, Swazy, or the rest of the fellas inside the trap house see him set trip about no female—especially one who'd fuck a dog. As difficult as it was to get that feeling of animosity out his system, he stood tall, playing his bitterness off.

"Come on, now. I'm a fucking boss in my household," he responded with false pride.

After the initial fanfare of the homemade porno died down, the dice game continued. With only two twenty-dollar bills to play with, Rico was quickly broke and left standing on the sidelines watching A.J. clean house. The combination of each roll the Alabama-born-and-raised visitor took, and the fact he'd felt like A.J. had got down on him earlier, had Rico fighting to keep his game face on. Asking Swazy to loan him a few dollars to get back in the game and getting turned down on his request pushed Rico to the edge.

"Oh, damn, Swazy, so you dick-riding with your cousin, huh? You can't give ya boy a couple of dollars to get back on? It's like that?" Rico felt he could make the next man act like he wanted him to do.

"Yo, dawg, I ain't got it," Swazy, instantly salty from working hard for his tips all night, fired back, shrugging his shoulders, standing amongst the crowd of guys. "And don't disrespect me like that!"

"Come on now, my dude. I just hooked you and this ho-ass nigga up on some pussy and head from old girl, and you tripping out on a few dollars. Damn!" Rico purposely let the handle of his pistol show.

"Slow your roll, motherfucker. You let Kilo get the pussy too. Now, was you over there begging his four-legged ass for some bread?" Swazy, strapped himself, was not the least bit intimidated. He'd had just about enough of Rico talking reckless and decided to put him in his place, gun or no gun.

"Begging? What?" Rico grimaced, acting as if he was gonna actually draw on his best friend and any other person in the house who seemed like they might want some.

"Nigga, you don't wanna do that. I'm warning you." Swazy refused to back down, showing his true Detroit credibility. "Ya best bet is to fall back and not jump out there with me! I thought we was better than that."

"Fuck you, Swazy." Rico, although unsure of the outcome, let his nuts hang and tried making his move.

"You heard my cousin, fool. Fall the fuck back. You past tense with that gangster routine." A.J. dropped the dice from his hand. Exchanging words then locking eyes, A.J. bum-rushed Rico, strong-arm taking his gun from him before he knew what was going down. "It's one thing to beat a female's ass, but make no mistake, homeboy, I'm a grown man—ya heard? Now let's see what you can do with that. I'll beat your local ass to sleep. Trust that."

Trading blows, attempting to fight back and hold his own, Rico received no help against the Southern stranger who had been treating the guys in the house, who'd been losing all night, to beer and weed. Truth be told, everyone in the crib shared the same view as Swazy. They were sick and tired of Rico getting high as a fuck, pulling out his gun, and getting rowdy. Now surrounded and unarmed, Rico got what he was looking for from A.J.—his brains half stomped out.

Eight long, grueling minutes later, A.J. had whooped Rico's ass for him, Swazy, every dude inside the trap house, and most importantly for Keisha, even though he did see her getting off with a dog. With the assistance of the guy whose house it was, he and Swazy dragged Rico out to his truck, throwing him inside to sleep off his high. With a black eye, a busted lip, and a deep gash across his jawline, Rico's normally handsome face, nine outta ten, would never be the same.

Chapter Eight

Lying defenseless in the pile of dirty clothes, face hidden. Keisha heard the heavy sound of Rico's Timberland boots getting closer. Feeling his evil presence standing above her, she clenched her fists as if she were preparing for battle.

"Turn over, ho."

"Naw, I'm not. I'm done." Defiant and fed up, she slowly shifted her head. "I'm fucking done!"

Rico still had his stiff dick out from taking a piss, and it showed no signs of getting soft anytime soon. Rubbing the permanent scar across his jaw with one hand and his meat with the other, he grew agitated. "Listen, Keisha, it's too early in the morning for your dumb ass to get tough. Turn all the way around, get on your knees, and come the fuck here. Right damn now. Crawl."

Cowardly reacting to the demeaning, demanding tone in Rico's voice, Keisha unballed her fist—doing as she was told. Down on all fours like Kilo, she caught a glimpse of herself in the full-length, white plastic-trimmed mirror that was nailed to the door.

What am I doing? This ain't me! I'm better than this! I know I am! Finally questioning the choices she'd made with her life, seeing firsthand what she'd ultimately become dealing with the likes of Rico Campbell, Keisha paused. *I should have killed him that morning! Because of him and that video, my whole life I used to have is fucked up!*

"Well, I'm waiting, you nothing-ass bitch. What you gonna do?"

Ironically, hearing Rico make that degrading statement caused her to think back to that very moment she was about to bash his brains in. He'd said that exact same thing.

Not making any unnecessary noise that might alert Rico to what she was about to do, Keisha's fingers and palms started to form moisture. With malice in her heart, she gripped the small statue in one hand and the butcher knife in the other. With an eagle eye, she slowly crept. Watching Rico's back, which was turned to her, go in and out with each passing breath, Keisha got excited. Each step had her getting deeper and deeper off into her emotions. Nervous and feeling out of character, Keisha felt a strange rage invade her soul. All the time she'd spent being involved with Rico, she never truly felt the urge to kill him. Today was different. She was at her wit's end. Today was the day she was ready to end his life and start her new one off in prison. She licked her lips then bit down on the corner, and her arm went upward. There was no hesitation or second thought. More than ready to get revenge on Rico, she smiled. Repaying him for all the pain and torture he'd caused in her life, Keisha swung the statue down with all her strength. Her sinister smile grew as it crashed it against his skull. With the quickness, she repeated the process once more. Before she could go at it a third, he was shouting out in excruciating pain.

"Urggggg . . . !" Rico, still dazed and dizzy from the beating he'd suffered at the hands of A.J, grabbed the back of his head. Instinctively, he started to squirm to halt any more blows. Not knowing what or who had hit him, he rolled off the couch and onto the floor. Hands and dreads now covered in gushing blood, he scrambled to stand to his feet but couldn't. Disoriented, he yelled out a few more times before Keisha decided to reply.

"You low-life-ass bitch-made nigga! Why in the fuck would you send that bullshit to my family, Rico? And to all my damn friends? Why in the fuck would you do that dirty-ass shit, huh? Why? That was some ole fucked-up shit to do to someone you claim to care about, let alone someone you hate!" The questions as to why Rico did what he'd done flew as she now felt empowered. After months of enduring his constant verbal and mental abuse, Keisha was not letting up one bit as she held onto the statue and the knife.

"I haven't done anything ever to try to hurt your ass. Not ever. And because you feeling some sort of way, you think it's okay to try to ruin someone's life. Just because you came from nothing and really ain't about shit don't mean you gotta hate on the next person.

"I don't know what I saw in you in the first place. My dumb ass was just looking for something, and you came along. I should've listened to my girls. Matter of fact, I should've left your crazy ass locked up the day you clowned at my parents' house. But naw, stupid me had to come get you. I loved you so much, and that love ain't shit but my downfall.

"Now I ain't got shit left in the world to hold my head up for. You destroyed that just like everything else you come in contact with. Rico, you ain't shit but a waste of skin."

"Urggg." Rico finally tried to speak once more.

"Seriously, nigga? For real? That's all the fuck you gotta say? Now, I'ma ask you once more why you sent that bullshit before I cut your ass. I'm done playing games." Waving the shiny blade, she wanted him to know she meant every single word she'd just said and that if it came down to more bloodshed to get answers, it would be his on the floor this time for a change, definitely not hers.

Using his bloody hands to move his scattered dreads, Rico squinted as he stared upward. "Bitch, look at my fucking face. You see this shit?"

Keisha was stunned, seeing the condition of his face. She knew that it was no sweet way in hell the blow she'd just given him to the rear of his head could've caused that much damage to his face. "What in the entire hell?"

"Yeah, Keisha, that's right, what in the hell." Rico fell back, allowing the light in the room to showcase the true extent of A.J.'s handiwork. "My shit is fucked up thanks to you."

Not letting the blood-stained statue, now a makeshift weapon, and the knife out of her sweaty grasp, Keisha eased slightly closer. Getting a better look, she was even more confused when he moved his hair. "Thanks to me? What in the hell are you talking about, thanks to me? I just hit you across the back of your stupid head. I know damn well that shit ain't do all of that. So once again, how is that thanks to me?"

Despite a black eye, a busted lip, a cut across his jaw, and now a huge gaping hole on the left side of his skull, he was cocky. Shaky and slurring, Rico tried his best to remain who he was, a trash-talking, manipulative asshole. "Thanks to you giving that country nigga that pussy in the kitchen, behind my back, he zoned out last night. He was all in his little feelings. But it's all good, though."

"What in the hell are you talking about now?" Keisha quizzed.

"You heard me, girl. Your new overgrown-goon, gold-tooth-wearing boyfriend got on one at the dice game. Like I said, he was in his feelings and bugged out like a li'l punk."

Keisha couldn't believe what she was hearing about a dude she'd just met and freaked with the night before. *Yeah, right. Whatever. This nigga must think I'm dumb. Ain't no guy just all of a sudden trip out over some female he don't know like that.* Knowing Rico and his constant games, she didn't know whether to believe him or not, but at this point, she couldn't care less. Like he claimed A.J. was all up in his feelings, so was she. Her main mission was to punish Rico for what he had done to her. Whatever he had going on outside of that was of no great consequence to her. It was one thing to humiliate, embarrass, disrespect, and altogether beast her like she was less than a human being. Pitiful as it seemed, she'd grown accustomed to that harsh treatment. It was almost second nature. But now, once again, like he'd done early on in their relationship, Rico brought pain, hurt, disappointment, and devastation to her parents and everyone she knew, for that matter. His verbal, physical, and constant mental abuse was now out of the closet. It was no more a dirty little secret they shared. It was public knowledge. If the God-awful video hadn't gone viral by now, she knew it was certainly well on its way.

"Okay, he was on one. Whatever. I don't give a hot shit." She raised her arm once more, feeling no sympathy. "Look at my face. It's messed up too. Besides that, what the fuck that got to do with you sending that bullshit to every damn body? Huh? What the fuck is wrong with you? Have you lost what little mind you got?"

Having been hit twice by the statue, Rico still struggled to regain his sight. Now, threatened with a butcher

knife an out-of-control, infuriated Keisha was swinging,
Rico had to think quickly. His first thought was to try
to get his gun and shoot or at least scare her. But that
idea quickly went out of play. He remembered A.J. had
taken it from him at the weed house, so that was out the
question. Secondly, he contemplated trying to overpower
and disarm her. Yet he felt like he'd endured enough
battle wounds within a twenty-four hour time span to risk
getting stabbed. Plus, Keisha wasn't one of those small
tiny framed females a guy could toss around. She was
thick and he realized as heated as she was, she was gonna
fight back. It wouldn't be an automatic easy win. Wisely,
Rico tried the one thing Keisha always fell for since day
one, his smooth charm and con man techniques.

"Look at my damn face!" Rico used his elbows to back
himself up against the couch. "That nigga was over there
talking mad shit about you. He was saying all type of
bullshit, and I was fed up. I wasn't gonna let no down-
South, green-eggs-and-ham, grit-eating nigga to try to
clown you. Fuck all that! I was defending your black ass."

"What are you talking about?" Keisha tilted her head,
giving Rico the side-eye as he tried shifting responsibly
for the condition of his face. "What you mean, defending
me?"

"Yeah, just like I said, defending you got my face all
messed up. Niggas ain't shit but some haters. A dude try
to show a fool some hospitality and they don't appreciate
it. Him and Swazy was over at the trap house saying how
you wasn't nothing but a hood rat and how you was ugly
as shit. Going in about how big you was and how you
couldn't be their wifey."

"What?" Keisha twisted her lips.

"Yeah, and when I stepped to them lames, they jumped
me. Him and Swazy punk ass. I done fed that guy and

smoked my last weed with him, and he turned on me. I guess blood is thicker than water. But it's all good, though." Rico kept his hand pressed to the still-bleeding gash in the rear of his head. With his shoulder-length dreadlocks now soaked and dripping blood, he continued to run his game on Keisha, telling her what she wanted to hear.

"I ain't tripping. It's all good. But now my face fucked up all because I was taking up for you. They some punk-ass niggas, especially Swazy's cousin."

Any other time, she'd be grateful for what he was saying, if indeed it was true. But Keisha was not dumb enough or naïve enough to get thrown off her square. She'd been through a lot with him and his bullshit lies, but not this time. She wasn't buying what he was selling.

"Okay, Rico. That's all good and all, and if it did all go down that way last night, good for you stepping up to defend some shit you created from jump. And once again, even if you were taking up for me with them, which I seriously doubt, why in the hell would you send that video to my people? Why? One ain't got Jack Daniel's shit to do with the other. See, that's what I'm talking about. That's what got your head cracked open, and that's what's gonna make me cut your black ass. Now, like I keep asking you, why? Why in the hell would you do some old slimeball shit like that?" She tapped her foot while waiting for an answer.

As she got closer up on him, Keisha's patience for not cutting Rico was growing thin. "My mother was crying. You made my fucking mama cry, you bastard. You betrayed me, and for what? I promise you for every tear my mother shed, you gonna give an ounce of blood."

"Hold up, Keisha. Hold the fuck up. I know I done did a gang of foul shit since we been kicking it, but let's keep this shit right here a hundred." Using his free hand, stalling for more time to get his self together, Rico continued his master manipulation techniques, trying to flip the script. "You stabbed me in the back first. I mean, like I said, let's keep shit a hundred. Why would you let that nigga hit it in my house like I'm some sort of lame? Explain that."

Keisha, although pissed beyond belief, couldn't believe what she was hearing. She laughed, rolling her neck as she responded to what Rico had just said. "Negro, are you fucking serious? You can't be. I know I must be hearing things. Excuse me, Rico, but didn't you just sit over there on that damn couch watching your so-called boys get the pussy? Was I dreaming last night or what? Correct me if I'm wrong." Irritated, she started cleaning under her nails with the long, sharp, shiny blade. "And ain't you the person that wanted them over here so bad when all I wanted to do was go to bed? Huh?" She stopped, sucking her teeth, giving him a cold, hard death stare. "You that same boss-ass buster calling shots, ain't you? That had all that madness jumping off."

Rico was seeing a side of Keisha he never knew existed. At a total disadvantage, he started looking around the room for something to knock the knife out her hand if she came any closer. "Wait, Keisha, damn. See, now you bugging. Don't you see what in the fuck you already did to me? I mean, you taking this bullshit way too far." Taking his hand off the open wound, he showed her the blood dripping from his fingertips.

Slamming the statue on the side of the end table, Keisha had listened to all Rico's excuses she was willing to take. Still clutching the butcher knife, she reached into her tracksuit pocket. Throwing her iPhone at Rico's head, she demanded he pick it up after he ducked.

"Crawl your bitch ass over there and get that shit! I want you to listen to all them voicemails. Read them out of order text messages. Is you fucking crazy or what? How in the hell is you gonna compare that hole in your damn hard head to what you did to me?" Wildly swinging the knife, she sliced his raised arm. "My mama was crying tears, nigga, over that scandalous shit. Real fucking tears. You put that crap up everywhere!"

"Bitch, is you crazy?" Rico flinched, trying to stop any more of Keisha's enraged attacks.

"Bitch?" she questioned as if she hadn't heard him correctly. With malice, she then swung the blade once more, this time missing. "I was wondering how long it was gonna take you to get back to normal. I should just kill your pathetic ass now. See, you ain't never gonna change. That evil is buried too deep in your filthy soul."

"Well, I'm waiting, big girl, with your nothing ass. I ain't gonna just keep sitting here and bleed out. What you gonna do?" Rico was growing tired of playing this cat-and-mouse game with Keisha, and it was starting to show.

"I gave you everything I had, and you just said fuck me. I lost my family, my friends, and every job I get behind dealing with your trifling ass. Well, I'm done. I can make it without you, and I will." Feeling liberated and tired of playing the victim role, a usually spineless Keisha stood tall for the first time in months.

Realizing his meal ticket might be truly serious about leaving and he'd have to actually get a full-time job or a hustle to feed himself, Rico swallowed his pride. "Okay, okay, listen Keisha, I know you heated, but how you think I felt when you gave that coon my pussy?"

"Your pussy!" Keisha, feeling empowered, no longer in denial, shook her head. "Come on now, guy, this ain't been your pussy since the night I bailed your black ass out of jail. You know, the night your surprise baby mama and me first met. So, guess what? You can just miss me with all that game you trying to spit. I'm good on all of that. You need to just say your prayers, 'cause you about to leave here for what you did to me and my mother."

Rico was speechless. Fully aware what she was accusing him of was true, he felt a surreal climate in the room. He'd played all his con man cards and was too physically exhausted to deal any more. Lifting his body up onto the couch, he used one of the fluffy pillows to stop the bleeding from his head. Closing his eyes, Rico decided to let Keisha do whatever she felt. If she got close enough for him to possibly make a move and take the knife away, then so be it, he'd do it. But as far as anything else extra, he was done. He had no more fight in him.

"You ain't got shit to say?" Keisha, knife clutched tight, bossed up, ready to pounce on the man she felt for months was her soul mate.

Interrupted by a series of thunderous knocks on the front door, Keisha and Rico both froze as Kilo started barking from the backyard.

"Who in the fuck is that?" Rico hissed, reaching for his gun before quickly realizing it was not on his waist as usual.

"Why you asking me?"

"It's probably you new boyfriend coming to save your black ass."

"Save me from what? What in the fuck can you do to hurt me any more than you already have? And F.Y.I., A.J. is not my boyfriend, but if he was, him or anybody I'd mess with is a come-up from you."

"So, now you and that country nigga on a first name basis, huh?"

"Fuck you, Rico."

"Naw, fuck you, tramp."

"Oh, we on back name-calling again," Keisha fired back as the barrage of knocks on the front door continued.

"Detroit Police Department! Open up!" Another series of hard knocks on the front door and voices seem to bounce off every wall.

Both looking at one another, Rico and Keisha were dumbfounded. Knowing their voices were louder than usual at this time of morning, it wasn't anything for their unemployed, ghetto-minded neighbors to call the cops for. Arguments that turn into murder, dudes' clothes getting tossed out the window, crackheads fighting over a rock, or a kid getting caught stealing a honey bun out the gas station was no out-of-the-ordinary occurrence. So, Detroit's Finest at the door was somewhat of a shock.

Wasting no time tucking the sharp-edged butcher knife underneath the cushion of the chair, Keisha snarled at Rico, who was pulling himself off the floor and back onto the couch.

"You lucky—for real—but I'm not done with you."

"Yeah, whatever, trick. We'll see." Rico, still delirious from the blow on the back of his head courtesy of Keisha, and extremely sore from A.J.'s ass-whooping, was now mouthy, even while nursing a hangover. Snatching the ashtray off the coffee table that had a couple of tails and a half blunt in it, Rico made himself scarce, leaving his woman to deal with the police.

"Yes, does Rico Campbell reside here?"

"Umm . . . yes, officer, he does."

"Well, is he here?"

"Umm . . . sorry. Not at the present. Is something wrong? Something I can help you with?" In light of what Rico had done to her, by right she should have stepped out of the way of the police, pointed toward the bedroom door, and begged them to handcuff his ass for whatever they wanted. She should have welcomed them to bury his no-good behind under the jail. But she didn't. No matter what, no one helped the police. That was how it was in Detroit and most hoods. The no-snitching code was always in effect, especially when it involved your own people. Besides, Keisha intended to lay down her own version of the law on him.

"Who are you?" one cop questioned as the other peered over her shoulder into the living room after noticing the obvious fresh bruises on her face. "What's your name?"

"Keisha. Keisha Jackson."

"Keisha Jackson?" The officer looked down at his small spiral notebook, then glanced back up. "Are you any relation to a Mr. Lorenzo James Jackson?"

"Yes, that's my father," she explained with a newfound panic and concern in her tone. "What's wrong? What's going on with my dad? Is everything all right?"

"Umm . . . yes and no."

"What do you mean, yes and no? Oh my God!" Her palm pressed against her forehead. Her heart started to beat faster. Running her fingers through her tangled hair, trying to gather it up in a ponytail, Keisha shook.

"Listen, you need to calm down." The nosey officer stopped trying to see if there was any movement inside the dwelling and coldly interrupted her rant. "It seems as if a bright-gold-in-color Yukon Denali registered to one Lorenzo J. Jackson was found two blocks over. Now, that isn't County Commissioner Jackson, is it?"

"Umm, yes, it is."

"You mean to tell me your father is County Commissioner Jackson?"

"Yes, I told you—yes!" She licked her dry lips.

"And you, his daughter, is living here?"

"Yes, I live here." Ashamed of her living conditions as well as her overall messy appearance, Keisha tried to hold it together.

The Tenth Precinct officer, still full of questions, looked around the outer perimeter of the house, as well as the surrounding burnt-out homes. Wondering what a girl from such a prominent and influential family was doing here, he continued to do his job. "Go figure that," he judged, knowing the crime-ridden area he and his partner patrolled on a daily basis. "Well, anyway, the vehicle was discovered crashed in the side of an abandoned building with the engine still running. Apparently, it also damaged three of four other vehicles on the street before its final impact."

Noticing for the first time since opening the door that her truck was not parked in the driveway as usual when Rico wasn't gone, she felt a new sense of rage overcome her body. "Oh my God!" She grabbed her chest with her right hand, covering her mouth with the left. This was one more thing in a long list of bullshit Rico had put her through since meeting him.

"Yes, well, that brings us back to Rico Campbell." The policeman holding the notebook revealed what Keisha immediately recognized as Rico's wallet. "This was under the front seat. The ID lists this as Rico Campbell's residence, not to mention some of the people whose vehicles are damaged reported seeing a man they recognized to be Rico Campbell fleeing from the scene on foot."

"Oh my God." Keisha shook her head, clutching her chest area once more. "Was anyone hurt?"

"No, just property damage. Mr. Jackson, I mean Commissioner Jackson, your father, has already been notified and the truck impounded. Now, once again, is Mr. Campbell home?" the officer asked, this time more sternly than the first. "And what exactly is his relationship to you and your father?"

"Well . . ." She hesitated with glassy eyes. "He's sorta my boyfriend."

"Well, is your sorta boyfriend home?" he sarcastically replied. "We need to speak to him. And by the way, what happened to your face?"

Distracted by the sounds of Kilo barking, Keisha stepped onto the front porch, shutting the door behind her. "Umm, I'm so sorry." She continued to keep her front up with the blatant lie. "He's not here. I don't know where he's at now. I haven't seen him since late last night."

Not completely satisfied with Keisha's answer, without a signed warrant to search the premises, the two Detroit police officers were limited by law in what they could do next. They had no other choice but to leave.

"You see how she looked? She must be a crackhead or something," one judgmentally remarked. "Probably on ecstasy, Molly, or some freaking other pill."

"Yeah, who would live here when her people got all that cash? Only a drug addict or a fool one."

Chapter Nine

"Yes, I'm here to see Commissioner Jackson." Led into the plush twenty-third floor office, Police Chief Armstrong thanked the young, attractive secretary before taking a seat.

Moments later, his old friend, frat brother, and golf partner entered the room. "Hey, Lorenzo."

"Hey now, Hank. How you doing?" They exchanged greetings and their customary fraternal handshake.

"I'm good, I'm good."

"How are Shelia and the kids?"

"They're doing fine—almost as fine as that young, pretty thing you got sitting out there answering the phones."

"Yeah, she is something special, ain't she?" He momentarily had freaky thoughts of his secretary's plump backside.

"What about your wife and Keisha? I haven't seen them around the club lately, or that cute cook you got over there."

"Aww, man, not so good, old friend, not so good."

"What? I'm sorry to hear that. What's the problem, if it's not too personal?"

"It's that same fool boy that I had arrested a few months back out at my house."

"Oh, yeah? Not him again. What was his name?"

"Rico Campbell."

"Yeah, that was it. Rico Campbell. Another wanna-be gangsta."

"I should've just followed my first mind and buried his ass under the jail instead of listening to my wife's fairy tale thinking that Keisha would eventually leave that hooligan alone."

"Calm down, Lorenzo, old buddy. Calm down. What in the hell has this kid done now?"

Sitting back in his oversized leather chair, Keisha's father took a deep breath before explaining what he'd heard from a reliable source about what Rico was putting his young, once innocent daughter through.

Being the chief of police, Hank Armstrong had seen and heard it all, but when he watched the shocking video of Keisha, a shy youngster that once played with his own children and he'd bounced on his knee, having oral sex with a dog, he was left speechless. With his jaw open, he could only rub his hand down the front of his face and stroke his beard; first, because of what his friend's daughter was doing, and secondly, his friend having the balls to show it to him.

"Hank, can you believe what in the fuck that monster has my baby participating in?" Slamming his clenched fist on the desk, the distraught father's fury could be felt two offices over. "One day she was a good girl—going to grad school, working part time, and hanging out with her friends. Now this, this, this—"

"How did you get a hold of this garbage, Lorenzo?"

"From what I can gather, it came from Keisha's cell, but you can clearly see her hands were tied. And if you noticed, she had bruises on her face. I know he sent it! He must have!"

Not wanting to say he was paying more attention to his friend's daughter's cunt and the way she was seemingly into what the animal was doing, Hank just nodded. "Well, umm, have you spoken to Keisha? What did she have to say for herself? Is she okay?"

"Yeah, Hank, apparently so. She tried calling me several times on my cell and twice here, but what is there to say? You tell me." He buried his face in his hands. "Strange thing is, I just saw her and that creep last night over at the Fox Theater, but I was kind of tangled up in something. But if I ever see him again, I don't know what I might do! I also just got a call about that bum tearing up the truck I let Keisha keep. Ever since she's met him, it's been nothing but a damn nightmare I don't know if I'll ever wake up from."

"Okay, Lorenzo, calm down. I know how you must feel." Hank truly couldn't imagine one of his daughters being such freaks but consoled him anyhow. "What can I do? You know the entire department and me are at your disposal. If you know where he's staying at, I can have a car swing by and pick him up—maybe the gang squad. You know they can teach his disrespectful ass a lesson or two."

"Naw, Hank, not yet." He looked up with hatred in his eyes and revenge in his heart. "I have something else cooking later on that's less traceable. But if not, that's definitely an option. But believe me, that joker is going to pay for humiliating my family. What if this gets out to the media? My career is over. I apologize for laying this madness all on you, Hank, but . . . "

"It's all good. And yeah, man, I guess you right," the chief replied, agreeing with the consequences of the controversial material being made public. "The news and every other vulture gunning for your job would have a fucking field day."

"Yeah, that's why I need that number for our 'friend' just in case, you feel me? Just in fucking case."

Hank knew better than to write the complete number down somewhere or, worse than that, text it, considering the scandal that had just taken place with the ex-mayor. Commissioner Jackson copied the first three numbers, in backwards sequence on the top of the page of his Bible and the last four on the back of the base of one of his golfing trophies.

After handling a small amount of city business, Hank left his fraternity brother to figure out his next move.

Keisha shut the door, not believing her luck in the past twenty-four hours. First, her so-called man forced her to have sex with two guys, which secretly she enjoyed, then jumped on her for doing it. Then he let Kilo eat her out, and once again, secretly, although the thought was disgusting, Kilo had given her better head than Rico could ever do. And forget him tearing up her raggedy truck that they fought over all the time; he sent that video to just about all her family and friends. Grabbing her cell off the floor, she scrolled down the SENT box. Keisha leaned back against the front door, seeing the devastating amount of people who he'd actually forwarded it to.

This snake! Why didn't I listen to everybody when it came to him? Why? Damn, why? I've been so stupid for so long. I've lost so much of myself. I swear I don't even know who I am anymore. His good-for-nothing ass has taken away everything from me, including my dignity, pride, and self-esteem. His rotten ass got me running around here like I'm worthless. And the bad part about it is I'm letting him treat me that way. I swear this is it.

Somberly, she was caught up in her confused emotions. Out of desperation to make amends before probably going in the other room, killing Rico, and going to jail for the rest of her life, Keisha attempted to get in touch with her already estranged father. Getting sent straight to voicemail on his cell, then repeatedly listening to his overly loyal secretary, Robin, claim he wasn't in the office, Keisha painstakingly got the point. Her father truly meant what he'd said in his message earlier—he was done with her.

I know my mother will listen to me! She has to! She has to understand what madness I've been going through over these last few months. Throughout her entire rocky relationship with Rico, Keisha's mother was always mentally supportive, if even from afar. With shaky hands, her finger finally pushed the SEND button adjacent to her mother's name. Within seconds, it was ringing. One ring, two rings, three rings, lastly four. Met with her mother's soothing voice message, Keisha was left with her already red and puffy eyes now burning.

Dang, not you too, Mother! In denial, Keisha wiped her tear-soaked face with the sleeve of her tracksuit and tried to reach her mother once more. Trembling after hearing the voicemail pop on yet again, Keisha was at a loss as she slid her weak body down the closed door.

Sandy! Keisha thought with a small faint grin and a glimmer of hope. *I know she has my back. She always does. She'll know what I should do. She'll talk to my parents so I can come back home. I know she will.*

Minutes after calling Sandy, her family's longtime chef as well as her friend and confidant, Keisha felt a sense of relief mixed with equal portions of shame, guilt, and embarrassment.

"Sandy, I don't know how it happened. Or even why it happened. I know he's no good for me."

"Then why don't you just come back home or at least get your own place? Why deal with a man like that?"

"It's hard. Rico monitors all my money. He spends every dime I get! I can't save anything. You don't understand."

"Come on. Please don't tell me that, Keisha! It's always a way to leave if you really want to. I'll help you."

"Sandy, you know I love you, and I'd never disrespect you in no type of way, but aren't you being a little hypocritical, telling me that?"

"Huh?" Sandy questioned, assumingly in the dark.

"You know what I mean, Sandy. The entire household does."

"No, Keisha, I don't. What do you mean?"

"Well, the way my father speaks to you, you should've been left, and you stay. I know it can't be the money."

Momentary silence was on both sides of the line before Sandy responded. "Keisha, my situation is much different than yours. You have options I could never dream about. Besides, I have to stay—I just have to. You don't understand."

"I know my mother relies on you, but—"

Sandy quickly changed the subject, not wanting to talk about her own painful life, but to try to help Keisha with hers. "Listen, I have some money I've been saving up. You know you're more than welcome to it." Nervously, she covered her cell, hoping not to be overheard by one of the other part-time staff that was incredibly loyal to Commissioner Jackson in hopes of getting full-time employment.

With no more tears left to shed, Keisha stood to her feet. Pacing the floor while also whispering, she soon found out her mother hadn't even attended the concert the evening prior with her dad or ignored her calls. Instead, she had taken more than her regular amount of sleeping pills and drank two strong double shots of liquor, trying to block out the bone-chilling memory of what she'd seen her daughter doing with "that awful four-legged creature," as she kept screaming repeatedly. Mrs. Jackson was knocked out and was dead to the world, which at this point was better to Keisha than having to face the backlash that was destined to come.

"Listen, Sandy, I'm glad we talked." Keisha felt hopelessness invade her soul, focusing on the closed bedroom door. "But I have to take care of something. When my mother wakes up, tell her I love her and I'm sorry I am such an embarrassment to her and my family."

"Wait, Keisha, don't hang up."

"I've gotta go." Keisha abruptly ended their conversation and headed toward the back for a showdown with Rico.

Commissioner Jackson rode down in the elevator in complete silence with a white business-size envelope in his hands. As the steel doors slid open, he tucked the envelope in his suit jacket's inner pocket.

It's more than one way to skin a cat, he schemed, walking to his city-issued vehicle. No sooner had his driver and bodyguard, Calvin, shut the door of the burgundy sedan than the embarrassed and still very much humiliated father took the documents out. Scanning them over, he handed his trusted driver a small piece of paper with an address scribbled on it.

"Remember it, then tear it up and toss it out onto the freeway," he ordered before placing a call to another close frat brother.

Doing as he was told, Calvin took a shortcut to the small bungalow home located on Detroit's far Westside.

"That's the house over there." He nodded. "The blue and beige house two doors down from the vacant lot."

"Very good." Commissioner Jackson frowned, causing several worry lines to appear in his brow. "Okay, Calvin. You can take me to the house first and then to the club. I have a very important meeting down there."

"Yes, sir."

Enduring the twenty-minute ride accompanied by bumpy, unmaintained city roads, Commissioner Jackson instructed Calvin to keep the car running as he entered his home and quickly returned.

"Okay, let's go. I have to get to the club."

Knowing from past experiences to do as he was told and not ask unnecessary questions, Calvin completely ignored the fact that Sandy, his boss's chef, was waving them down as if she wanted something urgent. When the man that signed his paychecks said, "keep driving," that's what he did, point blank period. If he said "kick a nigga's ass," then so be it. Being Commissioner Jackson's driver as well as bodyguard, his employer's wife and daughter both had his number on speed dial. So it went without saying he'd received the damn no-the-fuck-she-didn't video this morning when he woke up, along with everyone else in Keisha's contact list. However, he wasn't fool enough to mention it.

Chapter Ten

Keisha knew the lavish, carefree lifestyle she'd always been accustomed to up until meeting Rico was now lost forever. Her mother was disappointed, her father was devastated, and Sandy, who always had her back, seemed to have turned on her as well. And all of this was due to Rico and that video. Knowing she had nothing else to lose, she reached down on the side of the entertainment center. With deliberate, steady hands, her fingers wrapped around the steel baseball bat they always kept there. Rico would use it to callously hit Kilo across his backside if he got out of hand while he was walking him. But now, it would be Rico's turn to see how it felt.

One step, two steps—five steps to the closed bedroom door. Raising her foot, Keisha, blinded by rage and ready to battle, applied the most force she could muster. With a crashing sound of thunder, the flimsy door flew open. Stepping over the cracked pieces of drywall that littered the floor from the impact, Keisha called out to Rico.

"All right, all right, boy. We ain't done. You think that shit was a joke? You think I'm a joke?" Without a hint of fear in her body or voice, she quickly realized her soon-to-be intended victim was not in the bed, sitting on the chair, or even hiding behind the door prepared to maybe sneak her. Still gripping up on the bat's gray duct-taped handle, she checked the back door, which still had the chain on it. Drowning out the noise of Kilo's worrisome barks, Keisha headed to the only other place Rico could be—the bathroom. Glancing down, she saw the light shining from under the closed door.

This fool got me fucked up! She raised her foot once more.

"Naw, Rico, it ain't over! We ain't done yet!" Seconds after she caused the door to slam open, she was stopped dead in her tracks. "What in the entire fuck?"

Rico, lying defensively curled around the toilet, threw her mindset completely off. Expecting him to be waving a razor or maybe even a broken piece of metal towel rack to protect himself, she was stunned stupid. The sounds of him violently coughing up blood echoed throughout the cheap tiled walls. Not believing her eyes, mixed with the dark blood-filled mucus on the small but once-fluffy light green bath mat laid almost all Rico's long dreads. The long perfectly twisted locs he'd been growing since he was sixteen were now just some discarded hair ready for the trash. Now, being able to get a clear view of the still-very-much-leaking open gash on the rear of his head, Keisha started to feel a tiny bit of sympathy. After all, he did claim he'd gotten his ass stomped in fighting Swazy and his cousin A.J. for her so-called honor, as if she really had any left.

Confused, not knowing what to expect next, Rico struggled to turn over. Now facing her, Keisha saw a pair of shiny scissors grasped in his left hand—what he'd used to cut his hair. Looking past his bruises, staring in his eyes, she was at a total loss for words. For the first time since she'd met him, he had tears seeming to form.

"Rico?" She tilted her head to the side in total disbelief. "What's going on?"

"Huh," he replied, barely parting his dry lips.

Lowering the bat, Keisha stepped cautiously toward him. "Why you all down on the floor like that? I know you don't want me to feel sorry for you after what you did. My entire family and friends saw that bullshit." She nudged his leg with her foot. "Don't try to lay there and act like you the person hurt in all of this."

"Keisha, please! My head—please!"

"Your head? Rico, what in the hell is wrong with you? Did you just hear what I said? My life is ruined. Over. Done!" She ignored him reaching up for her as she stood on top of his once beautiful locs.

"Anyway, why you cut these motherfuckers?" She kicked them to the other side of the bathroom. "What, you trying to hide your identity or some stupid shit like that? Because if that's the case—sorry, brainchild. The police already know it was your dumb ass driving my truck, or should I say my father's truck? Some people around the corner already identified your always drunk ass."

Rico tried to sit up but collapsed back to the cold floor. "It wasn't like that." He exhaled, rubbing the rear of his head. "I'm just tired of being who I am. I know that was some bullshit what I did. I know. But I was so heated that you was in here freaking with that fool behind my back. I love your punk ass, and that's how you did me?"

Keisha was completely caught off guard by what Rico had just proclaimed. "You say what? I'm confused."

Seeing he was calming her down, Rico went on. "Yeah, girl, I love you. Just because you and me get off into that other shit don't mean I don't love you. How we supposed to get married one day and have kids if you gonna just go behind my back and just do whatever with whoever?"

"Married? Kids?" Keisha was dumbfounded at what she was hearing, but wide open. "Us? Me? You?"

"Why not? Because I'm not smart enough, or is it because I ain't got that major popping-off bread like your people?" Open head wound or not, scalp lumped up from A.J. manhandling and swinging him by his locs the night before, Rico was still good at running pimp game. He stayed winning. "Cutting my dreads is the first step in trying to change and flip the script onto some new shit and a new way of operating."

"Stop it!"

"Baby, I'm serious."

"Bullshit, nigga!"

"Keisha, you gotta believe me!"

"Why should I?"

"Because."

"Because what? All you do is lie and fuck over me."

"I know I've been bugging, but shit is gonna be different. No more threesomes, me making you do shit you ain't really into. No more. A nigga done. I swear I'm done."

"You must think I'm stupid. Just because I wasn't raised in the hood don't make me blind to the game. Besides, if I didn't recognize game when I first met you, I sure in the hell do now."

"Look, girl, it ain't no game. I love you. Flat out, I'm trying to just be with you and start a family and shit. Trust me, after last night, I know I ain't got nobody in my corner but you."

"Rico, stop saying that. Besides, your ass already got a family—your son and baby mama I take care of with my damn money. Or did you forget about them that quick?"

"Fuck both of them. I'm talking about us."

"Just like that, huh?"

"Yeah, Keisha, just fucking like that. I said I love you. Now, do you love me or what?" Rico reached up for the sink.

As his hand trembled, Keisha watched him like a hawk, not knowing what he was going to do when and if he stood to his feet.

"I ain't gonna keep begging you to stay with me. I love you girl. I want you to be my new baby moms. Now, you with me or not?"

Completely thrown off as well as feeling cut off from her own family, Keisha naïvely started to fall for the slick-mouthed bullshit Rico was selling as he slid back onto the floor. Always wanting nothing more than a man and a family of her own that would love and accept her unconditionally, she dropped the bat to the floor. No longer feeling threatened, she leaned toward the wall, praying what Rico was saying was the truth and not just the results of the head trauma he'd obviously suffered at the hands of Swazy and A.J. or the truck crash.

Whatever the case was, Keisha had nothing else or no one else to turn to except the original source of her pain. Having tried repeatedly to contact her parents, with no such luck, Rico's attempts to persuade her already brainwashed and mentally beat-down demeanor was like taking candy from a baby. Convincing Keisha he'd taken that outrageous, repulsive video of her and Kilo and sent it to everyone because he was extremely jealous and hurt became easier the more she thought about the way her father had treated her. She wanted acceptance, and Rico was now saying all the things she wanted and needed to hear.

Over the years, she'd had small glimpses of people, places, and events that never seemed to make any real sense. Within the past few months, more and more those glimpses had turned into dreams that soon turned into nightmares and many sleepless, confused nights. Instead of trying to figure them out, Rico demanded she just forgot about those "fucked-up, back-in-the-day mystery puzzle pieces" that were occasionally tormenting her and concentrate on making *them* more money.

Trying to process what Rico was saying coupled with a now splitting headache, Keisha started to have an anxiety attack. She didn't know what to do or what to think.

Naw, he doesn't mean what he's saying. I know him. He's lying to me. He doesn't care about me. He's just running game. He's just using me. I'm nothing to him.

Oh my God. My father said I was dead to him. He said I was dead. Oh my God, how did this happen? My father used to be so proud of me. He used to say I could be anything in the world. That I was going to be someone important. But this is what I've become.

Mother, I'm so sorry I disappointed you. I know you need me to be your strength, and here I am showing the world that I'm no more than common trash. Filth. . . .

Kim, you're my best friend. Why didn't I listen to you? Why? Why? You tried to tell me the first day I met Rico that he meant me no good, but I didn't listen, and now look at me.

Oh my God! Oh my God, please help me! Help me!

Kilo, stop barking! Shut up!

Oh, my head! My head is killing me! Please stop this pain. I wish I could be back at home, back at home in my own bed. Help me, God, please—help me!

The bathroom walls were spinning one way while the floor started to spin another. The oxygen level in the room seemed to decrease as Keisha fought to breathe.

He doesn't really love me! Why did he send that bullshit to all of those people? I can never show my face again. I might as well be dead. My life means nothing. I know why my family hates me so much. I'm worthless.

Confused and devastated, she felt anguished. Nothing was making sense to her any longer. Not thinking clearly, she wanted to leave the earth and all her troubles behind. She felt she had no other alternative. Rico had taken every single thing she'd ever cared about by vindictively filming that garbage. She had nowhere to go, no one to turn to, and seemingly no one that cared.

Keisha grabbed at her face screaming out. "Noooo!"

She stumbled backward losing her balance. The last thing she saw before striking her head on the corner of the open linen closet was Rico once again struggling to get on his feet.

It was scarcely mid-morning when Calvin, the driver, reached the destination ordered by his boss. Without being told, he adjusted the gun holstered on his hip and exited the vehicle. Watching everyone in his sight, including the ever-present bums and derelicts, Calvin opened the rear passenger door, allowing Commissioner Jackson to step out. Met by a few stares from people huddled at the bus stop located a few yards away from the canopied entrance, the still-very-much angry father made his way through the door, shaking as few hands of acquaintances as possible.

"I'll be ready to leave as soon as I take care of this business. Stay close by. I might need you." Shutting the office door of the club's owner, Keisha's father left his driver/ bodyguard posted on high alert.

"Hello, Lorenzo," Hakim greeted his buddy.

"Hey now, brother. How you doing?" He agitatedly sent another one of Sandy's persistent calls to voicemail.

"It seems a lot better than you."

"Yeah, well, you know how that goes. Shit rolls downhill when you got kids, especially daughters." He placed his cell back on his hip.

"Right, right," Hakim quickly agreed, pulling out his employee file list then picking up the desk phone. "Well, it looks like shit about to roll in another direction."

After him placing a call over the intercom, minutes later, Hakim and Commissioner Jackson heard a light knock on the office door. At the same time as the knocks, Calvin was calling his boss to see if he and Hakim were expecting visitors. Even though the club had its own security team on the clock, Calvin had his own priorities and interest to protect.

"Damn, Lorenzo, your guy doesn't miss a beat, does he?"

"Shit no." Lorenzo proudly cracked his knuckles and probably the only smile of the day. "That dude is as loyal and stand-up as a guy can be—tried, true, and tested."

Informing his driver to open the office door, Commissioner Jackson would soon come face to face with one of Hakim's employees, Lawrence Grant, the reason for his abrupt visit.

"Yes, sir, Mr. Reeves." Lawrence was eager to please his boss. "What can I do for you?"

"First off, you can remove your hat in my office," Hakim strongly suggested. "Then you can take a seat over there. My friend has some questions for you."

Glancing over to the other side of the room, Lawrence noticed Commissioner Lorenzo Jackson, whom he had seen momentarily the night before at the concert. At that very instant, his heart started to beat overtime, and his palms started to sweat profusely. He knew whatever the high ranking and powerful politician wanted with him, it wasn't gonna be anything nice.

"Umm . . . yes, sir. Not a problem." Doing as he was instructed, taking a deep breath, he marched across the room, sitting down on the dark-colored, butter-soft leather couch.

"Do you know who I am?"

"Umm—yes."

"Who?"

"Commissioner Jackson I think, right?"

"That's correct. Well, do you know why I wanted to meet with you?"

"Umm . . . no, sir. Not really."

"Come on, son. You have no idea whatsoever—not even a notion?"

Street smart enough to play dumb as the day he was born, Lawrence locked his fingers, trying to downplay his nervousness. "I can't say. I'm not sure."

"Okay, Lawrence." Hakim cut in, tired of the cat-and-mouse game taking place. "Trust me now when I tell you this. Right now ain't the time to be a wiseguy."

"Naw, Hakim." Lorenzo frowned, staring the young man directly in his eyes. "If I was him, I'd try my best to distance myself from what's about to go down too. Now listen. Lawrence, is it? I saw you last night talking to my daughter, her friend, and a guy over at the Fox Theater. Do you know who I'm talking about now?"

"No disrespect, sir." Lawrence swallowed the huge lump that had been stuck in his throat since entering the room. "I spoke to a lot of people last night. Mr. Reeves demands we greet every guest no matter what venue we're working at. Ain't that right, Mr. Reeves, sir?"

"Okay boy, that's fucking it. I swear for God." Commissioner Jackson raised up out his seat, coming completely out of character. "I'm done playing games with you, punk! You know Rico Campbell, don't you?"

"Rico?"

"Yeah, Negro, Rico! Stop acting deaf as well as dumb. I saw you talking to him and my daughter last night. You know Keisha also, don't you?"

"Oh, Rico and Keisha." He licked his trembling lips, not knowing what to expect next. After all, he did assist in beating down Rico, and worse than that, he and his cousin had just double-team fucked the man's daughter. "Umm, yes, I know them—I guess."

"Well, I got some goddamn questions about your friend, and I need you to answer them. You understand?"

Panicked, Lawrence, who his family and friends called Swazy, was terrified. He was months away from being off parole for a minor marijuana case and had bills to pay at his household. This was the wrong time to lose his job on the humble behind some dumb shit.

"Listen, sir, before you start. Let me explain what happened. Rico was drunk. He came to where my cousin and me were at, starting trouble. He stepped to us first."

"What?" Baffled with his outburst, Keisha's father sat back, listening to Swazy's account of what he claimed went on the night before.

"Yes, sir, I'm not lying. I know he's your daughter's boyfriend, but he got outta pocket. He swung first, so it was on."

"Is that right?"

"Yes, sir, it is." He continued spilling his guts as Hakim, sitting behind his desk, looked on confused at the verbal exchange his friend and employee were having. "I'm not gonna lie to you. Yeah, we was shooting dice and smoking weed, but he took it there first, pulling out his gun—so my cousin and me finished it. He made us choke him out. If he told you anything else, the nigga is straight lying."

Standing to his feet, pacing the room, sweat poured from his forehead. "Look, sir, with all due respect, he got his ass stumped outta frame for talking shit like he always do. So, if you gonna arrest me for protecting myself, or if I'm gonna lose my job, then fuck it. It's all good. That's just messed up, because he's your daughter's boyfriend. I got a family to feed. My girl is pregnant and due in a few months. I need this job."

Not getting an opportunity to get a word in edgewise about what he originally wanted to ask, Keisha's father took things in an entirely different direction than first planned.

"Listen, sit down."

Wanting to throw Rico further under the bus by telling Commissioner Jackson all the times his homeboy had kicked Keisha's ass or all the times the pair had been involved in freakery was tearing away at his self-survivor instinct. On the one hand, Swazy definitely needed this gig, but on the other, what if the enraged father found out he'd hit Keisha off a couple of times his damn self?

"I'm sorry, sir, I really am, but—"

"Listen, boy! Damn. Sit your talkative ass down!" Keisha's father yelled loudly, causing Calvin to open the office door.

"Naw, we're good, Calvin. Don't worry. This young man, Swazy, who resides on Riverview and Seven Mile, works for us now."

"Huh?" Confused the man knew his nickname and where he laid his head, a dry-throat Swazy sat back on the couch almost in tears. Watching Commissioner Jackson reach inside his suit jacket for what he assumed would be handcuffs, Rico's once-best friend saw his freedom flash before his eyes.

Chapter Eleven

Six days, nine hours, and twenty-five minutes later, a clean-shaven, bald-headed Rico was busy in the kitchen making a huge pitcher of grape Kool-Aid. As he stood in sagging jeans, wife beater, and unlaced Tim's slicing up a lemon, Keisha came into the room. With a smile of contentment on her face, she was strangely almost thankful over what had taken place the week prior. While not fully wrapping her brain around Rico's true motives for electronically fucking up her life, the fact that he had seemed to change his way of thinking over the past week was more than enough reward.

After she'd hit her head, blacking out, Rico managed somehow to get her to their bed. Not realizing how long she'd been out of it, she awoke from her nightmarish dreams of things she didn't truly recall happening in real life. The first thing she saw was a blurry sight of him, with a makeshift bandage wrapped around his own head. Devoted, with the I'm-worried-about-you face, he was posted at her bedside, holding her hand.

True to the statements he was making in the bathroom prior to that, he had seemed to be keeping his word. Waiting on Keisha hand and foot, Rico was running around the small rented house, acting like Keisha was the best thing created since hand-packed ice cream. Everything she wanted, including getting her cat licked, he was making happen.

After a long discussion, followed by what appeared to be a heartfelt apology, Keisha decided to try to get over it and let it go. Besides, at that point, he was all she had left. The rest of the world had abandoned her, so she felt.

Besides being aware of the police looking for him for reckless driving and destruction of property, Rico was still very much pissed off at Swazy for the bullshit he'd pulled at the dice game. Embarrassed to be seen outside the house, let alone off the block, he only crept to the gas station and the Coney Island Restaurant late at night. Any calls he received from Swazy or any of his other once-tightknit crew, he immediately shot straight to voicemail, not even bothering to listen to the messages. As far as he was concerned, their friendships were done. He was over dealing with them.

Keisha, just happy to have some attention, couldn't care less what his motives were for being so nice. She was feeling completely ostracized and cut off from her family and friends. Rico, conniving, convinced her to change her cell phone number and just make a new start. She deactivated her Facebook page and deleted her Twitter account. Her email accounts were closed as well. To show Keisha he meant what he was saying, Rico eagerly volunteered to do the same, vowing no female he dealt with in the past, the present, or even the future would have his new contact information.

Little did the couple know at that time, Keisha's father, Commissioner Jackson, was busy doing the same thing, ordering his overly loyal secretary, Robin, to change every phone number linked to him, excluding the office number, which, if his daughter was to call, she'd get denied access to him. Hell bent on making Keisha pay emotionally for what he felt was betrayal by dealing with the likes of Rico Campbell in the first place, Mr. Jackson made sure any possible way his only child had to get in touch with him was severed.

With contempt and malice in her heart, a half-naked Keisha finally found the inner strength she'd remembered having that morning, months ago, when she should've bashed Rico's head in with that bat. Now not in the mood to endure any more of her so-called man's sexual, physical, and emotional abuse, Keisha got off the floor. As Kilo rushed from the other side of the bedroom, excitedly jumping up on Keisha's side, she pushed him off his hind legs and back onto all four. In the midst of the dog's echoing barks, Rico stepped back, bending his hard dick back inside his jeans.

"Oh, peep game. So, you tough, huh?" Rico taunted, knowing they had been down that "I'm tired of you" road before. "What, you ain't trying to be a nigga's bottom bitch no more, is that it?"

"Rico, them foul-ass outlandish mind games you been playing is fucking over." Keisha tried closing her ripped blouse to cover her exposed breasts. "I'm over it. I swear I am. I'm done. I knew you wouldn't change."

Smushing Keisha dead in the face, he laughed. "Girl, you act like you call the shots. I done told you it's one boss around this motherfucker, and you looking at it. So, shut your mouth and get back on your damn knees."

"I ain't getting on shit. Fuck your fake ass!" Keisha screamed, causing Kilo to bark even louder. "I'm out this motherfucker."

Rico laughed once more, grabbing her by the throat and squeezing. "You think I'm playing? I can show you better than I can tell you." As he lifted her body with one hand slightly off the floor, she struggled to breathe. Using the other one, he pulled his still semi-hard dick back out. "I'ma teach your ugly big ass who's boss."

Wondering why she was fool enough to stay with him as long as she had, Keisha fought to stay conscious and alert, thinking about all the lies Rico had told, the money she'd spent, the family and friends that had cut her off, along with the degrading, crazy drama he'd put her through.

It was like any other Tuesday evening when Keisha got off the Davison Avenue bus. Blessed by finally finding a new job after posting her resume on Craigslist, she and Rico were getting along as well as could be expected. Both cutting themselves off from their family and friends— although Keisha's separation was involuntarily—was what it was. Besides the eight- to ten-hour days she'd put in at the downtown office, the pair spent their spare time together.

Rico, of course, had plenty of spare time. Refusing to get a job or leave the house to at least monkey-hustle up on a couple of dollars, every minute was spare time he spent smoking weed, watching bootleg DVDs, and playing video games, which Keisha sponsored. Rico might have been more attentive to his woman, including giving her some of the best nights of actually making love she'd experienced since they first met, yet his I-ain't-working-no-fucking-nine-to-five attitude was the same. That characteristic would never change, so Keisha would either have to deal with it or not. Left with only him in her life, she did.

Overly tired from an employment training class she was taking in hopes of rapid job advancement, cooking for Rico's lazy ass was not on her agenda. Desperately trying to stay ahead of the ever-mounting household bills, Keisha hated to spend money on fast food. However, today marked the one-month anniversary since she and Rico recommitted to each other. He seemed to be keeping in line with what they both vowed, so she had no intention whatsoever of rocking the boat. And Rico, selfish as he was, left with a hungry stomach and munchies, was sure to cause friction.

"Hello, Sam. How are you?" Keisha smiled, greeting the middle-aged Middle Easterner who ran the Coney Island.

"Aww, Miss Keisha." He returned the smile, cleaning both hands on his knee-length, grease-stained apron. "I am doing fine. You are a little late this evening getting off the bus."

Checking her watch, the only piece of expensive jewelry she wasn't forced to sell or pawn to make ends meet, she realized he was correct. "Sam, you always watch out for me every morning and evening. I appreciate it."

"Anytime, Miss Keisha, anytime. You know that is a rough neighborhood, and you're not like—"

"Don't say it, Sam." She leaned over toward the bulletproof glass so none of the other folk in the crowded restaurant would overhear their conversation. "I already know what you're going to say. And in reality"—she glanced at most of the foul-mouthed, ill-mannered patrons—"I can't say that you're wrong."

Placing her order, a double bacon cheeseburger deluxe with chili fries and a grilled chicken pita, she was told it'd be no more than ten minutes. Standing over to the far side of the doorway, Keisha read over the training manual from her job, hoping to do well on tomorrow's test. With her head down and her eyes focused on the pages, she failed to see two familiar faces enter the building, but almost instantly after hearing their voices, Keisha hesitantly looked up, locking eyes with A.J. first, then Swazy.

"Well, I'll be damned. If it ain't ole girl shawty from round the way. What it do, girl?" A.J. grinned, showing his gold tooth. "Where you been hiding?"

Keisha, still ashamed of what she let both of them do to her sexually, not to mention the fact she knew nine outta ten Rico had shown them the video of her and Kilo, just nodded her head without speaking.

"Yeah, hey, Keisha." Swazy stepped a little too close for comfort, making her lean backward. "Dang, sis, you can't speak?"

Now, with all eyes on her, she had no choice but to answer. Standing there like they would magically disappear wasn't going to happen. "Hey, Swazy."

"What about me, shawty?" A.J. winked, still smiling. "No hey for me? I thought we was better than that."

"Hey," Keisha replied, holding the coiled manual clutched to her chest.

Not completely sure if she knew what had jumped off that night of the concert after they left, especially considering the lies Rico was known to tell and the way he had Keisha wrapped around his finger, Swazy took the opportunity to set things straight. "Look, Keisha, can I holler at you for a few?"

"Yeah, I guess so." Knowing she had no other option since she was waiting for her and Rico's food to be ready, Keisha decided to hear him out.

Trying to find a small bit of privacy from the many nosey neighbors and prying eyes, the two of them headed toward the rear of the dining area. No more than two or three minutes into the one-sided conversation, she soon realized Rico had done it once again. He had played her. Not only were his claims about Swazy and A.J. talking shit behind her back untrue, but much to her embarrassment, she found out he was showing the awful video to everyone that came through the dice game that night.

"I saw his baby mama pushing a new whip, and she said she had seen the bullshit too!" Swazy threw in her face, not to hurt her further, but to bring home the fact that Rico was dead wrong. "Matter of fact, she got it saved on her damn cell phone, so it ain't no telling who she done showed at the strip club. You know she be out there."

Completely mortified, Keisha's inner soul started to ache. It was like the harshness of the coldhearted pain she felt the first moment she'd found out a month ago. Feeling the onset of a full-blown anxiety attack, the only thing saving her from probably passing out cold on the crowded Coney Island filthy floor was Sam calling her name, signifying her order was up.

As she made her way up to the window, Sam could easily conclude Keisha's overall demeanor had changed. Wanting to ask her what was troubling her, he decided not to. It was much too busy, and besides, his always-insecure second wife was working the cash register.

Leaving out the door, white plastic bag containing food in hand, Swazy and A.J. followed Keisha into the front of the building, letting her know that Rico, and Rico alone, was the reason he got his ass kicked. Swazy then informed her he had tried on several different occasions to get in touch with Rico so they could set shit straight, but his cell number was changed, and he didn't want to just show up at the crib unannounced.

She was still visibly shaken from what she just heard. A.J. stepped up.

"Listen, shawty, I meant what I said that night. You too good to be rocking with a weak cat like that soft punk. He ain't got your best interest at heart. You betta come down to the Dirty with me. I'm leaving up outta here tonight on that grey dog. I'll treat you right!" Writing his cell number down on a Foot Locker receipt he had in his back pocket, A.J. put it in her hand. "Whenever you get tired of that dreadlocked sucker, baby girl, call a real nigga. Remember, real rap, it don't matter how we started—it just matter how we end, ya heard." A.J. shook his head at how stupid and naive Keisha was as Swazy took his cell out his pocket to place a call.

Taking a shortcut across the litter-filled parking lot, disappearing into the hood, Keisha grew angrier with each passing step she took.

His no-good ass ain't never gonna change! I was nothing but being dumb again to have believed his lying, sneaky self! Taking up for me my ass! I knew it was too good to be true! Why I keep falling for his bullshit? It seems no matter what kinda bullshit he pulls, I still keep dealing with him. What in the hell is wrong with me? Why don't I want more for myself? Why don't I stop putting up with being treated like my life doesn't matter?

But this time, I'ma be strong. This time I'ma show him and prove to him that I'ma stand on my own and leave. I don't care if I gotta go to the shelter or be homeless out in these streets. I'm done being his convenient doormat!

With sweaty palms from the plastic bag she swung at her side, Keisha went home. The clicking sounds of Keisha's heels echoed off the broken concrete sidewalk then the lopsided raggedy wooden stairs to her front door.

"What up, doe?"

"What up, doe?" she answered in a questionable tone. "Are you freaking serious? Boy, please. Where in the hell you been? I ain't heard from you since you sent me that video."

"I been around. Just chilling, laying low. You know how it is." Rico lit his blunt, inhaling deep a few times before putting it in the ashtray on the coffee table.

"That's cool, but you had to change your number to do that bullshit?"

"Girl, whatever. So, check, word in the street is you got a new ride, huh? I guess the pole-swinging game ain't feeling the recession." Rico held his cell up to his ear with his shoulder. Using both hands on the controller, he tilted his body from side to side, trying to avoid getting out on the new game he was playing, courtesy of Keisha.

"What you got for me?" he asked.

"Who in the hell told your nosey ass what I'm pushing? Ya boy Swazy?" Ocean, Rico's baby mama, couldn't do anything but laugh at his brazen statement. "And FYI, dude, is you nuts? First of all, swinging on a pole ain't never, ever going out of style, and even if it was, I got a wet and juicy rent box between my legs, so a sista like me ain't never entertaining going hungry."

"I heard that. And FYI to your ass, Swazy ain't my boy."

"Yeah, well."

"Yeah, well, what about what I asked you?"

"What in the fuck you talking about now, fool?"

"You heard me, bitch, so stop clowning. I said what you got for daddy?" Taking it to the head, he downed the rest of his second forty-ounce for the day and was about ready for the third.

"Rico, please. Don't even play yourself. You must be on a serious one. You know those days of getting my bread are long motherfucking gone."

"Oh, is that right, Miss Shit Talker?" Belching, he sarcastically replied, putting the television on mute. "You wasn't blowing that garbage out your mouth a few months back when we was freaking with your girl from the club."

"Hell yeah, it's right. You better believe it. That was a few months back, and this is now," she yelled, feeling her true independence. "Matter of fact, I need to be asking your fake wanna-be pimping ass what you and that ugly bumpy-face ho you fucks with got for my son! She got some good head on her, but I needs that cash."

"Come on now, Ocean. You bugging."

"Boy, I ain't bugging. I'm trying to be straight up. What you got for my son?"

"Anyway, girl." Conveniently, he ignored her question and went onto more of his own. "How you get that ride? Put me up on game." He took the television off mute.

"Ain't no game. My new dude hooked me up."

"New dude?" Rico firmly questioned, calling himself getting serious. "Who you got being around my damn seed?"

"Boy, bye. Slow your deadbeat daddy roll. Ain't nobody around your son. My new guy, or should I say trick, is married. He just got that serious bread jumping off. He stays wearing a suit and tie. And even if my son was around the next motherfucker, so damn what?"

"Yeah, well, kill all that stupid noise. I wanna see you. How about that?" Rico's voice got louder and more demanding with each word he spoke. So loud, in fact, he failed to hear Keisha storming in through the front door. "I wanna see that ass tonight." Before he knew it, an overly aggravated Keisha was standing right over him, prepared for battle.

Chapter Twelve

"Commissioner Jackson, you have a call on line one from a Mr. Lawrence Grant. Do you want me to put it through?"

"Yes, thank you, Robin." He sat back in his oversized chocolate-brown leather chair. Lifting the receiver, he eagerly placed it to his ear, pushing the flashing light.

"Yes, Mr. Grant, what's the latest?" He spoke like they were old friends. "What do you have for me?"

"Well, Mr. Jackson, I mean Commissioner Jackson, sir, I just saw your daughter."

"Well, it's about time. I was starting to lose confidence in you. That initial bit of four-one-one you had on his personal life has proven to be a lot more lucrative than I anticipated, but still not enough."

"Please, sir, it's just that in between working and—"

"Listen, I'm not in the mood for any excuses. It's been a long day, and I'm running out of patience. The deal was you get me all the information about that friend of yours and my baby girl, and you keep your job and your freedom."

"I know, sir, I know."

"Well, what happened? Tell me. Was that dirty fool with her? What did she look like?"

Swazy went on to explain their surprise Coney Island encounter. Not everything said between the two was repeated, but enough to let him know Keisha was a little bit closer to kicking Rico to the curb once and for all.

"I told her I had been trying to get in touch with Rico and set things straight like you suggested, but she just brushed it off. It was like she was in some sort of a daze."

"Daze." The sometimes concerned parent sat up in his chair, listening attentively. "What do you mean, dazed? Like he has her on drugs?"

Swazy wanted to throw Rico under the bus again and lie, but knew if Keisha's father heard that about his daughter, it might push him all the way over the edge. It was one thing to have a freak, sloppy-seconds slut-bucket for a child, but a random-dick-slurping crackhead whore was another. "No, sir, not drug dazed. More like fed up, exhausted, what-in-the-hell-can-happen-next daze. Kinda like that."

Somewhat relieved in the answer, Commissioner Jackson informed Swazy to either step up his game of delivering valuable information that could help bring Rico to his knees or suffer the consequences. Only moments after ending that conversation, his secretary pranced into the office, telling him he had another call, this time from home.

"Excuse me." Robin, clearly irritated, gave him the side eye. "But Sandy is on the phone again—something about your wife. She claims it's important. Do you want to speak to her or tell her you just stepped out?"

"No, I'll take it. Thank you." He winked, now in a much better mood after speaking to Swazy. "And can you please shut the door on your way out?"

"In between your wife, Sandy, and that other thang that's been calling, it's always something," Robin mumbled underneath her breath before doing as she was told.

It's always motherfucking something. One day I'ma stop being his side chick and be wifey. And when that happens, I swear things gonna change around here.

"Who in the hell you talking to? Whose ass you wanna see so bad tonight?" Keisha tried unsuccessfully to snatch the cell out of Rico's hand.

"Damn, Keisha. Where in the fuck—" He was stunned, spinning around to avoid her hitting him across the back of his bald head.

"That's right, you lying sack of shit. I'm right here. And I just heard exactly what you said."

Quickly pushing the END button, terminating the call, Rico jumped to his feet in an attempt to explain. "Listen, Keisha, before you start blowing stuff outta proportion and trying to go hard."

She was still infuriated about her revealing conversation with Swazy. Catching Rico red-handed talking to some tramp was only adding more fuel to the fire. Ripping the plastic bag, she opened both white containers, throwing the food she'd just purchased onto the floor.

"Fuck you and this food!" She smashed it with the soles of her shoes while screaming. "I'm out working to keep a roof over both our heads, and you sitting your black ass around drinking, smoking weed, playing video games, and talking to bitches."

"Wait, Keisha, damn!"

"Wait for what? So you can tell some more lies like the ones you told about what happened between you and Swazy that night?"

"Swazy? I know you ain't say his name in this house. What in the fuck that snake-ass nigga got to do with jack shit?"

"Don't keep playing with my intelligence, Rico. I just spoke to him and his cousin."

"Oh, yeah? And did you give that country gold-tooth faggot the pussy this time, or was it just head again?"

"Oh, that's nice, but trying to flip the script ain't working this time around." Keisha's blood started to boil. "I know what he told me, and I sure in the fuck know what I just heard. All of this is too much."

"Look at your insecure ass wasting food and a nigga hungry." Rico, full of beer, had to piss something awful. Headed toward the bathroom, he continued to hurl accusations and try to deflect the guilt. "You tripping as usual. I don't know why I fucks with you. That was the weed man I was talking to." He slammed the bathroom door shut.

"What?" Keisha screamed out before noticing he'd left his cell on the couch. Without a second thought, she swooped it up. Finding the recent calls icon on the touch screen menu, she pushed CALL. Seconds later, a female's voice was on the line.

"Damn, henpecked Negro. That uppity, goofy bitch got you shook! I heard her getting off into that ass."

"Excuse me?" Keisha arrogantly fumed, ready to go in.

"Oh, damn. My bad."

"Who is this?"

"Who in the hell you think it is?" Ocean laughed, taunting Rico's girl.

"How should I know? That's why I asked. Now once again, who is this?"

"Now once again, who is this?" She mocked Keisha's white-girl, private-school tone. "This is Ocean, okay. Rico's son's mother. Now do you know who I am, or do you need to taste this sweet pussy again to remember?"

Immediately offended by what she'd just heard, Keisha went completely off. "Why in the hell are you talking to Rico? What are you two low-lives scheming on now?"

"Huh? Excuse you?"

"No, Ocean, excuse you. I'm tired of this bullshit."

"Then that seems like something you need to take up with Rico, not me. Y'all weak bitches kill me. Always blaming the next female instead of they man. If he fucks with me or any other chick, then that's on him, not us. Grow the fuck up or go kill yourself."

Just like that, Keisha was in an all-new state of mind. The light switch came on in her brain. Realizing Ocean was 100% correct and her true beef was with Rico, not the next female, Keisha conceded, easing up on her verbal tirade. "I guess you right, but Rico—"

"No buts." Ocean wasn't in the mood to let her mouthy attacker off the hook that easy and decided to really rub it in. "Look, girl, me and that fool you wanna call your man go back to sixth grade and hide go get 'em in the basement. I know he ain't shit. He never was."

"Well—" Keisha started to question but was stopped.

"Well what? Why did I have a baby with his slick punk ass? Why do me and him do what we do from time to time?" Ocean nonchalantly fired back. "Because he fine as hell with a big dick, that's why. But to have that buster as my man—girl, you a fool. Trust when I tell you don't no other bitch in Detroit wanna claim him but your dumb ass." She giggled into the phone, further agitating Keisha. "But I tell you what. If you ever wanna get down with me and my new man on some freak shit, I can straight hook you up. After all, I know firsthand your head game is on point. Or should I get Kilo? Rumor is he got some good head too."

"What?" Having had enough of Ocean's advice and insults, Keisha happily hung up jus as Rico came out the bathroom.

"So, you still out here bugging or what?"

"Naw, liar." Keisha threw his cell phone against the wall as hard as she possibly could. "I was out here talking to the weed man, Ocean."

Knowing he was cold busted, Rico tried to play it off as he bent down, picking up his phone. "Okay, so I was talking to my baby moms. So what? Big deal. You want me to not check up on my son? Is that what you saying?"

"Oh, yeah? Is that what you was doing? Or was you two discussing that video?"

"Stupid, look what you did." Rico acted as if he hadn't heard what she'd just said. "You cracked my damn screen."

"So damn what? I paid for the son of a bitch. Now you wanna explain what Swazy told me that I know is true? Or better yet, lie some more about Ocean? Which one is it?"

"Fuck it. I'm over this shit. Go fuck yourself or A.J., or better yet, Kilo." Stepping over the food smashed on the floor, Rico pulled up his sagging jeans, grabbed his house keys, and left out the front door.

Following close behind, Keisha called him a few names from the front porch before he bent the corner, heading God knows where. Wanting to call Kim and vent, she knew she couldn't. Having not spoken in close to a month, her once-best-friend-since-childhood told her never to dial her number again if she didn't leave Rico after the Kilo incident. And since Keisha hadn't, Kim lending an ear was out of the question. Her next thought was Sandy, or maybe her mom. Unfortunately, the few times she'd called home anonymously, to just hear one or both of their voices before hanging up, Keisha had come to find out all the numbers were disconnected or changed.

Trying to disguise her voice, calling her father's office didn't work either. His overzealous secretary, barely over her own age, recognized Keisha's voice and refused to put her through just like she was ordered to do. Having no one but herself for comfort, she looked at A.J.'s number and thought of calling him, at least just to talk, but quickly tucked the paper into her purse. Feeling sorry for herself, she cleaned up the mess on the floor before curling up in a ball on the couch and crying.

"Yes, Sandy. What is it now?" Commissioner Jackson stretched his arm outward. "It's already been a grueling day. I told you that last time you called. I hope you have better news this time."

With apparent hesitation in her voice, Sandy apologized for the constant interruptions but gently reminded her boss he'd told her to call him every hour or so with a household update concerning his wife's overly intoxicated, as well as medicated, condition. "I'm so sorry. I tried everything I know, but she's just getting worse. Her hands feel cold to the touch, and her eyes look weak when I hold the lids open."

"When will that woman learn? Mixing all those pills and martinis are for the white man—the Caucasians," he argued, knowing he had to call it a day and return home. "If I thought it wouldn't hurt me politically right now, I'd divorce her old ass."

Not knowing what to say next, Sandy remained silent. She knew since a small child and an early teen that Mr.

Jackson wasn't one to be argued with, told no, or kept waiting.

"Well, I'm calling Calvin for the car and will be there shortly. I know the maid is gone for the day, so I need you to make sure the bathroom in the far end guest room is clean. I'll be sleeping there tonight again. It's no need to try to deal with Mrs. Jackson this evening, is it?"

"No, sir," Sandy replied before he hung up.

Gathering a few files, he took a quick shot from a bottle he kept in his desk. Going into the outer office, Keisha's father was met with obvious shade from Robin, who was expecting overtime possibly in more ways than one.

"Well, you can just call it a night. I have to go home. And depending on a few things, I might not be in tomorrow. I'll let you know."

"Yeah, I heard." Her response was cold to say the least.

Sensing the young woman's attitude, knowing she'd been no doubt eavesdropping, Commissioner Jackson promised her a little something special in the days to follow if she put a smile on her pretty face. Motivated by money, Robin quickly obliged. When her boss stepped on the elevator and the door closed, she did what she always did—went into his office, sat behind his desk, and put her feet up.

One day, I'm going be calling all the shots around here. Using her foot, she knocked the picture of Mrs. Jackson off the desk and straight into the garbage can. *With that slut-ass daughter already out the picture, I know he's gonna need me!* Delusional in thought, Robin stayed in the office another twenty minutes, fantasizing about what could be—that was, if she played her cards right.

Chapter Thirteen

Hooking up with Ocean, Rico went with her and their son to Chuck E. Cheese. With Rico's pockets staying on empty, the entire evening of family time was sponsored by Ocean—by way of her older mystery man. Thanks to him, Rico was able to run around, with his son at his side, playing every game and putting him on every ride without giving two shits about how many tokens he was using.

"In between that new car and judging by that knot in your purse, it seems like you hit a serious lick with this so-called man. Where you meet his ass at anyway?"

"One night I was leaving the club, and he was just there." Ocean giggled, explaining the chance-encounter-turned-financial-windfall. "He was parked over near the fence with his headlights out. When I went to unlock my car door, he rolled down his window and flashed some cash! Shit—he scared my black ass, almost making me pee on myself."

Drinking a mug of beer, eating the last slice of pizza, Rico was amused by her story. "Oh, yeah? Then what?"

"What you mean, then what? Please, an hour later we was in a hotel room, and I was peeing on him."

"Oh, hell naw."

"Oh, hell yes, my nigga. Fair exchange ain't never a robbery." Ocean brushed her own shoulders off. "You

know how I do. I'm gonna get that money. I don't care
who I gotta fuck or suck to do it." Looking over at the
multi-colored ball pit their son was playing in, she began
to grin from ear to ear. "Me and mines gonna always be
okay with or without your deadbeat ass."

"Dig that." Rico low-key admired her go-getter attitude. To most, Ocean might have been considered a slut,
but in his eyes, his baby mama was a trooper and about
her paper.

Finishing the rest of their game tokens, the trio headed
back to the Westside neighborhood they both called
home. Ocean had to go to work later and insisted that she
and Rico part ways before she dropped their son off at
the sitter.

"For real, I don't need your broke, good-hating ass
hanging around the club tonight. You better go make up
with that low-self-esteem bitch you dealing with—the
one that made you cut them dreads."

"Maybe I will, but not now," Rico admitted with a
devilish smirk. "She can wait. Right about now, you can
just drop me off on Linwood and Davison."

Driving off, Ocean left her baby daddy right on the
corner. It was now dark outside, and he was still hungry
as hell despite the paper-thin pizza slices he had at Chuck
E. Cheese. Rico decided to grab a couple of original
wings and maybe an order of potato wedges from KFC.

Heading through the glass double doors, he was
shocked to see—who else, ironically—Swazy on his way
out of the restaurant.

"Damn, dawg. What up, doe." Swazy was the first to
speak. "Where in the fuck you been hiding?"

"Hiding? Whatever. I'm still in the game." Rico gave
him the serious fuck-you-faggot side-eye. "I'm still
pushing that bag."

"I tried calling your wild ass. Damn, guy, you cut your dreads."

"What?" Rico twisted his face in disbelief, tilting his head to the side. "Are you fucking serious?"

"Come on, dude." Swazy tried taking a cop, knowing he'd been waiting on an opportunity to make amends. "We go too far back to let some dumb shit come between us being cool. We was all high as fuck and drunk as hell."

"And what's your point, Swazy? Huh? That shit was foul—but I guess blood thicker than water, huh?"

"Come on, man. Think about it. You was wrong as hell pulling a gun on niggas—your boys and shit!"

"Yeah, where in the fuck is my gun anyway? I need—naw, I want that shit back." Rico's voice grew in volume as the girl working the cash register and a few other customers looked on.

"Yo, I been had it, but your ass went underground. After the hood was talking about you tearing up ole girl truck and the police coming by your crib, niggas ain't know what jumped. And everybody around here knows how Keisha is. They ain't asking her jack, and she showl in the fuck ain't volunteering a damn thing." Swazy tried defusing Rico's long-standing anger. "Come on, guy. Let's just squash this shit."

Thinking about what happened to him that night at the hands of Swazy and his cousin, and taking in consideration he knew Swazy had just dry-snitched him out to Keisha earlier, Rico's mind started working overtime.

"Yeah, all right, man. We cool, but your cousin, he straight grimy. Him and me got some unfinished business. That dude a full-grown snake."

Swazy gave him a playful shoulder bump while still holding onto a big bag of chicken. "Listen, guy. Ole boy about to hop on that dog in a few heading south. That's why I got this grub and a big-ass Faygo Red Pop in the ride. "I just gotta pick him up from this skank's crib on the Eastside, near Mack and Bewick, and drop him off at Greyhound. He taking that work back, so you know he gonna be ghost for a good while. Y'all can work that shit out later—like men."

"Oh, yeah." Rico schemed as his vindictive-toned words dripped from his lips. "Maybe so."

"Yeahm dawg. Why don't you hit me up in about ninety minutes and we can blow something up in the air? Maybe have a toast to them locs you cut off."

Hell bent on revenge, Rico agreed before Swazy left. Conveniently, he didn't mention him speaking to Keisha over at the Coney Island, so Rico played the game also and didn't either. After eating his food in the dining area, Rico headed home.

Noticing all the lights were off inside the house except for the bathroom, Rico crept through each dark room. Praying Keisha wasn't bold enough to be hiding with a frying pan or another bat to try to detach his head from the rest of his body, he tried to be as quiet as possible.

"I hear your two-timing, rotten bastard ass in this house, Rico Campbell. You ain't slick."

Rico paused, but only long enough to look for something in the hallway to defend himself. "Look, Keisha. I ain't come back here for all that nonsense you was talking earlier. I ain't in the mood."

With a jar of Motions hair relaxer in one hand and a comb in the other, Keisha stepped out into the hallway.

"You ain't in the mood?" She sucked her teeth and continued smoothing in the chemical. "Well, guess what? Neither am I. Matter of fact, I'm done talking about it. From this point on, you do you, because I'm damn straight doing me!"

"Oh, yeah?" Rico bossed up, sensing his money train was pulling out the station yet again. "What you saying?"

"Negro, please. I know that Detroit public school education taught you a little bit of common sense, didn't it?" Keisha dipped back in the bathroom, looking into the mirror. "But just in case it didn't, let me break the bullshit down for your stupid ass. Nigga, as of today, right now, this fucking second, me and you is through. Over."

For the past month, up until a few hours ago, bad-boy Rico had been on his best behavior where Keisha was concerned. He really hadn't been hanging out with his boys all times of the night. He truly wasn't calling Keisha negative, disrespectful names or putting his hands on her. As for kicking it with other females, besides calling Ocean earlier, he was innocent of even flirting with the next chick. However, if Keisha wanted it like that, to him, it was definitely not a problem.

"Okay, check this out, you ugly, fucked-up-in-the-face rat. You run around here in this hood, thinking you better than everybody. Well, guess what? Niggas be clownin' your fake ass and clownin' me for dealing with a fat-ass monster like you." Rico spit on the floor, showing his disgust for their relationship. "Every time I wake up and see that mug, let alone kiss you, I wanna throw up."

"Oh, yeah? Is that right?" Keisha felt tears swell in her eyes.

"Yeah, but hold up, you stankin' bitch. Don't get to crying now, Keisha. You wanted to man up, so man up."

"I'm only crying because I wasted so much of my time on an uneducated hood hoodlum like you. When I finish my hair, I'm gonna get dressed and find me somebody who appreciates me."

Walking away and into the bedroom, Rico soon returned with a stun gun he had hidden up on the closet shelf. "Okay, smart-talking, goofy trick with all the mouth. Get on your motherfucking knees and suck this big black dick before you leave. Then ask the next buster that kiss you out in them streets how my nut taste."

With a head full of perm, Keisha stood back, asking him if he was crazy. While she was reaching for a towel, Rico hit the button, making a small amount of electric charge buzz through the top. Realizing she had nowhere to run, Keisha tried to bargain and negotiate her way out of the potential violent situation.

"Okay, wait a minute, Rico." She threw both hands up, dropping the towel. "Why you doing this? Why? You the one that broke your promise. You the one that was talking to that stripper Ocean on the phone, baby mama or not. And you the one that took that messed-up video that ruined my damn life in the first place."

Seemingly mad at the world, Rico's eyes looked cold and lifeless. Gripping the black, rectangular-shaped handle, he hit the button once more.

"And guess what, Keisha? I'm the one that's about to get his dick sucked, too. So stop talking and drop down like I told you. Now!"

Having no other choice but to do as she was told, begrudgingly she eased her thick body down in between the sink and the bathtub. With the stinging feeling of the extra-strength perm starting to burn and irritate her scalp, Keisha opened her mouth wide, taking all of Rico in that she possibly could. As she slurped and licked the head and the shaft, he callously hit the button on the fully charged stun gun a couple of more times, causing Keisha to jerk her neck.

Just as he was about to bust, Rico took a step backward, sliding his pole out her wet mouth. Using his free hand, he took direct aim at her face. Completely amused at the sight of her on her knees, with white-in-color perm caked in her head and a wad of his cum oozing down from her barely open eyelids, Rico couldn't contain himself.

"Damn, you ugly. You one fucked-up ho. I swear for God, you busted." He cruelly meant every word he was saying. "I wish you could see your uppity ass now. Matter of fact—" Reaching in the back pocket of his jeans that were still down past his knees, he pulled out his cracked-screen cell. Holding it up, he dared her to try to hide her face as he took several pictures. "I can't see this shit clearly now, but fuck it, I bet the next nigga's screen ain't fucked up."

"Rico, please don't. Please!" Keisha's scalp felt like it was on fire. "I'm sorry. I'm sorry," she begged, still on her knees.

"Shut the fuck up, Keisha! That's your problem—you talk too damn much. For a whole month, I was posted in this raggedy motherfucker, and you got the nerve to be talking about giving the pussy to the next nigga. Bitch, please. Don't nobody want you but me. Your life is useless, ma. Remember that." He pulled his pants back up, zipping them. "And if you keep talking slick, even I ain't gonna want that ass. You know what? Fuck this bullshit and you. I'm out." Pissed off, Rico took the money for the rent from Keisha's purse. For her sake, luckily, he didn't see A.J.'s cell number folded up, or there'd be no telling what he'd do next. Irritated, he left the house with Keisha still in the bathroom on the floor, scared to move.

When, and only when, she was sure he was gone, she turned the shower on full blast. Not having time to even take her clothes off, Keisha jumped underneath the strong pressure of the cold water. Exhaling, she felt the relief of the burning chemical rinse out her almost-ear-length hair. Tightly closing her eyes, letting the water wash away Rico's sperm, she prayed he wouldn't let anyone see the pictures he'd just taken. Raising her hand up to wipe some of the water from her face, she felt huge clumps of her hair falling from her head and onto the shower floor. Seeing it clog the drain, Keisha slid down the wet walls and sat there in disbelief over the mess she'd made of her life.

Rico met up with Swazy at a mutual friend's house. The girl, whom they had both banged at one point or another, was always down to get high, drunk, or fuck, so chilling over there to daybreak was definitely not a problem. After she was passed out cold, Swazy and Rico continued to get high. Still trying to feel each other out, the once-closer-than-brothers best friends curiously asked questions about each other's recent dealings.

Rico, on a mission, had one thing and one thing only in mind, and that was to fuck Swazy's street credibility over like he'd done his that night at the dice game, and then ultimately put a bullet in his cousin's head. So, of course, every question Rico was asked, he answered carefully.

This boy think I'm a fool. He ain't said jack shit about seeing Keisha's ugly ass up at the Coney Island. Rico suspiciously smirked from across the room. *He probably wanna hook his cousin up with my meal ticket. Sneaky motherfucker. That's why he keep bringing her and me up.*

Swazy, on the other hand, had his own agenda. Not really giving a fuck about Rico truly forgiving him, low-key the only thing he was interested in was information about Keisha and how Rico's relationship with her was going. Commissioner Jackson was pressuring revoking his probation and getting him locked up if he didn't hold up his side of the bargain. From the first time he met him and from several phone updates, Swazy could easily tell Keisha's father was not to be played with and far from a joke.

Chapter Fourteen

The following day, to no surprise, Rico hadn't come home. Keisha wasn't shocked. Truthfully, she was glad. Most times he did that crap, she'd be up practically all night, worried, but not this time. As she washed her face, looking into the mirror at the huge bald spots and fresh sores on her scalp, she prayed he was dead. That way she wouldn't have to be strong enough to leave him; he'd just be dead and gone. Already running late for work, she struggled to find a way to do something, if anything, with her hair, or what was left of it. Yeah, Keisha had plenty of weave lying around the house: a multitude of buns, ponytails, and spare pieces in various colors and lengths. However, she was working against the clock. She'd been late a few other times, and her boss had already given her the serious side-eye on more than one occasion.

Damn, I need to hit the beauty supply real quick. Continuing to get dressed, scarf wrapped around head, she was soon out the door, heading up to Davison. Passing the White Castle, she decided to get a small coffee to wake her all the way up.

Searching through her purse for some change, she realized the envelope with the rent money inside of it was missing.

That good-thieving son of a bitch! Instantly infuriated, Keisha was at a loss for words. She was gonna use some of that money to get herself a wig until she could figure out what to do next with her hair. *I gotta go to work. I can't lose this job. I can't!*

Marching across the street with a determined attitude, Keisha proudly entered the Korean-owned neighborhood beauty supply like she often did. Unlike most of their hood clientele, Keisha never whined or complained about the prices of the more expensive packs of hair or other products. She just paid with a smile. So, when she headed toward the rear of the store, neither Tommy, the owner, nor Sue followed. The ho-ass house nigga they had guarding the door even remained seated, eating his breakfast. Desperate, without so much as a second thought of what she was about to do, Keisha quickly chose a wig that she thought would suit her, snatched it off the faceless head and stuffed it in her purse. Looking up in the security mirrors, she walked back toward the front, confident no one saw her.

"You didn't need any help?" the guy at the door asked when she breezed past.

"Naw, I'm good. I just wanted to check a price." When she stepped on the other side of the door, no alarms ringing or buzzers buzzing, she was relieved.

With his plastic fork in hand, the guy followed her outside. "Hey, since I let you go on that wig back in there, why don't you let me get your number?"

"Huh?" Keisha momentarily paused, more than shocked she was busted. "Umm, I don't think so."

"Come on now. I know you don't think you better than me, do you?"

"What?" Keisha tried to keep it moving, praying the police were not on their way.

"Oh, my bad. I guess you just do dogs now and not humans."

"What?" She could not believe what he had just said to her.

"Yeah, that's right. I saw the video at the dice game that night," he yelled across the street as she shamefully lowered her head. "You just another cum dumpster from around the way trying to stunt all VIP."

After using the bathroom inside of the early-morning crowed Coney Island to put on her stolen wig, a mentally drained Keisha bashfully borrowed five dollars from Sam so she could catch the bus to work and back. Claiming she'd left her wallet at home and didn't have time to return and pick it up, Keisha promised to pay him back later that evening. Having somewhat of a secret crush on her, Sam had no problem whatsoever helping her out.

Getting on the bus and finding a seat, Keisha pulled out her cell phone. With a cloud of doom seemingly looming overhead, she went down her contact list. Stopping at K, she hit Kim's number. Needing no more than a shoulder to cry on and a compassionate ear to listen, she called her childhood friend, hoping for both.

"Hello, Kim?"

"Oh, hell naw," Kim smartly replied. "I know you ain't calling me, stranger! What do I owe this unexpected pleasure?"

"Kim, please, girl. I need to talk." Keisha tried not to break down crying, finally hearing her best friend's voice after a month's time.

Cold in tone, Kim asked her the million-dollar question, waiting for the two- million-dollar answer. "Well, did you leave that fool the fuck alone or what?"

Within a few seconds of dead silence, Keisha finally found the courage to speak. "Umm . . . naw, not totally, but—"

"Girl, bye." Kim sucked her teeth loudly before hanging up in Keisha's face, leaving her to fight back the tears the rest of the way to work.

Rushing in the building and luckily into an open elevator, Keisha tried her best to dip into the training session with the least commotion as possible. She had msised more than two thirds of the presentation. Her boss, who was sitting near the back door, motioned for her to step out into the hallway. Then he asked her to follow him to his office.

"Well, Miss Jackson," he said judgmentally as he sat down behind his desk. "This is the sixth, or is it seventh, time you've been over an hour late since you've been hired."

Stumbling over her words to explain, Keisha promised, if given another chance, she'd not be late again. "Please, sir. I need this job."

"To be perfectly honest with you, considering the unemployment rate in Detroit, let alone Michigan, I would think that if our Human Resources Department gave you a chance, you'd try your very best to take advantage of it."

Frantic, fearing he was about to terminate her, Keisha stood to her feet. Seductively walking over toward the desk, without warning, she leaned over so he could see her breasts. While his eyes were glued on her cleavage, she took a chance, not knowing how he was going to react, and made her way in front of him. While he was still seated, mesmerized by what the much younger female with the extra-wide ass in the tight-fitting skirt was doing, Keisha dropped to her knees like she had on so many occasions with Rico. Using her teeth, she unzipped her boss's pants. Before he or she even knew next, the extremely successful company's CEO was getting an impromptu blow job of a lifetime.

As his white-shaft, pink-tipped dick tried its best to stiffen and his eyes rolled to the rear of his head, neither he nor Keisha noticed his wife suddenly come into the office. At least twenty years his junior, she, bizarrely enough, didn't react how Keisha assumed she would. Obviously a freak herself, she got down on her knees and helped her husband's employee suck him off. Minutes later, the boss enjoyed the sight of both women on his couch in the sixty-nine position.

Needless to say, Keisha had the rest of the day off, and her tardiness was overlooked.

If Rico wanna not come home and fuck everything that hops, jumps, or skips, it's nothing! Two can play that game! Back in total freak mode, she allowed a random man sitting on the bus to discreetly ease his hand underneath her skirt and finger her until she reached her stop. At this point, Keisha was out there.

It was morning time at Commissioner Jackson's house, and after a long night, Sandy was beyond tired. In between dealing with both Mr. and Mrs. Jackson, she was exhausted. Normally one of the other people employed there would help her out. After all, she was only supposed to be doing the cooking, like her mom had for so many years till her death. But since Keisha's abrupt relocation away from the home, Sandy had been doing more than her share. Demanding more privacy than usual, Commissioner Jackson let most of the folk working for him go. Sandy, being there since birth, was the only one he felt he could truly trust. Even though, against his orders, she'd let Keisha inside the house to get some of her personal belongings, Commissioner Jackson knew Sandy wouldn't have the nerve to really betray him against any outsider.

Mrs. Jackson had always been a social drinker; however, after her only child left, she barely left her bedroom, and on the occasions that she did, the distraught mother wouldn't be seen without a wine glass in her hand and a strange, distant gaze in her eyes.

A few months prior to Keisha meeting Rico, Mrs. Jackson flew to a secret location to get pampered and supposedly a tummy tuck. Yet, when she returned, her husband, never one to mince words, constantly belittled her, saying the doctor that performed her surgery should have his medical license taken away because she was still fat. Hearing no encouragement, after multitudes of insults, Mrs. Jackson increased the amount of painkillers she was prescribed and started trading other pills with her inner circle of equally prescription-addicted well-to-do housewives.

Knowing nothing else since birth but that household, Sandy clung to Keisha's mom after her own mother's death. Basically living alone in the guest house, Sandy also had a room in the main house. Depending on the mood inside the home, she would float back and forth. Sandy and Mrs. Jackson always seemed close in the past, but since the pills, the drinking, and the missing part of her heart, Mrs. Jackson blamed everyone, including Sandy.

Extremely devoted to the entire family, as the days passed, Sandy started to feel resentment build up as well. Just a little over thirty years in age, she'd given up more than just her days and nights cooking for the family. Truth be told, she'd made the ultimate sacrifice, and as far as she was concerned, both Commissioner Jackson and his wife owed her at least common courtesy and respect, if nothing else.

"Good morning." Sandy entered Mrs. Jackson's gloomy bedroom with a breakfast tray in hand. "You didn't eat much last night in the way of dinner, so I brought you some toast and a cup of coffee. You need something."

"Go away, Sandy. Please. Just let me be." Mrs. Jackson's hands trembled as she twisted the cap off the orange plastic bottle. With dark circles surrounding her eyes and thinning hair sticking up, she took a shalow breath, trying to clear her raspy throat. She swallowed several pills without so much as a sip of water. Sandy tried her best to intervene but was stopped with a barrage of hateful comments.

"Look at you. Running around here trying to act like you care about me. You don't care about me. None of you do. I see all of you whispering about me in my own damn house. I'm not crazy," Mrs. Jackson, with her blood boiling, slurred with contempt and treachery in her heart for the entire world. "Nobody knows how I feel. Nobody. Not my husband, and certainly not you. I need Keisha back home at my side."

Sandy stood there at first, silent. Holding the tray in her hands, she finally spoke out. "No disrespect, Mrs. Jackson, but how can you sit there and say that? I miss Keisha just as much as you. Sometimes even more."

"I knew it was only a matter of time," Mrs. Jackson hissed, leaping out the bed. Under the influence of liquor and countless days' worth of pills, in bare feet and a dirty gown, she could hardly stand. Truth be told, she needed to be under a doctor's constant care, but lately she refused any treatment of any sort.

Unstable and weak in the knees, she staggered toward the much-younger, always-loyal employee. She slapped Sandy across the face.

"After all I've done for you. How dare you throw that up in my face? How fucking dare you!"

Holding the side of her stinging jaw, Sandy didn't say a word about the unprovoked attack, both physically and verbally. Setting the tray she was still holding on the nightstand, she just walked out the room, down the stairs, and out toward the guesthouse.

"Hey, Sandy. Good morning." Calvin was mannish. He grinned, standing next to the car's passenger door. Thinking about the few times he'd hit her off, his manhood jumped. "Damn, girl, how was your evening?"

"Whatever. Leave me alone." Sandy huffed in tears, arrogantly storming past as he watched her ass jiggle from side to side.

I don't know how much more of living this lie I can take! she thought.

"I guess it's true. The more bitches, the more the problems," he speculated at her apparent temperament, knowing sooner or later he'd luck up and get the pussy again.

Moments later, Commissioner Jackson, who ran his household like a modern-day dictator, emerged from inside the dwelling. Briefcase in hand, he got into the rear seat of the vehicle. With Calvin driving, he returned numerous missed calls. One from Swazy, with a very interesting update about the night before, and about five or six being from a jealous- hearted Robin, wondering if he was coming into the office.

Dealing with his wife's over-the-top dramatics the night before had the always overly flirtatious husband at the end of his rope in their long-standing marriage.

If it wouldn't hurt me politically, I'd leave that woman!

Chapter Fifteen

With a newfound self-serving attitude, Keisha came through the front door feeling absolutely no regrets whatsoever about what had taken place at work between her boss and his wife or the stranger on the bus. Matter of fact, both sexually charged scenarios played out repeatedly in her mind, causing her pussy to get moist. Once again, wanting nothing more than to get her freak game on ten, at this point, Keisha didn't care who or what could get her where she needed to be.

Finding Rico sitting on the couch, playing his video game like nothing happened between them, was of no major surprise. He was arrogant like that. Keisha was over that awful character flaw and came to accept it as normal.

Hitting the pause button, he turned around, ready to hear whatever bullshit she was about to spit. Suffering from the same type of sudden, brain-splitting migraines his girl was constantly having, he wasn't trying to hear her nagging.

To his astonishment, Rico sat back, stunned, mouth wide open. Without encouragement, Keisha hiked her skirt up over her ass, dropped down, and started blessing his mic. At first, he felt like she might have been planning on biting his shit clean off, but he was so overcome by her dedication to making him bust, he relaxed, grabbing the rear of her head, causing the wig she was wearing to slide backward and eventually fall to the floor.

Strangely, when she was done, Keisha announced that as far as she was concerned, they could go back to their old ways. In her own words, she conceded they were much more content as a couple when they were involved with some sort of freakery.

Knowing he wanted a little peace before he planned his next move or found another dumb-ass female to step in and take Keisha's place, Rico eagerly agreed. As a show of good faith in what she was proposing, Rico let her take his cell phone and personally erase the scandalous pictures he had taken and saved. Digging in his pocket, he even gave back what was left of the rent money he'd stolen out her purse.

Back in her slut mode, Keisha urged him to call a female over to the house so they could all have a party. Call anybody but that smart-talking baby mama of yours." Keisha played with herself as Rico watched, living in the celebration that she was apparently falling back in line.

"Don't worry, Keisha. Ocean's ass is on some other shit. Right about now, she thinks she's bigger than the game."

As Rico continued to choke Keisha out, he shoved his dick in between her legs. With each thrust, her extremely weak body slammed against the wall. She thought about the past couple of days. She knew it was only a matter of time before the good times they recently had would finally end. Rico's attitude and disposition were growing colder and more distant. It was like she could do no right at home. It didn't matter what she said or did; he was on edge, practically biting her head off. Rico claimed he was just feeling sick most of the time, but in Keisha's eyes and heart, the reason for his brutal backsliding didn't matter. The old Rico Campbell was back in full effect.

On a good note, however, no sooner had she and Rico started back being overly promiscuous than her job performance seemed to increase and her boss grew more and more impressed. This earned her a slight promotion and wage increase. It was like the more sexual partners she engaged with, the higher that her confidence level leaped. In fact, Keisha tried repeatedly to get in contact with both her parents, Sandy, and even once-best-friend Kim. When she was shot down each time by disconnected numbers, ignored calls, not returned texts, and her father's extremely rude secretary, Robin, Keisha still kept her composure together without falling apart.

Rico was feeling the pressure of the streets calling him back. Staying either in the house, or sometimes hanging with an overly nosey-as-fuck Swazy was growing old. His girlfriend was due to deliver at any moment, so Swazy's hanging all night was about dead anyhow. And sure, Keisha returned to freely indulging in all his sexual fantasies, but that wasn't enough. Her knowing about and sharing in all the extra pussy he was getting was quickly playing out also.

Before Rico knew it, he was back to sneaking around with his baby mama. Ocean was getting money hand over fist from her main trick. She told Rico, although the older married man was a straight-up freak and his pockets were deep, no amount of little blue Viagra pills he took could keep his dick as hard as Rico's could get. So when they fucked, they fucked.

Chapter Sixteen

Distracted from bringing Rico down and Keisha back begging at his doorstep for forgiveness, Commissioner Jackson was spending his recent days concentrating on the upcoming election. Knowing he was almost neck and neck with at least one other candidate, every single move the county commissioner made for the next thirty days had to be carefully calculated. He was especially hard on his staff. Robin, Calvin, and everyone else on the payroll was putting in extra-long hours.

Swazy, of course, days away from being a new father, was ecstatic as well as relieved, not feeling the intense pressure that Keisha's father and his driver-bodyguard, Calvin were putting on him for information about Rico. At this point, one thing and one thing only mattered to Mr. Jackson, and that was being re-elected to office. Keisha and her turbulent life would have to wait.

Bringing a hot cup of coffee to her boss and Robin, Sandy returned to the kitchen to prepare an evening snack for Mrs. Jackson. Having gotten over the insulting words and allegations, Sandy's loyalty to Keisha's mother was un-rocked. With a tray in her hands, she walked by the home office, listening to Robin rant and rave about how she would have redecorated this room and that room if this was her house.

This little bright-skin tramp got some nerve coming in here talking like that. Parading through here in that tiny skirt like she's running something! Sandy angrily thought, climbing the staircase. *If Mrs. Jackson was well, I know she'd rip that hussy's hair out from the roots. I wish I could just find Keisha and tell her that her mom needs her.*

Not bothering to knock, Sandy opened the always-dark room, finding Mrs. Jackson damn near coughing up a lung. She was drastically losing weight, seemingly with no hope to live. Sandy was forced to take action. Commissioner Jackson had strict orders inside the household that no family business was to be discussed, brought up, or mentioned whenever they had visitors. Robin, although Mr. Jackson's personal secretary, was still considered an outsider to inner household dealings. So, Sandy alerting him to his wife's physical or mental condition in Robin's presence would be considered against the rules.

"Fuck him and his rules." Sandy wasted no time running down the steps and marching into the office.

"Excuse me, Sandy." Mr. Jackson looked up from a small pile of papers while Robin, who was leaning over him, adjusted her blouse. "Didn't I tell you I didn't want to be interrupted?"

"Yes, but—"

"No buts, Sandy. Can't you see we're busy?"

"Busy?" Sandy raised her eyebrows in a suspicious manner. "Well, I need to speak to you, sir. It's very urgent."

"I guess good help that follows orders is hard to find, huh?" Robin smartly replied, acting as if she was frustrated with Sandy's insistence and even her mere presence.

Sandy had endured enough of Robin's over-the-top comments and the dodging of putting her calls through to Commissioner Jackson at the office. Coming all the way into the home office, closing the door, Sandy cornered the slick-mouthed Robin.

"Listen, you wanna-be little whore. I don't know what you think you're doing, but if you ever try to come in between me and this family, I'll fucking kill you." With clenched teeth, Sandy's eyes bulged. "Are we clear?"

"Whatever." Sucking her teeth, Robin maneuvered her way out the corner of the room, dismissing Sandy's irate threat as a joke. "That hood talk doesn't mean anything to me. Why don't you go cook something? Make a bed, dig a ditch, or whatever it is you do around here. Poof, be gone."

"Oh, for real? Well, in a hot minute, I'm gonna be kicking your narrow ass around here. How about that? If Keisha was here, I swear for God."

"Listen, listen!" Mr. Jackson demanded, coming in between the two. "I don't have time for this. As much as any man enjoys a good catfight, I'm not in the mood. And Sandy, what did I say about mentioning that name under this roof? Now, what in the hell is so damn important?"

Practically begging the once dutiful husband to go upstairs and see firsthand Mrs. Jackson's downward-spiraling health condition, Sandy was left stunned and speechless as he ordered her to just keep monitoring his wife and wait until after the election to take Keisha's mother to the doctor. It was bad enough he'd not been in to check on Mrs. Jackson's physical well-being in days, claiming he himself had been feeling under the weather and didn't want to spread germs, but now he wanted to deny her much-needed medical attention.

"Please, I think we should do something now. She's getting worse," she whispered discreetly as they walked. "She needs help. I don't think she looks well."

"Sandy, don't disobey me. As long as you've lived in this house, you know I don't like that, don't you?" Mr. Jackson raised his voice, yanking at her wrist. "Now, please do as I wish. I don't want to ask you anymore."

"Yeah, Sandy!" Robin yelled, now out of the office as well and posted at the bottom of the stairs.

"Robin, stop telling her how to do her job and do your own. You're starting to be more trouble than you're worth. Now, let's get back to work."

Needless to say, Sandy was pissed he was handling her and the dire situation the way he was. Not only was Mr. Jackson ignoring the fact that his almost non-responsive wife needed help, but now he was allowing Robin to feel she was someone that she wasn't—a boss.

If he thinks I'm going to sit around here and remain silent, he's a bigger asshole than I always thought he was. Disappearing back up the stairs, she ducked into Keisha's old room, looking at all of the pictures, different awards, trophies, and other accomplishments the young lady whom she'd always been so close to growing up had accumulated. *Don't worry, Keisha. I know how hurt you'd be if something or someone was to bring harm to Mrs. Jackson. It ain't shit stronger than a mother's love for her child.*

Laying Keisha's eight-by-ten framed high school graduation picture down with the entire family on it, including her and the recently-proven-to-be-shady character Kim, Sandy picked up the receiver of the house phone sitting on the white desk. Moments later, the operator at 911 reassured Sandy help for the commissioner's wife was on the way.

Unlike the neighboring Detroit, seemingly seconds later, lights flashing and sirens blaring, an ambulance pulled up in the circular driveway of the suburban home. With no other choice but to play the devoted husband, an infuriated Mr. Jackson informed the EMS technicians he'd follow the rig in his own car.

"My driver Calvin is away on personal business. Just let me grab my car keys, and I'll be right behind you guys." The commissioner put on his best concerned act, worthy of a year's free pass with the weed man. "Please hurry and help my dear wife. She means everything to me."

Before pulling off past the crowd of nosey neighbors, including a reporter for the local newspaper, Mr. Jackson demanded in no uncertain terms that Sandy pack all of her belongings and vacate the premises before he returned.

"If you think I'm playing around this time, Sandy, you're sadly mistaken. Pack your belongings and get the hell out. You can go find Keisha for all the hell I care. You two are just alike. Sluts!"

"You don't have to worry about me. My entire life you've treated me like shit on a stick. I'm tired of being a second-class citizen around this madhouse any goddamn way," Sandy huffed. Vindictively, she was now in tears. "But one day, somebody gonna repay you for all the cruel things you do and the inhumane way you treat people."

Wow, this night couldn't be going any better if I planned it. With a smug expression on her face, Robin, nothing more than a hood rat on the come-up, got into her vehicle and followed behind her boss, just in case he needed a shoulder to cry on. *First Keisha, now Sandy. Fuck what you heard. All I need is for that old, dried-up bitch to die tonight, and it's on and popping.*

Chapter Seventeen

"Okay, Rico. Enough is enough. This is the third time this week you hanging out in them streets." Keisha followed behind him as he attempted to get dressed. "Correct me if I'm wrong, but didn't you make a commitment to me, to us? You said things were never going back to before."

Rubbing lotion on his chiseled chest, Rico stared into the mirror. Putting on his blue jean shorts, he made sure the top of his boxers were showing just enough as he fastened his belt. "Look, Keisha, I don't wanna hear all that lip, so fall the fuck back before you see the old Rico Campbell for real."

"I knew the way you was acting was coming to an end. I knew the bullshit was only a matter of time," she yelled in his face. "I knew it. I knew it. I knew it."

"Damn, girl. Why is you bugging? You acting like you straight-up crazy."

"Naw, you the crazy one, three times this freaking week."

"What you trying to say? I know you ain't saying I'm trapped in this son of a bitch like some fucking prisoner on death row."

"What?"

"You heard me."

"You stupid."

"Naw, Keisha, you the stupid one. I'm a grown man, and you standing your dumb ass here asking me why I'm going out."

"Oh, it's like that?" Keisha took a couple of steps back before Rico knocked her over, grabbing for his boots. "All I do is work and try to hold you and us down, and you back to running around like you ain't got no woman. How grown-ass man is that?"

Rico laughed, slipping his T-shirt over his head. "Damn, girl. Maybe I might send you back home for some training. You talking like some old hood rat now."

"Is that right?" She planted her hands on her hips.

"Hell yeah. You always been ugly as a fuck, but at least you was kinda smart."

"Damn."

"Yeah, damn is right. So dig this: instead of sweating me and where I'm headed, why don't you pick up a book or something? Get your fucking mind right."

"If you leave out that door—"

"If I leave out that door what? Are you threatening me again?" Rico cuffed her up real quick, rushing her toward the wall. "Okay, Keisha, you want the old me back? Well, here the fuck I am. Enjoy the ride." With that being said, he let her go, grabbed his keys, and walked out, leaving the door wide open.

Keisha was once again left looking dumb as a fuck. It was no doubt about it she was one of those silly females her and Kim used to talk cash shit about back in the day. Her self-respect and self-esteem couldn't get any lower. It was like she was watching some sad-ass movie or a soap opera.

Wanting to make amends with her once-best-friend Kim and hopefully get some advice on getting out of this relationship with Rico once and for all, Keisha dialed her number. After a few attempts, she realized either Kim's cell was turned off or she was being sent straight to voicemail. Whatever the situation was, Rico's forever victim desperately left at least three heartfelt messages. Curling up with a blanket on the couch, looking just as messy as any rat in the hood could, Keisha prayed Kim would return her pleas for help.

"Why this stupid girl keep calling me?" Kim mumbled underneath her breath. Shaking her head in disbelief in who and what her childhood BFF had become, she continued to shop at one of the many Somerset Mall stores she'd been hitting up hard over the past few months for a forever-updating wardrobe. Strangely, she'd been losing weight and attributed it to missing her friend.

"I know I'm more than out cold for some of the stuff I've been doing this past year, but damn, at least I'm getting money behind the bullshit," Kim reasoned for the grimy ultimate betrayal she'd been secretly participating in. "And now Keisha leaving messages. Probably about how that bastard been dogging her some more and she still won't stop fucking with him. She crazy."

An hour or so later, the mall was near closing, and Kim headed toward valet parking. Waiting for the attendant to bring her vehicle to the door, Kim finally listened to Keisha's messages.

Damn, this time it seems like she means it, but knowing her, this is just another time he dogged her out and she feeling momentarily lonely.

"Who knows?"

Kim got in her car and headed back toward the city. While she was driving, a song came on the radio that she and Keisha used to ride to. Feeling temporarily guilty, she picked up her phone, calling Keisha's father. If he was in a good mood, maybe, just maybe, he could be reasoned with and persuaded to forgive his child.

Three rings in, a more-than-familiar voice answered.

"Yes, hello, Commissioner Jackson's phone. How can I help you?"

"Excuse me?" Kim was more than shocked to hear Robin's voice on the line.

"Yes, I said Commissioner Jackson's phone. Is there something I can help you with?"

"Robin?"

"Yes, this is Robin. And who is this may I ask?"

"You know who in the hell this is. Look, Miss Thang, put him on the phone," Kim demanded with a serious attitude. "What you doing answering his personal line anyway? You doing too fucking much."

"I'm sorry, but the commissioner is indisposed at the present. Is there anything I can help you with?" By the caller ID, Robin knew it was Kim, Keisha's best friend, and started to act extra with it. "Any messages or requests?"

"Okay, Robin, you sneaky little bitch. I don't know why you have his cell or what you trying to prove, but whatever the case is, I'll call him back later. It's very important I speak to him tonight."

"Not a problem." She giggled, further adding fuel to the fire. "And I'll make double sure to not tell him that you called with your fake very important matter." Robin sneered as she terminated the call. Smug in her position, still down at the hospital on a hopeful death watch of her boss's wife, Robin went back to daydreaming what her life could soon be.

Rico had no remorse for the way he treated Keisha or any other female he encountered. It didn't matter how fat or skinny, how tall or short, how cute or ugly—he dogged them all. The only factor he sometimes cared about was money. Even he'd stand down for money if the price was right. But now in his mind, Keisha was about done in the money department. She was beginning to be way more of a liability to him instead of an asset. In between all the emotional bullshit and trying to get him to change who the fuck he was, Rico was about done with Keisha. He'd made up in his mind after tax time and he spent her refund check, he was gonna be out once and for all.

"Hey, girl. What up, doe?" Rico smiled when Ocean pulled up in front of the Coney Island. "What took your ass so long? That nosey Arab Sam was getting on a nigga's last nerve."

"Come on now, guy. Don't play yourself. I said I was coming, so fall back." Ocean wiped sweat from her forehead as Rico got in, shutting the car door. "Besides, I feel sick as a dog."

"What in the fuck you being sick got to do with me?" he callously replied, reclining the passenger seat. "I'm still trying to hit that pussy."

Pulling up at Ocean's newly leased riverfront apartment, the pair went inside. Wishing he could get Ocean back under his spell, Rico grew jealous of his own son and all the new clothes and toys her new trick had purchased him. Turning on the sixty-inch LG flat-screen television mounted on the wall, Rico stripped down to his boxers. Ocean, feeling dizzy, went into the bathroom to throw up.

"I'm feeling sick as a motherfucker." She staggered out into the living room. "For the past week or so, a bitch been going through it."

"Oh, hell naw. Let me find out that duck you fucking with got you knocked up, or one of them lames from the club."

Ocean was definitely not in the mood to argue. "Look, fool, besides you and ole boy, I ain't banging nobody raw dog, so."

"So it damn straight ain't mine, so don't try it."

"Boy, please." Ocean managed to laugh. "Ain't nobody trying to have another baby by your deadbeat ass. Trust me, if I was knocked up by you, I'd give that shit back to God with the quickness."

Fighting through her illness, Ocean and Rico fucked like wild animals, with him trying to prove a point that no nigga on the earth could take his place between her pussy. Ocean was in shivering chills when he finished.

Barely able to stand, she got a text message from her "friend" that he wanted to stop by later that evening. Ocean found the hood-rat, chickenhead, on-the-prowl strength to drive Rico to the nearby Greektown Casino and drop his broke ass off.

"Here's cab fare, baby daddy. Do you. I'm ghost." She mustered a smile before screeching off back to her apartment to change the sheets before her old trick got there.

Knowing plenty of females that worked and also hung out at the casino, Rico headed inside, ready to make a night of it.

Maybe I'll call Swazy's fake ass and see can he get up from under that pregnant slut of his! And fuck that whining ho Keisha! I'll deal with her when I get back to the crib.

Chapter Eighteen

The Here and The Now . . .

"I can't take this anymore. I'm done. I'm done. I swear for God I'm done. I'm not dealing with you or your nonsense anymore. We through." Keisha tried to break loose but couldn't. "I'm better than this. I'm better than you and everything you stand for, which is nothing!"

"Shit, you tired? I'm tired of your damn mouth that never stops running," Rico hissed, bending her back over the dresser as Kilo, tongue hanging out to the side, looked on. "I was gonna wait until April when you get them taxes back to stop dealing with your simple ass, but naw, I'm good. After this last hot nut in your back hole, trust me, I'm the one done. You can bounce. You can take your nasty ass back to your funny-looking mother and that wanna-be boss father of yours. You worn out anyway. I got another upgraded model begging to take your place. She's slim, fat ass, and pretty as fuck in the face. I definitely gonna be glad to see you leave."

Who in the hell does he think he is? No matter how much of his ruthless and rotten garbage I accept, he always goes one step beyond that. Nothing he says or does shocks me anymore. He has no home training and it shows. But now he is gonna feel my wrath.

Reaching her hand out for the can of oil sheen that was knocked over on the dresser, Keisha was fed up. She'd had enough of Rico's Dexter-Linwood area mentality and everything that went with it.

"Look, don't say anything about my parents. If you weren't so jacked-up in the head, you'd realize you just messed up the best thing that's ever going to happen to you: me."

She suddenly twisted her body around, and Rico was left with his wet, shitty dick sticking straight out in the air. In the same movement, Keisha aimed the oil sheen directly at his face. Before Rico could prevent it, she sprayed the chemical-based mist directly into his eyes.

"Urgggg!" he screamed out, pressing both hands to his face. "Keisha, I'm gonna kill you. I promise, you done really messed up this time. I'ma stump the blood outta your ass."

"I hate you, Rico. I hate you and everything about you. You ain't worth a female like me, and I was mad stupid for allowing this to go on this long." Keisha reached for an oversized bottle of perfume, and like she'd done with the statue, slammed it down across the rear of Rico's head. Seeing him being dazed and temporarily blind, she seized the opportunity. Wasting no time, she grabbed her purse then shoes as he struggled to make it to the bathroom.

As she attempted to run by him and out the front door, Rico snatched a hold of her blouse, ripping the sleeve.

"Noooo! Get your freaking hands off me!" Raising her bare foot, Keisha kicked him square in the nuts. Knocking over a chair, she bolted toward the door as Kilo continued to bark.

"You done lost your mind, you stankin'-pussy slut. I'm gonna fuck you up. On everything I love, I swear to God you dead." Doubled over, with his shorts down to his ankles, he fell to the ground. Still a trooper, Rico made it to the sink, splashing handfuls of water up to his burning eyes. With the water still running, he got a washcloth and pressed it to the small gash on his head.

When I catch up to Keisha, I'ma make her pay for all this.

At five twenty-six in the morning, the crackhead zombies had just gone in after prowling all night. The few working people in the nearly deserted neighborhood had yet to leave their homes. It was one of those kinda-quiet-in-the-hood times before the total evil of darkness turned to partial good of daybreak. Keisha took full advantage of the time, cutting through vacant lots without anyone seeing her. With every barefooted step Keisha took, she swiftly realized she had nowhere to go. Since dealing with Rico, she'd cut everyone off. Not bothering to take the time to put her shoes on, she felt the soles of her feet getting small cuts and abrasions. But that didn't matter. At this point, she'd cut off both her feet and hands if that meant being away from that monster.

Seeing the neon light from the Coney Island Restaurant flashing, Keisha headed in that direction. Glancing over her shoulder, she prayed Rico wouldn't find her before she at least flagged a cab. Looking a hot ghetto mess, Keisha finally entered the deserted building.

"Oh my God! What has happened to you?" Sam, the Arab owner, knew Keisha well enough to know something drastic had taken place. Every morning, he'd have her large cup of coffee, two sugars and two creams, waiting because she always seemed to be running late. In his eyes, Keisha wasn't like the other hood customers he'd encounter daily. She had a good education and surprisingly knew a great deal about his Middle Eastern culture.

The only thing Sam found puzzling was why Keisha kept company with a man as uncouth as Rico. He would see him parade all sorts of random females around when his "wifey" was at work. The evening before, he'd just seen him hop into a sports car with some young female. He'd also hear Rico talk about his woman like a piece of trash to all his friends. Shamefully, Sam had also seen nude pictures of Keisha, as well as the infamous dog video on Rico's cell phone.

"Sam! Sam! Please help me!" With shoes, purse, and a dead cell phone in her hands, she acted as if a monster were chasing her. And in her eyes, there was. Hysterical, Keisha broke down in tears. She didn't know where she was going, but she knew she had to get out of the neighborhood and away from Rico. "Sam, can you please call me a cab? Please hurry!"

"What is wrong, Ms. Keisha? Were you robbed? Why don't you have your shoes on?" Sam, having a soft spot for her, took a chance unlocking the dead bolt on the bulletproof security door. "Come back here with me. I call police for you! Your nice blouse is ruined, too. Who do this thing to you? Where is your boyfriend?"

Before Keisha could answer any of his many questions, Sam motioned that Rico was coming across the parking lot.

"Oh, never mind. Here he is. I see him coming now by the alleyway."

"Oh, no, Sam, please hide me! Please! Please! Please!" Keisha ducked down underneath the counter merely seconds before an infuriated Rico entered the restaurant.

"Yo, Sam. You seen Keisha? Did she come in here with her no-good ass?" He rubbed at both eyes, still trying to focus.

Caught in the middle of what was obviously a domestic situation, Sam's Islamic beliefs forbid him from keeping another man's wife away from her husband; however, he knew Rico's shady character and decided to lie.

"Keisha? Umm . . . no, I have not seen her this morning. Maybe she got on bus already."

"That girl think I'm playing with her." Rico sinisterly peered out the huge window, searching for any sign of his renegade girlfriend. "I'm gonna beat the hot piss outta her when I find that trick. . . . Spraying that bullshit in my goddamn eyes. Do my shit look red or what?"

"Please calm down," Sam begged, feeling Keisha's hot breath blowing at his pants zipper, causing his heart rate to increase. "Yes, they are a little red, but maybe that's from smoking the weed, huh?"

Rico laughed at Sam's last comment, but he was still on a mission to beat Keisha's ass. He had no idea Keisha was perched down under the counter and continued airing his business out. "Yo, Sam, I should've traded that big-foot wildebeest in a long time ago. You done seen the type of top-notch females I usually fucks with sliding through here with me. If she wasn't cashing a brother out so swell, I would've been sent her packing."

Squinting from the oil sheen still burning, Rico looked back out the window. Seeing there was still no sign of Keisha, he continued to dog her out. "Shit, but real rap, where I'ma find a tramp dumb as her, paying all the bills so I can have the next dime piece lay up with me while she at work? That bullshit is the American Dream. If she only knew how many females I done banged in our bed or on that couch. Hell, a nigga like me even had some of them bitches coming over cooking me breakfast as soon as Keisha went to work. She might think she's book smart, but that be the ones who don't have one clue about the streets."

"Man, that's wrong," Sam lectured, rubbing his long goatee. "Keisha is a good girl. A real good girl. You shouldn't talk about her like that. She goes to work every day to help you and her. She is a good woman to you. You don't deserve to have her. You better straighten up and love her correctly."

"Man, fuck Keisha. Fuck her entire existence. I'm the treat in that big girl's pathetic life. You see, my sand nigga brother, I got that good dick that drives these bitches out here crazy. And she ain't no different. As soon as I put this thang on her, she was my slave. And as for love, I never loved her ass. It was nothing but game from day one. I'd cry over losing my dog more than her. Like I said, fuck Keisha and everything about her. A mack like me out here trying to live my best life. Her tramp ass getting in the way of that, but I got her covered."

Rico's words cut like a knife. It was one thing to speculate how someone felt about you, but to hear firsthand was another. The heartbreaking truth hit Keisha like a ton of bricks. She didn't know what to say or what to do. She wanted to curse him out, but she knew it wouldn't do any good. Knowing him, he'd probably just gain enjoyment out of knowing he'd hurt her even more. Stunned, she stared at Sam's zipper and the seemingly huge bulge behind it. Listening to Rico unknowingly confess to all

the dirt he'd done over the months, spitefully Keisha
reached up, slowly pulling Sam's zipper down.

I hate him! I hate him! I hate his ass!

With Rico just on the other side of the counter, Sam
remained as quiet as possible as Keisha's hand took out
his beige-colored, pudgy, six-inch dick. Shifting his
weight from foot to foot, his eyes twitched with excitement from her touch. Wanting to yell out in his native
tongue, Sam glanced down just in time to see Keisha ,
with ease, throat-fuck his now rock-hard meat. A virgin
when Rico met her, he'd taught Keisha the art of being a
true freak of the week.

Every word coming out Rico's two-timing mouth
pertaining to all his female conquests was met with
Keisha slurping, slobbering, and licking Sam's hookup.
Having no panties on from earlier, she fingered herself,
rocking to the beat of Rico's cruel words.

I hate his ass! I hate his ass!

Soon using two fingers to satisfy her own pussy, she
tasted a warm, sticky fluid escape from the tip of Sam's
throbbing pink head just as she climaxed. She knew at
any time Sam was at the brink of blessing her with his
foreign cream.

"Look, dude, I'm outta here. I gotta go find where my
meal ticket call herself hiding at," Rico hissed, heading
for the door. "And, oh yeah, if you see Keisha, tell that
cum-drenched goon to take her punk ass home. I'll be
waiting for her to clean up all that mess she made."

"Okay, Rico, I'll tell her." Cradling the black female's
head while she sucked him off better than she sucked
both his wives combined, Sam was indeed seconds away
from exploding full blast in between Keisha's jaws.

No sooner had Rico left the Coney Island than Sam snatched Keisha up, laying her face down on a pile of cardboard boxes in the corner of the restaurant. Shoving his dick in her, his fantasy of doggy-style fucking a black girl was finally fulfilled. Asking Allah for forgiveness, Sam gripped her ass, watching his dick go in and out. Seconds later, he yelled, letting loose a heavy load of nut in Keisha's wet hole.

He stood to his feet. Cum was still dripping from the tip of Sam's head. Swallowing his dick like a true champ, Keisha polished it off and didn't waste a drop.

No words were passed between the two as Sam zipped up his pants then wobbly-walked, reaching for the cordless phone to call his overly promiscuous friend a cab. Keisha, not the least bit ashamed of what she'd just done, took a small stack of napkins off the counter, wiping her face dry. Minutes later, a yellow Checker Cab pulled up, blowing its horn twice. Sam smiled, handing Keisha one of his employee T-shirts to cover her torn blouse and five twenty-dollar bills out the register. Taking a complimentary early edition newspaper off one of the tables, she left out the door. Watching her get in the cab and pull off, Sam prayed she'd leave Rico alone for good; however, he knew women, no matter what race, were all weak for a man.

All Keisha wanted to do was go beg for her father's forgiveness and hopefully move home. Seconds after she gave the taxi driver directions to her parents' suburban house, something strange happened. The cab ran over a huge object, forcing it to stop just as Keisha read the newspaper's shocking headline: COUNTY COMMISSIONER JACKSON'S WIFE RUSHED TO HOSPITAL.

"Oh, shit! I swear to God I didn't see him! The guy was putting something in his eyes and just walked out in front of me. I didn't see him. He just came from out of nowhere. Oh my God, you saw him just come from nowhere too, didn't you, miss? I just pulled out," the panicked driver defensively explained as he jumped out of the driver's side.

While extremely disturbed and worried about the headlines she'd just read, Keisha also got out the cab to investigate. Glancing over her shoulder just in case Rico was around and still in pursuit, she tried to hold her composure. With the newspaper still clutched in her hands, she walked to the front side of the vehicle. The cab's lights were still on, even though the engine was off. Standing near the hood of the cab, her heart raced.

After all the bad luck she'd suffered over the past year, God had finally given her a blessing. To her surprise, it was Rico. He was laid out in front of the cab with a bottle of Visine clutched in his hand. Although the cab wasn't going at a high rate of speed, it had still managed to run over Rico's lower torso. Ironically, to get the redness from the effects of the oil sheen out his eyes, the liquid had distracted him.

Somewhat dazed from being struck, he moaned in discomfort. While a small amount of blood trickled out the corner of his mouth, his lips started to quiver slightly. The alarmed driver did his best to beg Rico to remain calm, but it was to no avail. They were both in shock as Rico used his last bit of strength to yell out.

Not able to form any more words or speak, Rico focused his eyes to see, of all people, Keisha. Having been dragged a few yards, in excruciating pain, he fought to reach his arm up toward her, but he couldn't manage to do so.

Keisha immediately saw the shape her once-beloved was in and cautiously eased to his side. Towering over him, she peered down in disgust.

"Look at you, Rico. You're nothing but a miserable human being. You deserve to be right where you are at, on the ground near the gutter you came from. I'm embarrassed that I even let you drag me down. I know I've been a fool so many times for you, but this time I'm awake. This time I'm never coming back."

Keisha meant every single solitary word she was saying as she bent down. Now on one knee, she started to smile. Bringing her face close to Rico's ear, she started to whisper in sheer excitement.

"Guess what, nigga? A.J.'s dick was way better than yours. Hell, so was Swazy's. And for that matter, my boss downtown was about his business in the fucking department as well. The only thing good about having sex with you is when you finish, I don't have to feel you touching me anymore. Your repulse me; believe that. I hope you lay here and bleed the fuck out. You don't deserve to live. You don't deserve to be around normal people. You a fucking animal!

"Now, as the ambulance or morgue comes and scrapes you off this ground, just remember I'ma be back at home living the good life. No more struggling. No more being dogged by you. And no more being held under your wicked spell of madness. I'm done. I'm free of living like you and yours. Now, nigga, I pray you rot in hell, you waste of skin!" Keisha made sure no one was looking as she spit in Rico's face before standing up. To add more insult to injury, she kicked him in the side of his head before walking away from the accident scene.

Rico couldn't respond. He couldn't move. His stomach felt far worse than it ever had in life—even when he had alcohol poisoning. Every part of him wanted no more than to smack the fire outta Keisha for all the things, true or not, she'd just said. But instead, he was forced to remain motionless, with her saliva slowly sliding down his jaw. Suffering from what seemed like two broken legs and leaking from the rear of his bald head, Rico had no choice but to wait for an ambulance. As he swallowed his own blood, in the back of his mind he knew he'd catch up to Keisha sooner or later; that was, if he lived to see the sunrise. After all, in Rico's way of thinking, she was nothing more than a low-esteem, dumb-ass female that would be back on his line as soon as he snapped his finger.

Hailing another cab that happened to be riding down Davison Avenue, Keisha jumped inside, giving the driver the same instructions she'd given the first. Using the aid of the few streetlights that actually worked in the city of Detroit, she read the rest of the alarming article. The first-hand account of Mrs. Jackson's late evening emergency was given by someone Keisha recognized as one of her neighbors, so she knew it was true.

Seeing how it didn't identify what hospital she was rushed to, Keisha knew it was best to just head to the house, and if nothing more, at least Sandy would tell her where her mother was at. Her dad could change all the phone numbers he wanted to, re-key every lock in the house, and order every person that was in his inner circle to keep her away from him and her mother because of her promiscuous ways, but this was an altogether different situation and circumstance. Keisha was no stranger to how her father, the great Commissioner Jackson, had another personality in public than private, so if she showed up at the house unannounced without his advanced approval, it'd be no way in sweet hell fire he'd deny her to visit her own mother.

Chapter Nineteen

Enlisting the aid of Keisha's step-by-step directions to the secluded home in the gated community, the cab driver pulled up to the place his disheveled passenger claimed was home. Collecting a few more dollars added to the twenty-dollar deposit the early-morning rider was forced to put up, he slowly left out the circular driveway.

With her purse and the newspaper tucked under her arm, Keisha immediately noticed the house appeared dark. Moments from daybreak, her first mind told her that in all probability, her dad and Sandy were down at the hospital at her poor mother's bedside. However, after a few more steps, she took notice of her father's car. Then she noticed two strange vehicles inconspicuously parked around the side of the huge house, near the kitchen door.

Wow, I wonder whose cars are these, she pondered with each step. *Maybe it's some new people Father has working here to help Sandy out.*

Putting that out her mind, she then concentrated on the task at hand. Keisha tried her luck, praying just on the humble that the kitchen door was left unlocked. Trying to twist the knob to the left and then the right, Keisha crapped out. It was definitely locked. Knowing good and well her father might deny her entrance, she searched over near the garden area, finding a broken half of a brick the gardener must've discarded.

I hope the alarm doesn't go off. But if it does, oh well, so be it. I'm done caring about what's right and what's wrong.

Holding the stone tightly, she closed her eyes to avoid injury. With all her strength, Keisha smashed the lower corner of the glass-windowed door. After a second delay, the loud sounds of the alarm failed to go off.

Yes! Thank God, it isn't on!

Sticking her hand inside, she turned the two handles from the inside, gaining entry to the house. Once inside the dark dwelling, she was like a wild lion in search of its prey. Keisha ran up the stairs two at a time to her parents' room, calling out for her father. Bursting through the door, she quickly discovered that their bed was empty.

Dang, maybe he's in one of the spare rooms asleep.

After checking all four of those, Keisha went into her old bedroom. Momentarily swept back in time, she remembered who she was raised to be and, tragically, who she'd become since dealing with Rico. Then and only then, for the first time since the cab she was originally riding in struck him, she wondered if Rico was dead or still alive.

Whatever! I'm home now. My father will take me back into his good graces, and the nightmare with that asshole will finally be over.

With wishful thinking, Keisha snatched one of her many stuffed animals off the bed, hugging it as she twirled around.

Now, if I can find out what hospital Mother is in, I can go to her. It's probably just her blood pressure. Now that I'm back home, I can help Sandy take better care of her.

Not bothering to changed her ripped and torn clothes or even put on a pair of panties, Keisha straightened out the employee shirt Sam had given her after blessing his dick the best she could. Determined for information, she headed down the stairs, out the kitchen door, and toward the gatehouse that Sandy called home.

Marching past the two strange vehicles, Keisha slowed down, then paused altogether. Something strange caught her eye. She took notice of a tassel from a graduation cap dangling from one of the car's rearview mirror. However, because it was parked in the shadow of the house, she couldn't make out the school colors clearly. Yet, she was in a rush and had no time to spare. Stopping to get a better look inside one of the mystery cars was the last thing on her mind. Keisha was on a straight-up mission to get some information on her mother's present whereabouts, as well as the true verified ailment that sent her away in an ambulance, making front-page news.

Seeing a light on in the bathroom, Keisha assumed the family chef and her longtime confidant, Sandy, was just getting up and would definitely be able to shed some light on what happened. Not wasting time to knock at the front of the gatehouse, Keisha knew for certain the far rear entrance near the rose bush was unlocked. Years ago, Keisha had locked herself in the gatehouse as a small child, and her father ordered that the door that was hardly used was to have no locks on it whatsoever.

"Sandy! Sandy! It's me!" Keisha bolted through the threshold, yelling out as she passed the open bathroom door. Seeing no one was inside the candle-scented domain, excitedly she ran into Sandy's bedroom.

"Sandy! Sandy! Wake up! It's me, Keisha! Wake up! I need to know about my mother!" Flipping the light switch on the wall upward, Keisha froze dead in her tracks. Totally speechless, she couldn't believe her eyes. It was as if she was in a dream or a nightmare and everything was going in slow motion.

"Keisha!" The equally stunned words rang out from Sandy's bed. "Just what in the hell are you doing here?"

"What?" Keisha could hardly speak. The words couldn't come out as her throat instantly grew dry. She was almost speechless.

"Have you lost your mind? Don't what me, young lady! I said what in the hell are you doing here? And what in the hell do you have on?"

Almost in shock, Keisha didn't know what to do or say next. It was as if someone or something was holding her.

This can't be happening! Not now! It can't be!

Thinking about her poor, sick mother lying in some hospital bed suddenly gave her a small bit of strength.

"Father, are you fucking serious? How can you sit there and ask me some shit like that? Look at you! How can you do this to my mother? I'm ashamed of you! This is some old crazy shit you see in the damn movies. Not for real!"

"Are you serious? This can't be my life right now. You are ashamed of me? Isn't that wild, all things considered. Look at you standing there. Standing in the middle of the floor, looking like something the cat drug in. And you have the nerve to cast judgments? I'm the one that's ashamed and have been for some time. So, how dare you even take that hypercritical tone with me? You disgust me. And now that I think about it, didn't I tell you not to bring you self back on my damn property? And here you stand."

"Father, are you serious right now? I will take what-ever fucking tone I choose in a situation like this." Keisha refused to back down. "This right here is some straight-up bullshit! Where is my mother at? And how long this scandalous garbage been going on with these ratchet pieces of trash?"

Keisha's father, stark buck naked, seemed to have no worldly remorse for what he was caught doing. Wedged in the middle of two sheet-covered females, he acted like what his daughter discovered was of no great importance, even when it was compared to her defying his orders to never step foot back on his property again.

"Who are you to bombard me with questions? Let alone raise your voice and curse," he sneered as Robin grabbed at a small portion of the sheet to cover her breasts.

"And you, Robin." Keisha pointed with contempt and malice. She was ready to attack as her anger increased. "I've known for a long time you wanted my father like he wasn't married. You ain't about shit. I should kick off into your whorish ass for my mother right damn now. Not to mention all the times you lied when I called the office trying to speak to my dad—ole devious, homewrecking bitch! I promise on everything I love, you gonna catch these hands. Watch."

Feeling secure that her boss really loved her, even though he'd never even slightly mentioned the word, Robin giggled, acting like Keisha was a joke. She casually waved her hand, dismissing any of the high-pitched vows of violence directed at her. "Yeah, all right, girl, please. Ain't nobody trying to hear all that married crap. If he doesn't care, why in the hell would I? Matter of fact, instead of posting up in here, playing the role like some tough girl, go get with your long-in-the-tooth mother. Have her step her game up like your good-fucking-a-dog ass. Then maybe she can keep a man." With no true shame in her game, Robin climbed out the bed. Naked as the day she was born, she grinned as if this entire situation was a joke.

"You dirty bitch!" Keisha balled up her fist, ready to do battle.

"Now, now pump your brakes and watch your mouth. Is that any way to speak to your soon-to-be stepmother? I don't wanna put you on punishment or cut off your allowance. Aww, damn, I forgot. You already are cut the fuck off. My bad."

Just as Robin was brazen enough to bend down and pick up her clothes off the floor, it all popped off. The new hood-driven-in-attitude Keisha strong-kicked the small-framed secretary dead in her face twice.

"Bitch, you got me all the way fucked up. You best watch your mouth when speaking to me, especially about my mother. If you think you're woman enough to take her place, then try it! Sucking my father's dick ain't a form of transportation to the top of the food chain. Only thing you guaranteed to get is this ass-kicking. I'll have your heart beating real fast."

"Aww, please, Keisha. Either step up or shut up and play your position, because I'm growing weary of your little threats."

Enraged that Robin was discounting her feelings, Keisha was soon delivering a few more kicks, followed by a combination of punches to the side. Keisha tossed Robin about like a rag doll. She never gave the big-mouth female a chance to get even one hit in. Keisha dominated Robin, then finally allowed the disorientated homewrecker to stumble to the bathroom for refuge from the well-earned beating.

Keisha frowned, watching the injured female run for her life after teaching her a life lesson. Turning her attention back to her father, who was now putting his boxers on, Keisha hissed. She then continued to grill him on his illicit actions and obvious indiscretions.

"How could you, Father? How in the hell could you do what you've been doing?" Her voice was piercing, bouncing against the thin walls of the gatehouse. If there ever was a time that the normally timid daughter wanted to be heard, today was that day. "I'm confused. I'm messed up in the head right now about this bullshit. Have you lost your mind? Mother being sick is all in the newspaper, and you're here in bed with females like it's no big deal? You just acting like your vows mean nothing. Oh my God, I can't stomach you or this!"

"Newspaper?" Ignoring the more-than-valid questions, Commissioner Jackson, up for re-election, demanded Keisha compose herself and calm down. He kept in mind all the noise she was making in the otherwise tranquil neighborhood. Although it appeared to be quiet, he knew better. It was no telling who was up.

"Damn, okay, Keisha, you beat the poor girl up. You got the best of her. You proved your point that you could beat her up. You win, okay?" He motioned toward the bathroom, where an injured Robin was no doubt hiding. "You made your damn point. Now, please be quiet. Lower your voice right now."

"Don't tell me what to do, Father! My mother is in a hospital, and you're posted up in the bed with not one, but two other women. I guess I can be thankful at least you had the common courtesy not to do this foolish bull-shit in mother's bed." Being involved in more than her fair share of threesomes and other sexually promiscuous behavior over the past year, Keisha was the last one to pass judgment, but this was just plain wrong.

"And Sandy," she sobbed, looking at the female cowering under the sheets in obvious shame. "How could you do this? My mother trusts you. She loves you, and I love you too. How could you do this to both of us? Oh my God, Sandy, I thought you were my friend. I'm so hurt. How long has this been going on?"

Keisha eagerly anticipated locking eyes with Sandy. She wanted to hear her explanation of the ultimate betrayal. Her entire being wanted to know how Sandy could be so black-hearted.

With uncertainty, the corner of the sheet finally lowered. What was once a secret was no more. On this day, all her father's dirty little exploits would be exposed. It was of no big surprise what Robin's intentions were. She'd made them disrespectfully clear since day one. But this—this unveiling—almost knocked the emotionally drained daughter off her feet.

"Keisha, I'm so very sorry. I am your friend. I swear I am. I just got caught up."

"Oh my God! Oh my fucking God! This must be some sort of damn nightmare I'm in. I must be dreaming." Keisha's eyes grew twice their normal size as she shook with anger, ready to attack once more. "This can't be real. Oh, hell naw. Kim, how could you? Of all people, how could you do this bullshit?"

Lowering her head in shame, Kim struggled to find the proper words. She prayed this day would never come. Keisha's supposed best friend had crossed the line. Clenching the sheet couldn't conceal the embarrassment. This offense was far worse than sleeping with Rico or a boyfriend. That code was still intact. Kim was sleeping with Keisha's dad—her mother's husband.

"Oh my God, Keisha, I'm so very sorry. I don't know why. Things just happened. Shit just got outta control. I never planned for it to go this far." Kim tried pleading her case with her childhood playmate. She knew at this point it was nothing she could say or really do to explain why she was just found in the bed with Mr. Jackson and Robin, yet she knew she had to at least try.

"Please forgive me, best friend. I'm sorry. I swear I am. Please forgive me. Please! I don't know why I allowed myself to be involved in this. I swear I know I was wrong."

Keisha was livid. She was seeing red. Having been through hell and back over the past year, nothing had prepared her for this shock or pain. Not Rico putting his hands on her countless times as if her life didn't matter. Not being forced to abandon her family. Not being humiliated by the guy at the beauty supply or asked by A.J. to go down South and be one of his whores. So what everyone had seen a dog have oral sex with her, or she slept with her boss to save her job? It was way too many awful, gut-wrenching occurrences to relive as she stood in a daze.

Keisha stood motionless, taking in what she was seeing. With a lump in her throat, she wanted to throw up and almost did. The stunning disloyalty of the moment ran through her veins. She felt like someone had savagely socked her in the stomach. Her world was in a shambles. Minute after minute, more and more surprises were being revealed to her.

The young woman who once had a perfect life couldn't catch her breath. Feeling the oncoming effects of one of her excruciating migraines, she fought to focus. Keisha turned away, not wanting to actually see what was reality.

Her best friend was involved in an outrageous three-way relationship with her father, of all people.

Finally, she found her voice. "Wow, Kim, so is this why you haven't wanted to answer any of my phone calls or respond to any of my text messages? Damn, I can't believe this bullshit. Kim, oh my God, not you of all the females I know. Wow, really." Unsuccessfully, Keisha tried to run her fingers through her badly tangled weave. "I'm fucked up right now. I can't lie; this is almost the worst thing that has happened to me in my entire life. Rico was right. My life don't matter."

"Hold up, Keisha. Please wait. I told him about your messages just last night. I swear I did. I promise." Kim sobbed crocodile tears while attempting to explain her terrible transgressions. "Tell her, Lorenzo. Didn't I tell you? Please tell her. I'm not lying!"

"Damn. Wait, Lorenzo?" Keisha barked at Kim calling her father by his first name like they were equals. "Wow, really. But I guess why not, since y'all two, I mean y'all three, is fucking! I guess first names is the order of the day. Shit, while you at it, why don't you call my father bae or boo?"

"Listen, will you please both keep your voices down? How many times do I have to tell you that? Are you both insane?" Mr. Jackson once again insisted, thinking about his Republican news reporter neighbor. "People around here don't want to hear this mess, so stop giving them possible headlines to use against me."

"You might need to stop talking to me, you damn rotten-ass cheater," Keisha forcefully shouted as Robin, now fully dressed, eased the bathroom door open, peeking out. Her mouth was busted. "All three of you aren't shit! Doing this bullshit to my mother! I swear I'm ready to kill all three of y'all!"

Wrapping herself in the sheet, Kim stood near the bed. "I know you're pissed, Keisha, and I'm sorry. I know if it was me, I'd be heated too. I wanted to tell you that night at the Fox Theater when I was there with your father, but I didn't get a chance."

"The concert?" Keisha's already scattered mind flashed back to the night of the concert. So much drama had taken place that evening it was easy to do—but painful to relive. It dawned on Keisha that that was another reason she hadn't seen her mother that night. Obviously, it was because her father's offensive, lying ass was there, out in public low-key with her best friend. "I can't believe you! This shit been going on that long? Wow, y'all both some real slimeballs."

Lowering her head in disgrace, Kim went on with her spontaneous confession. "I was going to tell you the next day, but that idiot sent that video to everybody and, well, you know the rest. It was chaotic from that point on."

"Yeah, you right. I guess it was never the appropriate time for my best friend to announce that she was having sex with my damn father." Keisha had heard and seen just about enough. She was drained. "Whatever. How could you, Kim? You went on vacations with us since we were kids. You spent nights over here all the damn time. My mother treated you like a daughter, just like she did Sandy. Matter of fact, where the hell is Sandy? Do she know about this circus of filth? I know she couldn't know y'all here in her place!"

"Okay, Keisha, okay. Calm this tirade down. You've proven your point. And don't worry where Sandy is. She's not here making a spectacle out of herself like you, so let's leave it at that."

As Mr. Jackson tried to gain control of the explosive emotional situation and do damage control, Robin took the opportunity to dart from the safety of the bathroom. From there, she bolted out the front door. Her next stop, no doubt, the hospital to get X-rays for her possible broken ribs courtesy of Keisha.

Not wanting to get the same brutal treatment as Robin, Kim nervously held the sheet tight. Completely embarrassed, not knowing what else to say in the way of apologizing to her so-called friend, she just cried. Gathering her clothes, Kim rushed out the door, barefooted, onto the gravel. In the brisk, early-morning air, she opted to get dressed in her car, which was a short distance from the house and Keisha's obviously well-warranted wrath.

"So, okay, my wicked-mouth offspring. You wanted some attention. You wanted to show out and let everyone know you can fight. Well, now it's just you and me. Now is your chance."

Keisha, who was just as loud as a person could be in that situation, now had a lump in her throat. At a loss for words, instead of a grown woman who'd been through sheer hell the past year, she felt like a small child. It was if all the years of downgrading insults were at the forefront. All of her father's sneers and snickering at her shortcomings were present. She felt meek, not empowered.

"Yes, Father, it's just me and you. There is no one left to put on an act for. Now, will you please tell me why you're doing mother like this? She loves you. She'd never do something this treacherous to you. She doesn't deserve any of this. And FYI, you're the one who is wicked!"

Commissioner Jackson took in all of what his daughter was saying; however, he wasn't moved, not one bit. In any normal circumstances, he would have to stand mute and accept his scarlet letter. But that humbleness was void. Instead, he flipped the script. He wanted—no, demanded—some answers himself.

"Look, before we go any further in you grilling me like some low-income, first-year prosecuting attorney, why are you dressed like this, in a Legends Coney Island shirt and a torn skirt? And what's wrong with that face and hair of yours? You are a disgrace to this family's name."

"A disgrace? Family? Are you serious right now?" Keisha took a deep breath, thankfully realizing she had a right to be heard. "How fucking dare you speak to me like that! As many times as I tried reaching out to you . . ."

"Lower your damn voice I said." Mr. Jackson's expression was cold, as if he were talking to a stranger in the street, not his daughter. "I don't know why you insist on being so damn disruptive—acting ghetto. You've been misbehaving since you were a small child."

Keisha tried the best she could to fix herself up, yet at this point, it was what it was. "You can just go easy with the name calling. I've had more than enough of that this past year. And stop trying to stall your explanation. I wanna know what your problem is."

As he stood there in his loosely hung boxers, Mr. Jackson's snide laughter filled the room. His condescending, black-hearted stares shook his daughter's very being, which he took delight in.

"So, Keisha, did you just meet me or something? When will you learn that I don't like questions or those that ask them? And if you are attempting to make me feel some sort of guilt or remorse about my actions tonight or any other night, you can just forget about it."

"But—" Keisha tried to speak but was cut off.

"But nothing. And if you're here to find out about that drunkard, pill-popping mother of yours, then you can just go crawl back in the gutter hole you been living in with that abusive filth you call a man. Matter of fact, where is that lowlife pimp boyfriend of yours? He's not outside in a stolen car waiting for you to beg me for some spare pocket change, is he?"

"Father!" Keisha's feelings were hurt, and it was written all on her face. Not the fact that he'd brought up Rico, who could be in the hospital or dead in the middle of the road, but the fact that he was so mean-spirited and uncompromising on his attitude.

Dealing with the general public, Commissioner Jackson was known for taking a hard line with issues and had a zero tolerance attitude. Immediately, he saw the weakness in his child's eyes that was hard to disguise. With no repentance, he took the opportunity to bring her down a few more notches.

"Look at you. You have the nerve to come in here passing judgment on people, and you look like something the cat dragged in—something that's been dead underneath the porch for days." Mr. Jackson gripped up on his manhood like some rebellious teen on the corner talking shit to his homeboys. "My daughter, Keisha Marie Jackson, the biggest hood slut in town. Ain't that a bitch? I wasted money paying high tuitions at the best schools for nothing. Expensive dermatologist treatments, all those designers clothes and purses you wanted. What a goddamn fucking waste." His verbal assault continued as the tiny amount of Keisha's self-esteem Rico left her with, started to crumble.

"I'm ashamed of you. The entire family is. Why do you think your mother stayed up in that bedroom like a zombie waiting for the devil's orders? She'd rather die than face the fact her daughter is you!"

Devastated by his words and accusations, Keisha felt her legs grow weak. What her father was saying, face to face, was far more hurtful than anything Rico had or could have said. Sure, he'd been behaving as if she hadn't existed for months, but his words never cut so deep.

Unsteady physically as well as emotionally, Keisha leaned on the nearby dresser for support. "How can you say those awful things, Father? How can you? I wanted to come home so many times."

"Yeah, well, the truth of the matter is you didn't. I guess in between fucking that no-good bum and his four-legged hairy companion you forgot the way, huh?" Mr. Jackson had no shame in how he was making her feel. "And by the looks of your present state, it looks like you just went a few rounds with that animal before you showed up here!"

Totally defeated, Keisha pleaded, "Father, can you just tell me where Mother is? Please?"

"I'll tell you what." He tilted his head to the side and folded his arms. "I'll tell you about that sick-in-the-head mother of yours, but the question is how bad you want to know."

"Huh? What do you mean?"

"I mean, I think after all the money I've spent over the years on you for what seems like nothing, you owe me!"

Completely confused as to what the man she'd always respected and looked up to meant, Keisha remained perfectly silent while his spiteful intentions went on.

"Well, Daddy's little bad, slutty girl, how bad you want to know?" Commissioner Jackson dropped his arms to his side. Once again, he then used his hand to move his now hardening dick to the side of his boxers. "And you might want to hurry up with your answer. The last I checked, your mother was damn near coughing up a lung. She's probably taking her last breaths in a dark hospital room by herself as we speak. So, what's it gonna be?"

No stranger to men and what that meant, Keisha was dumbfounded. What her own father, of all people, was suggesting, was uglier than any nightmare or thought she could ever think of. Pure hell. If what he was saying was indeed true, her mother could be minutes, maybe seconds, away from dying. Dealing with Rico, she'd done plenty of downright ridiculous, degrading, and scandalous things sexually to please him as well as herself, but this—her own father—sucking his dick would top them all.

"Father, you can't be serious. Have you lost your mind altogether? I don't know who you are anymore. Do you hear yourself? Do you even realize what you're asking?"

"Come on now, Keisha, I know you haven't forgotten the special times we used to have in your bedroom when your dear old mother was passed out."

"What? What are you talking about?" Keisha started experiencing the worst migraine she'd ever had. The more she looked into her father's dark, cold eyes, the more confusing childhood memories flashed in her already tormented mind. Fighting the pain of what incestuous actions he was eluding to, she pleaded one last time.

"Please, Father. The article in the paper didn't say. Please. I'm begging!"

Looking at his watch, a self-righteous Mr. Jackson took his stiff dick out his boxers. "Okay now, Keisha,

I already told you, your mother is probably taking her last breath right now, and you here negotiating about what you do best," he remarked casually, as if his wife's impending death didn't matter one bit to him. "The best place for you to be is on your knees, pleading for my forgiveness. And guess what? If you do a good job, Daddy might let you come back home. You do wanna come back home, don't you?"

Keisha considered her few options and the high stakes at hand. First and foremost, she'd give anything in the world to see her mother, who was once so proud of her, possibly one last time and let her know how terribly sorry she was for all the grief she'd caused her over the past year. And secondly, the harsh reality was, she was broke and fucking homeless. If that jackass Rico did survive being hit by the cab, going back to him and his overly abusive ways was completely and totally out of the question. Keisha desperately felt she had no choice. Her back was against the wall. Her father, as usual, was the winner. Sick to her stomach, Keisha's inner soul ached as she eased over toward him, dropping to her knees.

Chapter Twenty

When I find that good-for-nothing thot, I'ma beat her like she stole something. Her ass got me out here early as hell on some dummy mission looking for her. The damn sun ain't even up, and a nigga tired as shit. I swear I'ma stump a mud hole off into Keisha's fat ass.

Rico had just left out of the restaurant after speaking to Sam. After finding out his sexual meal ticket was not inside, he'd given the Middle Eastern owner a disrespectful earful. Rico had not only referred to Keisha as everything vile he could think of, but he confessed some of his dark secrets as well. As if he were a soldier on guard duty, Rico marched throughout the dimly lit area back and forth. Hell bent on making his supposed woman pay for the offense of finally standing up for herself, each step he took was filled with malicious intent.

I know I should have never let that bitch outta my sight. I should've never let her get a damn job. A nigga like me should've kept the ho slanging that pussy at the crib. As soon as she gets out and talking to these motherfuckers, she wanna get cocky. She wanna start with all that Oprah, I-am-woman empowerment bullshit. Well, fuck Oprah, Keisha, and the next ho out in these streets. If a bitch gonna fuck with me, she gonna come all the way correct and bow down. A bitch gonna submit or get her ass handed to her.

Caught up deep in his feelings of superiority, Rico came out of the gas station, shaking his head. Sam had not seen his girl, and neither had Hassan. Twisting the tiny top off the bottle of Visine he'd just got on credit, Rico picked up his pace in search of Keisha. He wanted revenge for the stunt she'd pulled and wasn't going to rest until he checked behind every dumpster and under every parked car. He realized it had taken him a few minutes to get himself almost back together back at the house, but she couldn't have gotten that far. Keisha was book smart, but definitely not street smart, no matter how much he'd tried to train her.

Tilting his head backward, he kept it moving as he lifted the small plastic red-eye relief. Using his right index finger, he slightly pulled down on his lower left lid area. With two quick squeezes, the cool-feeling liquid filled one eye. Head still tilted backward, Rico blinked, allowing the Visine to do its job.

Before he could wipe away the excess fluid that was dripping down his cheek, Rico was abruptly knocked off his feet. Before the evil-minded tyrant knew what was taking place, his body was snatched onto the ground. Whatever the source of the impact, he was now on the concrete pavement being dragged a few yards. By the time the unannounced drama ended, Rico felt the heaviness of what he would soon discover was a vehicle rolling over his lower body.

Urgg, what in the fuck? What just happened? Shit! What the fuck!

In a mere matter of seconds, Rico went from searching the parking lots and back alleyways for Keisha to being sprawled out in the middle of the street. In an enormous amount of pain, his eyes being red from the chemical-based spray was the least of his problems.

My fucking leg! What happened? My stomach! Fuck!

He was dazed and disoriented. Not paying attention to where he was walking had just gotten him hit by a cab. With the wind knocked out of him, he struggled to speak as he felt the heat radiating from the bottom of the vehicle. Ironically, he started to shiver. Chill bumps covered his injured body. This was more pain than he'd ever experienced since birth. Growing up in the hood, an average kid, teen, or grown-up, was subject to just about anything going wrong to make them suffer physically. However, God or the devil had spared Rico from this unplanned agony—until now.

What in the entire fuck just happened? Why I am so fucking cold? Urgg, my damn back.

As his mind tried to overtake the pain to focus, he couldn't. His lips couldn't seem to form words as two pairs of feet neared him.

"Oh my, oh my. I'm so very sorry. But I didn't see you. You came from nowhere. Why you not look?"

Rico then realized he had been run over. He'd actually been struck. It was coming back to him—he was just walking, putting that shit in his eyes, then bam! Infuriated, he wanted to leap to his feet and fight the driver for what was an accident, but he couldn't move his legs.

"Nigga!" he yelled out to the Middle Eastern driver. "You got my shit all fucked up."

"Please, please, young man. I'm so very sorry. I didn't see you. I swear I didn't. I'm calling you an ambulance right now."

Rico wanted to reply but couldn't. Small amounts of blood started to fill his mouth. Seconds later, he was gagging, choking, and struggling to breathe. As the pure blood turned into a thick mucus mixture, Rico's tongue started to swell. Just as he thought his pain and rage could not grow anymore, the bad-boy tyrant saw another pair of feet approaching. In the midst of all that was taking place, he locked eyes with Keisha. Now more than ever he wanted to speak. Being run over by a cab hadn't magically changed who he was. He wanted to tell her about herself and warn her that her ass was kicked as soon as he could manage to get up.

Here this stankin', no-good fat bitch is. I wish I could just smack the dog shit outta her. It's her damn fault I'm out here in this street fucked up in the first place. If she would've just bossed up and took all this dick and the ass-kicking that went along with it, shit would've been Gucci. But naw. That was too much like right. She wanted to get all up on her high horse. Shit! Damn! Fuck, my legs is numb and my stomach is burning like they on damn fire!

Rico felt emotional and physical damage just as he had made Keisha feel since she became his so-called woman. He was already plotting his revenge for her early-morning defiance.

Now here this bitch come. Probably trying to kiss a nigga ass and apologize. Ole miserable, worthless ho. I'ma make her pay for this bullshit.

Keisha stood towering over Rico. Caught up in her feelings, she took a few seconds to gather her thoughts. After all she'd been through back at the house and all she'd overheard him just say inside of the restaurant, this was it. This would be Keisha's day of reckoning. Here Rico was, laid out in the middle of the street, obviously too injured to move. Without further hesitation, she bent down.

Rico's reddened eyes widened. Now only inches away from his face, she had her say. After calling him out for the piece of filth and waste of skin he was, Keisha spit in his face before kicking him on the sly. Rico lay there, helpless, with his eyes wide open to see Keisha stroll slowly away.

After what seemed like an eternity, the ambulance finally arrived. Upon getting placed in the back of the flashing-light rig, Rico saw Sam and a few more neighborhood folks standing around, no doubt judging him by the looks plastered on their faces. If he wasn't busy throwing up his own blood and in a huge amount of unbearable pain, he would have shouted out for all of them to suck his dick.

The bright lights in the triage area seemed to burn Rico's eyes. Each time he found the strength to crack them open, tears poured out. The once self-proclaimed hood warrior and Casanova was drifting in and out of consciousness. He was mumbling a few words that sounded as if he were speaking in tongues. Having his clothes cut from his body, he could only lay there and pray to the devil who he seemingly worshipped. With needles being shoved into his veins to draw his blood, IV bags being hung and blankets rolled around to stabilize his legs, Rico was ready to surrender his will to live. Even with the strong meds they immediately pumped into his system, no relief was seemingly near. If he could speak, Rico wanted to beg them to just let him die. Right before he passed back out, Rico heard one of the nurses ask if he had a wallet on him so they could contact his next of kin.

Chapter Twenty-one

Having just seen Kim wrapped in a bed sheet, parked over on the side of the road getting dressed seemed surreal. Pulling over herself, she didn't know what to expect in the way of an explanation. Sandy couldn't believe when Keisha's supposed friend horribly confessed to her what had just taken place back at the gatehouse and how long the mind-boggling affair had been taking place. The closer she got to the estate, the more Sandy could feel her heart beat at a rapid pace, not knowing what was going to happen next.

Holding the steering wheel as steady as she could with sweaty palms and shaking fingers, Sandy turned into the circular driveway. Bringing the car to a screeching halt, the now-ex-chef to the Jackson family jumped out of her vehicle, leaving the engine running and the driver's door wide open.

"That's right, daddy's little bitch. Close those eyes and open up. Suck me off like you've been doing Rico all these months. Show me some of that wild passion you had for that dog."

Hearing Mr. Jackson's brass-toned voice echo from the rear of the small gatehouse, Sandy knew he and Keisha were in the bedroom. Rushing toward the room she'd slept in since a child, Sandy was overwhelmed with disbelief, finding Keisha submissively on her knees in front of her half-naked father.

"Have you lost your fucking mind altogether? What in the hell!" Sandy snatched Keisha up by her forearm, practically throwing her across the room, landing her on the floor.

Directing her rage at Mr. Jackson, Sandy held no punches. "How low will you sink? This doesn't make any kind of sense! You're a fucking animal! You need to be locked under the damn jail!"

Mr. Jackson's manhood started to shrink as he slid it back inside his dark-colored boxers. "Just what are you doing here, Sandy? Didn't I fire you?"

"Fired?" Keisha puzzled from the floor while thanking God for Sandy coming to her rescue.

"Yes, Keisha, this bastard that calls his self a man—a father, a husband—had the nerve to not only fire me, but allow his wife to slowly kill herself."

"Bastard?" Mr. Jackson laughed at her choice of words.

"What?" Keisha rose to her feet, overlooking her father's callous attempt at sarcasm. "Sandy, where is my mother at? Please tell me you know. Please!"

Infuriated by the lewd act she was fortunate enough to interrupt, Sandy gave Keisha the answer for which she was willing to sacrifice the last bit of morals and dignity she had to offer in exchange.

As the two embraced, Sandy informed Keisha that no matter what, she would not see her out in the street. Having saved the majority of her wages throughout the years, Sandy wasn't rich, but she was a far stretch from being destitute.

"Keisha, please don't worry. You don't have to be beholden to any man, especially him," Sandy snarled at her ex-boss.

Seeing firsthand that the strong reign he'd held over the years at his household was slipping away, Commissioner Jackson went berserk. "Sandy, just who in the fuck do you think you are, trying to come in between me and my daughter? After all I've done for your ungrateful ass."

"Ungrateful? Nigga, please! You should be in jail just like the fuck I said. But instead, you've got everybody in and around the county thinking you this high and morally correct individual, and you ain't shit but a full-grown snake."

"Shut your damn mouth."

"Naw, shut your fucking mouth. It's been enough silence and secrets around here for two or three lifetimes."

"You little bastard."

"There goes that word again." Sandy stood tall, with contempt in her tone. "So, I'm a little bastard, huh?"

"They say God don't make mistakes, but you—" Mr. Jackson had the look of the devil in his eyes. "I'm glad your mother isn't here to see the little smart-talking, disobeying ratchet tramp you've become." He shook his head, smirking at the thought. "You think I don't know about you sneaking Calvin in here those late nights, giving him that worn-out pussy? I know every fucking thing that goes on around here."

"All of the different women you've had throughout the years, cheating on your wife, you've got a lot of nerve talking about me, or anyone else, for that matter. You sick in the head."

"Me? Sick?" he mocked, ready to slap Sandy into acting right. "How dare you?"

"You should be ashamed of yourself. Mrs. Jackson is lying in the hospital bed with full-blown AIDS, and you still out here fucking the next bitch. Or should I say bitches? All without condoms, knowing you."

"AIDS? Yeah, right." He quickly dismissed his wife's shocking condition as just Sandy trying to scare him.

"You heard me! AIDS—full blown, the doctors said after you and that self-serving opportunist Robin left the hospital. And if she, Keisha's so-called friend Kim, and the rest of the young dumb females you sneak around town with know like I know, they better get tested."

"Like I said, Sandy, your mother is probably in hell burning extra hard for who and what you are: a bald-faced liar! But guess what? One thing for sure, two things for certain—your mother was one of the dumbest whores I knew, but the trick could scramble a mean egg or two. That's besides sucking good dick."

Running up to him, Sandy raised her hand, bringing it down across her boss's face. "Don't you say shit about my mother. Not shit! You ruined her life—our life!"

"Me? Ruined her life? Are you serious, or are you on the same prescription drugs as that one over there's mother?"

Keisha had heard enough. As far as she was concerned, Sandy and her disrespectful, predatory father could argue about the past all day and half into the night. She just wanted to get to her sick mother's bedside as soon as possible.

"Stop it! Stop it! All I want to know is where is Mom at?"

Mr. Jackson dismissed Keisha's words and kept in on Sandy. "I don't know why I've kept you around here as long as I have. I knew from day one you were going to be trouble. But I was trying to be nice—trying to do the right thing."

"You no-good motherfucker. Trying to be nice? Trying to do the right thing?" Sandy screamed the words she'd wanted to say for years but was forbidden to even whisper in the dark. "You kept me around because I'm your damn daughter! Your first born!"

"Daughter!" Keisha shockingly yelled to the two of them. "What you mean, daughter? Sandy, what are you talking about? What are you both talking about?"

"What in the entire hell? You stupid bitch. You dumb little stupid bitch." Mr. Jackson started quickly putting on his clothes so he could get Sandy out the door and off his property before she did any more damage to his already tarnished reputation.

The big, dark family secret was now on the table. It was no more trying to tiptoe around facts. No more of making up stories to cover the awful shame that dwelled in the walls of the once seemingly normal dwelling. Enough was enough.

No longer holding back the truth, Sandy decided it was time to be completely honest with Keisha. Taking a deep breath, she braced herself for the drama she knew that was sure to follow.

"I don't know how to say this, and after all the years I've practiced, it's still hard. I didn't want you to find out like this. I swear I didn't."

"Okay, and . . . "

"At this point, it's no easy way to put this, Keisha, but just I'll say it. Your father has been sleeping around on your mother for years. Matter of fact, more damn years than I can care to even remember. Let me just say Robin and Kim aren't the first, Keisha. They are not the second or even the third or fourth. There has been what seems like hundreds of random females this no-good monster has flaunted practically in Mrs. Jackson's face. Well, maybe not hundreds, but damn near close to it."

"I get all of that, Sandy. He ain't jack shit. But you said daughter. I heard you." Keisha was baffled. Her mind was spinning, not knowing what she'd hear next. "What did you mean? Why did you say that?"

"This no-good piece of trash raped my mother, Keisha," Sandy sadly revealed, answering the million-dollar question of the evening. "When she was young, he raped her. This rotten-intentioned monster knew she didn't have any family to turn to. He knew she was out here in the world alone, so to satisfy his own needs, he kept raping her until she got pregnant with me."

"Shut your fucking pie hole, you damn slut. You just like your no-good mother, running off at the mouth and don't know when to close it." Mr. Jackson raged at hearing his awful past thrown up in his face. Wasting no time, he started with the blame game and his own accusations to try to justify his horrid actions.

"Now, first of all, you need to get your story and facts straight. I didn't rape that little ghetto-breed slut."

"What? Have you lost your entire mind?" Sandy swiftly protested, ready to do battle to protect her deceased mother's character.

"Shut up, you ungrateful bitch! You wasn't here to know what happened way back then. That hotbox girl ran around here in those tiny, tight skirts, bending over, trying to be seen. So out of pity, I did her a favor and noticed her." He laughed, having a momentary flashback. "That good-slaving dead bitch wanted every inch of this dick I gave to her. Old Deep Throat was happy carrying my baby," he proudly announced as if it were a badge of honor. "I did her a favor. I gave her and you a roof over your heads, no charge. And look at you standing here running off at the mouth!"

"You damn no-good pedophile rapist! How dare you speak about my deceased mother like that? You need to be stopped. Matter of fact, you need to be behind bars somewhere until you rot!" Sandy balled her fists tightly. With the heart of a lion, she began to swing. Twice delivering blows to his chest, she finally hit her mark, making contact with his jaw.

Mr. Jackson ultimately had enough. Swiftly, he retaliated, all the while smirking with satisfaction. Snatching Sandy up by the collar of her blouse, he swung her around the room, tossing her from one side to the other. he let her feel his power as a man that was still intact despite his age.

"Stop it! Stop it! Oh my God, stop it," Keisha once again begged, trying to intervene before being knocked off her feet and onto the floor.

In amazement that Sandy was in fact her sister and not just the family chef, Keisha didn't know what to do next or who to help as the two did battle—her father, who once loved her but had just made her perform oral sex on him, or her newly discovered sister, Sandy, who'd always showed her love.

"This is too much! This is crazy! Stop it! Stop it! Take your hands off her! Father, no! Please, noooo! You're hurting her!"

Despite her father's pleas to keep the noise down, the time for being silent was no more. He was doing and had been doing more than enough to scream about. Keisha's passionate cries of mercy could soon be heard in the early-morning calmness that surrounded the gated community. She stood helpless. It was as if her father had transformed into some sort of heinous monster right before her very eyes. Watching his strong hands practically squeeze the life from Sandy's body, his apparent illegitimate daughter, Keisha felt another sharp pain engulf the right rear portion of her head.

Overwhelmed and confused with what to do next to stop his attack, Keisha grabbed one of her childhood spelling bee trophies that Sandy always strangely cherished. Clutching it in her hands, she cried out for him to take his fingers from around Sandy's throat. Quickly, it became apparent her father was not listening to her pleas. With all her force, she vindictively sent it crashing down on their father's head. She repeated the heartfelt motion several times, until his blood started to spill from the huge gash in his head and onto the carpet. With hatred for Rico and every other man that had deceived, fucked her over, or just plain told a white lie, Keisha felt empowered, relieved, and justified. Her best friend Kim's betrayal, along with the tragic fact that Sandy revealed her mother had AIDS, was only fueling her violent rage against her father.

With the now-broken trophy still in her hand swinging, Keisha had snapped. She was out of her mind. Forcefully, she had to be stopped by her neighbor from across the street. Thank God, he had been outside walking his dog and had overheard the loud commotion from the rear gatehouse. Ironically, he was the one who'd written the newspaper article about her mother being transported to the hospital. By nature of his profession, the nosey reporter had stood at the doorway for a few moments, listening to the sordid family turmoil before finally feeling the need to come in and halt what sounded like a life-or-death confrontation. Thank God he did enter the premises, because he was able to not only bear witness to what he had heard but what he'd seen with his own eyes.

After the longtime neighbor called 911 on his cell phone for an ambulance as well as the police, he stepped outside on the roadside to flag them around to the rear gatehouse. Sandy, gasping for air, was left on the floor, holding her throat. Another few seconds of Mr. Jackson choking her, she would've been dead and reunited with her deceased mother.

Keisha, still astonished at what she'd heard her father and Sandy claim, was close to blacking out herself. The news that Sandy wasn't just the family chef but her sister was overpowering to her very being.

"Is it true, Sandy?" Keisha asked, cradling her in her arms in utter shock and denial over the revelations made. "Please tell me if what he and you said is true. Are you my sister? Did he really rape your mother? Did he?"

Finding the energy to lick her dry lips, Sandy spoke barely louder than a tiny whisper. "I wanted to tell you for so long, Keisha, but Mrs. Jackson and that monster lying over there thought it would be more than you could stand."

"My mother knew about this?" Keisha questioned, hearing an ambulance in the far distance. "And she stayed with him after all of that? How could she? Why was she that stupid?"

"Don't judge her, baby. How have you stayed with Rico? Look, Keisha, she turned a blind eye to a lot of things he did because he had her self-esteem so low, she thought that treatment was what she deserved." Sandy coughed in between her words, still holding her very sore neck. "Your father—I mean our father ain't shit! I hope he bleeds out and dies over there for all of our sakes! God forgive me, but he doesn't deserve to live."

Throughout the confusion, she knew Sandy was not wrong. Keisha knew that was the same way Rico had treated her and she had accepted it. Maybe that's why she chose to stay with a man that cruel and heartless. He was just like her father—a self-serving tyrant.

"Sandy, I believe he raped your mother, and I'm not condoning it at all. But I want you to know, if you are my sister, I'm happy. I've always loved you like we were family anyways. I mean it. So it is what it is. We can both deal with that later. But, Sandy, can you please tell me what hospital my mother is in? That's where I want to be right now. I know she needs me."

Sandy knew there was more to the story—much more. And since she was dead in the middle of confessing the dark family secrets, she felt it was time to let all the skeletons out the closet.

"No problem, Keisha. You're right. You do need to be at Mrs. Jackson's side. But I just have to tell you one last thing Mrs. Jackson turned a blind eye to. She, I mean we, have been all deceiving you. It's more to the story than what I just told you."

Not knowing what in the hell Sandy could say next, Keisha braced herself as the ambulance sirens got closer. "I know, Sandy. I heard you. My mother has AIDS. It doesn't matter to me, not one bit. I still love her, and as soon as we can, we can both go to her side."

"No, Keisha, it's about that pedophile animal laying over there." She motioned toward a hardly conscious Mr. Jackson—their father. "He is a monster. He has no soul. He is as black-hearted as they come."

"Sandy, oh my God, what is it?" Keisha was running out of patience.

Sandy took a deep breath. "Not only did he rape my mother; he raped me also when I was just twelve years old."

"What!" Keisha screamed out as the EMS technicians came bolting through the doorway with her neighbor leading the way. "He did what? Noooooo, are you serious? Naw, Sandy, why? Oh my fucking God!"

Sandy knew she'd gone too far to go on without revealing the entire truth to Keisha. In spite of the strangers in the room, she felt it was best to get it all out in the open once and for all. Mr. Jackson had to be exposed and the air cleared. Still whispering, Sandy bravely confessed the unthinkable.

"He raped me when I was only twelve, and I got pregnant."

"Pregnant!" Keisha couldn't believe what she was hearing. "What? Are you serious right now?" She was stunned at the monster her father truly was.

"Yes, Keisha, pregnant. He forced himself on me more than once, and I got pregnant."

"Oh my God, no! Sandy, no! So my father made you have an abortion?" Keisha's eyes grew wide, awaiting her response. "He made you kill your own baby? How could he be so mean? I can't believe him or any of this."

"No, Keisha, I had the baby."

"What? You did? You had a baby?"

"Yes, I did."

"Oh my God—what?" Keisha cried for her newfound sister's pain for having a baby and not being able to raise him or her. "Where is the baby? Do you know? Was it a boy or a girl that you had to put up for adoption?"

"Yeah, I know where the baby is and has been. That asshole and Mrs. Jackson took the baby from me."

"They did?"

"Yeah, they took my baby and raised her as their own."

"Huh?" Keisha fought to make sense of what she was hearing. "What—as their own? I'm confused now more than ever. What does that mean?"

Sandy took another deep breath. She knew the fallout from what she was about to expose next would be crucial, to say the least. "Keisha, all of what I've been telling you is hard. Trust me. I swear I didn't want the truth to come out like this."

"Just say it, Sandy! What are you talking about?"

"Okay, Keisha, try to stay calm. The truth is, not only are you my sister, but you're also my daughter. I'm your real mother—your birth mother. You are my child."

"My mother? What in the hell are you saying? No, it couldn't be! I'm confused! What? My mother! Why you say that? It's not true! My mother! Naw, Sandy, stop all this lying. First you said you were my sister; now you saying you my mother too! How could that be?"

Seeing Keisha's bewildered facial expression and all her barrage of questions, Sandy remorsefully continued. "Look, baby, I know it's a lot to take in right now, but let's just thank God I got here and came inside when I did, or you might've been the next in our twisted generation to have his baby! He's a monster, Keisha, and I hope he dies for the damage he's caused to all of us and every female he's ever come in contact with over the years!"

With the police now entering the small gatehouse, Keisha was completely overcome with confusion over what Sandy had confessed. She felt the room spinning. Her heart was broken, and Keisha's soul felt shattered.

To make matters worse, the jaw-dropping announcement from the EMS technicians that her father was dead sent chills throughout her entire body. Overcome with numb emotion, it was too much to bear. Not wanting to face the tragic reality of what her life truly had become, she buried her face in her hands. Keisha grew increasingly short of breath as her head felt as if it was going to explode. Seconds later, the once-carefree good girl blacked out.

Chapter Twenty-two

Months later . . .

"It's really funny how life is, isn't it?" Sandy, after getting the results of a paternity test, smiled. She and an extremely skinny, thin-haired Keisha walked out the courthouse. Hand in hand, deemed the two sole heirs to their father's small fortune, all was well with them financially. They could travel anywhere, eat anything they desired, and shop until they dropped.

Still, there was a dark cloud that hung over their heads, one that all the money in the world couldn't give you back if God saw fit—and that was good health. Having gone to a doctor, Keisha had a complete physical as well as an intensive mental evaluation done. Every test that could be administered was. Sandy, a worried sister and mother, was eager to finally be able to openly take care of her child the way a mom should.

After it was all said and done, the truth was revealed. The diagnosis was sad but all too clear. It was discovered Keisha's blind devotion to Rico and many other people in her life was a chemical chromosome imbalance. The doctors easily attributed that illness due courtesy of their father's incestuous actions and Keisha's conception. With that medical news, on the top of another, Sandy and Keisha still tried their best to remain upbeat and optimistic.

Tragically, her mother, Mrs. Jackson succumbed to death a week later from AIDS she contracted from her husband. If it wasn't for Sandy, Keisha would've been crazy with grief and denial when, ironically, she found out she, like her parents, was infected with the wicked disease.

"You're so right. A year ago, I was half out my mind, just straight acting a fool, but now things are finally starting to look up. Despite my health issues, I'm just glad to be done with Rico once and for all. Why I let him do all the things he did to me and why I stayed, I don't know. It all seems like a bad dream, one I couldn't wake up from until that terrible day."

It was nearing the anniversary of Mr. Jackson's untimely death on the gatehouse floor. After finally regaining consciousness, Keisha had been immediately handcuffed and arrested. She was brought up on manslaughter charges for her father's death. A long, drawn-out criminal trial could have taken place, but it didn't.

Fortunately, her nosey reporter neighbor, in exchange for an exclusive story, testified that he'd been at the doorway listening. He testified to the jurors and judge that he'd overheard Commissioner Jackson and Keisha that early morning. He informed them that not only had the deceased victim threatened to physically attack both females, but that he also heard him confess to several other unimaginable crimes.

When the jury took into consideration all the corrupt actions that were discovered, they were appalled. The prosecutor fought to keep most of the family's ugly secrets and skeletons out of the trial, but Keisha and Sandy weren't having it. They, along with Keisha's defense attorney, wanted the entire world to know what a house of horrors Mr. Jackson was the head of. That, coupled with all the various allegations of the commissioner's promiscuous behavior and other inappropriate affairs at the job, were brought to the forefront. If he weren't deceased, he could have been charged with several other crimes stemming from people finally brave enough to speak up.

The neighbor felt as if he'd hit the mother lode of all stories. With the deal he'd made with Keisha, he would stay busy for months. He was elated to write several heart-wrenching articles that were award-worthy. In no time flat, Keisha Jackson, accused murderer, soon had the people on her side. That was all she needed to tip the scales of justice. Once a loser, she was now a winner. If only temporarily.

Life was life. It never proved to be easy. There would always be storms, and although she beat the case, her storm wasn't totally over. Her blessing of being acquitted and avoiding a life sentence seemed pointless. Keisha couldn't feel free to live in the celebration with what was now looming over her head.

Originally, Keisha and Sandy couldn't figure out how she contracted the deadly disease. However, after discovering Kim, now also sick, depressed and shunned by her family after them finding out about her scandalous affair with Mr. Jackson, it made sense. Her being HIV positive, all the puzzle pieces started to fit together. It didn't take a rocket scientist.

It seems that Robin was not only sleeping with her infected boss, but she had also been secretly banging his loyal driver and bodyguard, Calvin, as well. When Robin found out what she was facing, she lost her mind. She couldn't cope with the disease and the stigma of having it. In a matter of weeks, she committed suicide by jumping off the high-rise office building where she once worked.

Calvin, on the other hand, tried to be a standup guy. He knew he had messed up his life and wanted to take full responsibly. Not only did he bravely confess to his wife, who divorced him, but to the stripper, Ocean, who was his new mistress.

Sandy was blessed and knew it. She was relieved she'd stopped having sexual relations with Calvin long before he hooked up with Robin or the infamous Ocean. Her wise decision saved her life from being in the deadly twisted triangle of filth Calvin had created.

From there, connecting the dots of the deadly disease didn't take much effort from Sandy or Keisha. It was simple. Ocean, of course, was still fucking Rico. That was a no-brainer. To make matters worse, come to find out, she was pregnant. After the devastating news Calvin told her about probably being infected with HIV, she wasted no time giving that toss-up baby back to God. Still dancing at several Detroit strip clubs, possibly exposing tricks to HIV, she refused to be tested, saying she ain't wanna know.

Her son, Rico's son as well, had no great interest to visit his father, who was left completely paralyzed from the cab hitting him. Day after day, barely eighty-nine pounds, he lay in the dark room of the hospice, praying for death to take him away from the internal pain of full-blown AIDS. Yet, as they say, God don't like ugly, so Rico Campbell, who treated Keisha no better than shit on a stick, amazingly kept breathing and suffering.

Keisha knew Rico transmitted the disease to her, and she, in turn, possibly infected A.J., who, exactly like Ocean, turned down every opportunity to be tested. Keisha knew nine outta ten times he took the virus directly back down South with him. So, what started up North in Detroit was going to cause plenty of people down the way unwanted grief, tears, and denial.

After sitting back and thinking, Keisha easily accepted the fact that she definitely transmitted the virus to Swazy, Rico's road dawg. Swazy, who was no angel by far and a willing participant in all the scandalous bullshit exploits, passed it on to his newborn. With an immune system that couldn't withstand the serious rage of the disease, the baby only lived six days with the curse. Sadly, Swazy's girl died in complications from childbirth. Thank God she never found out her man wasn't about shit.

It wasn't a good six months later that Keisha discovered she'd given Sam the awful gift of death. Going on with his daily life, he had no idea what was wrong when he started feeling out of sorts. He just chalked it up to catching a cold and prayed that Allah would heal him. Sam naively transmitted it to both of his wives. When it was discovered, he shamefully moved his family back to his country so they could die in their own motherland.

Keisha's boss and his wife never did find out the source of the deadly linked chain that struck both of them with HIV. Since they lived a swingers' lifestyle, there was no telling how many people in the city and places that they traveled to that they spread the disease. The possibilities of the reach was unreal.

Mr. Jackson's continued legacy of unprotected sex was a seemingly vicious, never-ending cycle. Generations to come would be affected by one wicked man.

Chapter Twenty-three

Calvin

"Baby, your cell phone is going off. And at this time of morning, I don't even need to ask who it is. Does that man ever give you a break?"

Calvin's wife turned over, pulling the blanket over her head. Since the two of them had been married, it was as if she never had a full eight hours of sleep. Her husband was loyal to his job. And he was extra loyal to his employer. When Commissioner Jackson called, Calvin jumped. This time was no different.

It was a little shy of six a.m. when his cell rang. However, unbeknownst to her, this time it was not her husband's boss interrupting their sleep, but Robin. Even if the devoted wife did happen to answer and it was Robin on the other end, she would pay no major attention to it. She would chalk it up to Commissioner Jackson having his private secretary do his summoning of her spouse.

Without bothering to look at his screen, Calvin just snatched up his phone. Yawning twice, he headed to the bathroom. After placing it on the sink, he turned to hit the hot water knob on the shower. He then jumped into the warm, steamy mist. As he got done, he reached for a towel. While drying off, Calvin's cell rang once more. When he looked, all he could do was shake his head.

"Yo, why in the hell you calling me this time of morning? Have you lost your damn mind?"

"Oh my God! Oh my God! Calvin you have to get over here to the house. Please hurry up!"

"Robin, first of all, calm the fuck down. Secondly, what you mean, get over to the house this early? What's happening?"

Robin started to stumble over her words as she nursed a busted lip. "It's Keisha. She just came over and started going crazy. She was trying to kill me. I swear for God I'ma press charges on the little tramp!"

Calvin was completely dressed and on his way out to the car when he finally got the entire truth from Robin. He was at a total loss for words. He knew she was sleeping with the commissioner. That was no big surprise to anyone, probably even his wife. But having a threesome with him in Sandy's bed of all places was far over the top—even for Robin's constantly conniving ass.

Driving toward the house, he dialed his boss's number a few times but got no reply. With no traffic out that time of morning, he arrived quicker than normal. As he drove onto the property, he was stopped by a marked police car with its lights still flashing. Not knowing what exactly to make out of all the commotion, Calvin knew by the looks of things it was nothing nice.

After showing the proper credentials, he was let onto the inner edge of the property and questioned by a detective. As he was giving him a statement, he glanced over to see Keisha being led out in handcuffs. Making eye contact with Sandy, who was trailing close behind, he knew that his boss certainly was dead.

As the days went by, the news of Mrs. Jackson's death filled half of the newscasts. The other half was occupied with Keisha's murder of her father. With all of that attention to their personal lives, Calvin soon discovered that Commissioner Jackson had AIDS. He knew that nine out of ten times that meant Robin had been infected. And of course, since he was sneaking behind his boss, having sex with her, he was at risk. Finally getting his nerve up, he got tested. He encouraged Robin, as well as the little hotbox he was screwing, a dancer named Ocean, to get tested as well.

When the results came back, Calvin was devastated. He was indeed touched by the long hand of the devil he had been playing so recklessly with. This was a hard pill to swallow, but one he couldn't keep to himself.

He wanted to make sure of what was what before he sounded the alarm at home. He'd done a lot of fucked-up things throughout the years to disrespect the vows of his marriage; however, not warning his wife of an impending death sentence would not be one. Calvin waited for her to come home from work one evening and sat her down. With tears in his eyes, he confessed all his wrongs. It was dead silence in the room before his devoted wife stood. Once on her feet, she slapped him twice before packing a bag, never to return home as his loving spouse.

Swazy

It didn't take long for the news to circulate. The ghetto was like that. If someone got evicted, the block knew before the bailiff showed up with a dumpster. If someone's lights or gas was shut off for non-payment, the neighbors could easily tell you what the occupants had done with their bill money. Even if a person did something good, someone was watching and ready to give a hood report on all the details.

No sooner had Rico finished calling Keisha a rotten bitch than the lady a few doors down knew. Matter of fact, she watched Keisha flee the house. A few minutes later, she witnessed Rico dart out as well. She had just posted about it on social media when she heard an ambulance siren. All she could do was shake her head when it was discovered Rico had been hit by a cab. One of her daughters was friends with a girl whose soon-to-be baby daddy ran with bad-boy Rico. The nosey neighbor texted her daughter, and just like that, it spread like wildfire.

Swazy was half asleep when his girl started to nudge him. Trying not to hear what she was saying, he forced himself to wake up. He knew she was near her due date and didn't want to miss a beat. Dragging himself out the bed, he took a morning piss before hearing her out. While part of him wanted to say fuck Rico and his bad luck, the other wanted to find out what exactly happened so he could go back and report to Commissioner Jackson.

Ensuring his woman was okay, Swazy got dressed. Not knowing what to expect, he headed down to the nearby hospital. It was only two to choose from, and luckily he'd picked correctly. After going through the metal detectors, he stood at the front desk. Before long, a patient's advocate emerged, asking his relationship to Rico. Of course, Swazy lied, claiming to be his brother. Moments later, he was informed that Rico had been rushed to emergency surgery and if there was any other concerned family members or person in charge of making critical decisions, now would be the time to call them.

Swazy lowered his head, fearing the worst. Knowing this type of information would be valuable to Commissioner Jackson, Swazy placed the call. After several rings, the voicemail came on. Not wanting to be accused of holding back anything he'd found out, Swazy left a text to return his call as soon as possible. He had no idea whatsoever that call would never come. At least he'd made an attempt.

As the days went by, it was hard not to hear the shocking news of Commissioner Jackson's untimely demise at the hands of his own daughter. Feeling no sympathy for the deceased man, Swazy was overjoyed to be out from under his overpowering wrath. As far as Keisha's fate went with facing manslaughter charges, it was what it was.

It was as if the once-happy-go-lucky crew was destined to suffer. Soon Swazy came to discover that Rico, who was in a medically induced coma, had contracted the HIV virus and that made receiving proper treatment more difficult than normal. No longer feeling any emotion for his once-best-friend's well-being, he switched it over to himself. The ugly truth, or what could be, was haunting him daily. If Rico had the deadly disease, chances were that he could have it as well, especially since they had both grown in the habit of having sex with the same females—Keisha included.

It was no way he could get in touch with her, so he finally manned up. Swazy went to a free clinic on the far side of town. As he waited for the results, he grew sick to his stomach. He wasted no time in calling his cousin to give him the threat of the tragic disease, but he wasn't trying to hear anything about HIV, let alone the possibility of him having it.

Swazy waited for a call from the clinic. Constantly, he kept checking his cell. While pacing out in the park, he lit a blunt to try to calm his nerves. Before he could get a good buzz going, he heard the loud ringtone from his front pocket. Answering it, he threw the blunt down, racing back to his car. It was his girl. She was in full-blown labor and being rushed to the hospital. Breaking the speed limit, he got down there just in time to see his baby being born and his girl ironically die. The doctors were baffled. Up until the moment the baby was born, her entire pregnancy seemed normal. Then, just like that, her blood pressure skyrocketed and her sugar level spiked. It was nothing they could do. As Swazy stood speechless and stunned, his newborn was whisked away, also suffering from some sort of complications.

Once again, the loud ringtone rang out. Answering it in tears, Swazy discovered he indeed had the "package." It would be the first and only gift he would ever give his daughter, who died six days later. His life would never be the same, and he blamed Rico.

I knew if I kept doing dumb shit with him it was gonna get me fucked up. Now my girl and my baby gone. My life might as well be over too.

Ocean

"I swear for God. I just wish them damn people from the health department would stop calling me. I don't know what in the fuck they wanna tell a bitch so bad, but I ain't interested. Ever since I had that damn toss-up baby abortion, they been on my head. But it's all good in the hood. I know how to handle that dumb bullshit!"

Ocean walked into the Metro phone payment center. Digging in her purse, she pulled out a balled-up stage-hustle twenty-dollar bill. Tossing it in the small slot, she demanded the clerk change her number. After writing her information and PIN down, the deed was done. She would now be free of anymore unwanted calls from the clinic. There would be no more random hangup calls from bitter bitches whose man she was banging, past or present.

Most importantly, Calvin could not contact her about his claims to have HIV. It was bad enough she heard Rico was cursed with it. As far as Ocean was concerned, that was on both of them and their bad luck. Sure, she had unprotected sex with the pair, but so what? She felt fine. Her arms worked. Her legs still moved, and her head game was still on point. Taking all those things into consideration, to Ocean, it was business as usual. She was back on the pole, swinging and tricking at night just as soon as her flow was manageable. Her main concern was to feed her son and pay her bills, nothing more and definitely nothing less. Allowing Rico to lay eyes on their child was the last thing she was thinking about. Besides, the way she heard the streets talking, he didn't have that much time left on the earth anyway.

Maybe that meal-ticket bitch Keisha will use some of her dead daddy's money to get that bum a miracle cure. Shit, she just beat a murder case, so I know she Gucci! Ocean smirked as she went on to secretly infect another unsuspecting guy she met at the strip club.

Rico

"You know it's a sin and a shame to be this young."

"Yeah, you are so right. To be this young and not have not one person care enough about you to come visit."

"Girl, or at least place a call to see if you're dead or alive."

"This dude must be grimy as hell."

"I'm not sure, but the lady with the long weave that works on the night shift said this is that guy that was linked up with ole girl that killed her daddy but still ended up with all his bread. Shit, I heard he got a little son that the mother ain't brought to see him either."

"Wow, then he is a slimeball when your baby and baby momma ain't fucking with you in the last hours. And shiddd, we already know when he leave this earth where he going."

The hospice caregivers carried on their conversation as if Rico were not laying paralyzed in the bed just a few yards from them. They had no filter whatsoever. Day after day, it was the same routine for them on their job. Patients would come into their facility, oftentimes in an ambulance. However, it was only one way they left. Well, truth be told, two. One, in a fancy funeral home hearse, if you had insurance, or two, tossed in a body bag only to be transported in the back of the dark-colored county morgue vehicle if you were financially broke or unclaimed. Either way, death was imminent. For the workers, it was just a job. For the patients, it was their final taste of hopefully some sympathy and comfort on their final journey to either heaven or hell.

I hate I'm in all this pain. Every part of my fucking body is hurting. I feel so weak I can't even lift my arm. And my damn legs been felt like they wasn't there. That dumb-ass cab driver fucked me up for real. Shit! I know I

done did some shady shit to people over the years, espe-
cially some of them bitches, but this shit right here—this
shit right here I don't wish on my worst enemy. And every
single day these same hoes come up in this son of a bitch
talking cash shit. I wish I was my old self. 'Cause if I was,
I'd have both they asses on they knees, sucking on this
dick.

And all them ho-ass niggas that claim they was my
homeboys, where the fuck they been? Why at least
Swazy ain't done showed his punk ass up? He probably
somewhere playing house with that stuck-up pregnant
bitch of his. That nigga straight pussy. Always talking
about he just trying to live his best life. Fuck all of that.
Fuck living your best life with one female. How that
bullshit work?

Rico had been through just about every medical
procedure a person of his limited financial resources
could have. Seeing how he was broke, there weren't
many. That fateful morning he was struck by the cab,
emergency room doctors tested his blood for all sorts
of abnormalities. When it came to light he had HIV,
a lot of things changed in his care. Moreover, when it
came out in the news reports about him and the way
he'd treated Keisha Jackson, all bets were really off with
most. Even though most professionals take a sworn oath,
people are still human and, of course, judgmental.

If that tramp Keisha would not have been trying to go
for bad that morning, a nigga like me would have been
out in them streets getting money and pussy. And that ho
got the nerve to not have brought her stankin' ass here,
wherever the fuck here is, to see about a nigga. But it's all
good. I'm hurting like a motherfucker. Every part of my

body feels like it's on fire. And I know it was that ho that gave me AIDS. She probably was fucking behind my back like all hoes do. I was good to that girl, and she think she got over. But it's all good. We gonna meet again. I know if I don't get on that bitch Keisha head in this lifetime, I'ma damn sure kick her ass in hell. She got that much coming, ole fat bitch!

Chapter Twenty-four

Pulling up at the Metro Airport terminal, Keisha and Sandy got out of the Uber. After tipping the driver extra, they gathered their luggage. The lines were long to check their bags, but neither cared. They would be living their lives as if they were golden. Life was much too short, and Sandy didn't want Keisha to forget to smell the roses when at all possible.

Making it through the security checkpoint, Sandy found a nearby bench to put her shoes back on. Keisha made a quick trip to the bathroom. She had been urinating more frequently and had developed a terrible cough. Swallowing even small amounts of water was becoming difficult at some times, but Keisha was tough. After all she'd been through with Rico, a murder trial, and burying both parents back to back, nothing could break her. She would fight until the end.

Soon the pair boarded a private flight to a tropical island. It was rumored amongst the new age generation doctors that certain experimental drugs were being used to treat the HIV and those cursed will full-blown AIDS. Prepared to use all of their father's inheritance if need be, the once-sloppy-seconds-minded female closed her eyes tightly before the plane took flight. Silently, she prayed her sexual exploits and her stupid ridiculous loyalty to Rico and his "good dick" would not cost her the ultimate price unprotected sex often did—someone's life.

As she opened her eyes, she saw Sandy's face and reassuring smile. Reaching over, she placed her hand on top of hers.

"After all I've been through, I want to live my life right. I want to go places. See things."

"Don't worry, baby. You will. God has your back, and so do I."

Sorrowfully, a few months after arriving on the island, Sandy stood by the edge of a beautiful beach, sobbing. She had just buried her sister and her daughter—Keisha Marie Jackson. Sandy trusted in God's ultimate plan, and she knew in spite of Keisha's troubled life, she didn't die in disgrace. She believed her daughter went to walk in the light. Unlike Rico and Commissioner Jackson, heaven was her just revenge.

The End

Note from the Author

We all know a Keisha, that one stupid female who, no matter how much you try to school her silly ass, she just keeps letting a Rico dog her out. Whether she's spending all her income tax check on the bum, using her food stamps to feed his greedy play- the-video-game-all-day behind, or not paying her rent to make sure he has the new Jordans. Hell yeah! I already know! Lol . . . As fucked up as she living, the bird still think she stay winning! Imagine that!

Well, guess what? Newsflash! The Ricos of the world are giving the good men and great fathers a bad name . . . but do the Keishas care? HELL NO! If they even think the no-good rat bastard is giving the dick to the next female, they want to kick her ass! You stupid bitch! Kick your own ass for not letting that jumpoff take that burden off your hands!

Stop turning a blind eye, living in the moment just to please the next person. Getting infected comes from ignorance. Black, white, yellow—HIV is colorblind! Rich, poor, middle class—AIDS doesn't check W-2's! I know not having intercourse isn't the answer to the spread of the disease. People gonna get it in till the day they die! However, safe sex is! Just think if half of the men in this story wrapped that shit up! The moral to this rant . . .

Love Yourself First!